Domain

by

Douglas A. L. Smith

Smith Cottage Publishing

Copyright ©2020 by Douglas A. L. Smith
ISBN:978-0-578-89817-9

*To the brave soldiers
of whom the wars they've fought
have never ended.*

"And this we do also: we have consultations, which of the inventions and experiences which we have discovered shall be published, and which not; and take all an oath of secrecy for the concealing of those which we think fit to keep secret; though some of those we do reveal sometime to the State, and some not."

Francis Bacon

"The New Atlantis"

Prologue.

Quinton takes a deep breath. It's only a switch. All of life is a matter of combinations. He just happens to be a very specific combination of dark and light. That's all this is.

A different combination of dark and light.

Except he's the one creating it.

He nods to his assistant, permission to initiate transmutation, and watches through the empty glass chamber as the lights flicker and a fleshy form takes shape. Attached to the chamber is a cylindrical tube-like structure, the size of an oil truck tanker. The sleek body glistens silver with a hint of charcoal lurking beneath, vibrating with a visible incandescence. The techs call the machine and chamber configuration *Thor's Hammer*, a visual reference more relevant than objectively understood.

His heart pounds with a rise in velocity parallel to the hum of the machine. With each new layer of flesh that culminates into a recognizable form, his hope accelerates. At first, the idea was to start with something simple, and expand from there. The process worked in grade school, and it seems to be universal. Humans have this tendency to overthink things. To sensationalize. After all the work that's been done in science, the formulations, the speculations, the theories, life comes down to two things.

On, and off.

Eternity is found at the threshold of every room, static potential awaiting its transformation. Life in this world is nothing but a swarm of light switches. Endless combinations of dark and light, patterns reliant not only on biology but more so, belief.

The ante is ever increasing. He understands the lackluster of cloning at this point in science. No more cloning. No more sheep. The time is ripe to create new things. At least, that's what the *Eidolon* said. *Raise my children,* he recalls the deity's message, *I'll show you how, and you can rise to be one of us.*

He didn't think it was possible to create, especially outside the dynamics of genetics and biology. The concept simply didn't make sense from a human perspective, but then again, he wasn't communicating with a human.

When will you tell me your name? He projects the thought to the room. He can feel the Eidolon form to his right, watching the scene as it unfolds, invisible to everyone including himself. A human like shape vibrates inside the chamber now, but not just any human. This creature is half-human, half-god. The ancients called them Rephaim, a term older than the Bible. The mystery of this magnificent creature can only be understood by references in mythology, an often overlooked part of history that most have rejected as fable.

When you're successful. The Eidolon replies, a voice only in Quinton's head.

Skin forms on the Rephaim, a pale white speckled with brown. The creature pulses as though hit with a resuscitating pad.

"That's too soon," He turns to the other tech. "Campbell, shut it down!" He barks.

A young man in a white lab coat holds a tablet, stylus in mid stroke. A patch adorns his breast pocket in white and blue with the words *Kelim Tekhnologies* embroidered in a clever pyramidal design, the *el* having emphasis. He hesitates, unsure of how to proceed.

"Did you hear me, Jason! Shut the thing down!" Quinton reaches over and grabs the tablet from Jason, anxiously jabbing at the screen with his finger. Everything important is on this one device. The passcodes. The science. The blueprints for the machines and the manuals for running them. The entire process is recorded and controlled by this one simple piece of technology. Of course, there is a backup, but only two people have access to it, let alone knows where it is. Quinton is one of them.

"Sorry, sir." The tech snaps out of his shock and rushes over to a monitor attached to the machine, then punches in a code. "Ready when you are sir." He holds a cautious finger over the keypad.

"Campbell, just do it!" Quinton yells, his voice subdued beneath the vocal jittering of the giant beast in the chamber. The Rephaim sprouts long red hair on both his head and face, his wide mouth peeled back in guttural pulsation of interrupted bellows. Like a premature newborn whose lungs have yet to develop, the beast gasps for air and swings his massive arms. A second row of teeth protrudes rapidly behind the first, and the Rephaim clamps down his jaw on his own tongue, spurting blood onto the glass chamber wall.

Quinton watches in subtle horror as his creation convulses into a collapse, naked and motionless on the chamber floor.

It's time. The Eidolon whispers in his ear. He jerks, relying on the disastrous scene as an excuse for the sudden jolt. Behind him, a door opens.

That was a failure, Quinton projects back, *how could it be time?* A bead of sweat rolls down his back, reminding him of the inevitable end to the real project that only he knows about.

"Quinton," a voice hesitates in the back of the room, beckoning him to turn. Byron Dempsey, the facility's Project Manager, holds out a reassuring hand. "It's a simple fix, remember?" He squints behind black horn-rimmed spectacles, accentuating deep crow's feet across his temple. His thinning gray hair is slicked back in a lazy pompadour, the same style he wore it forty years ago but with less pomade and even less vigor.

Rob Comins stands back with arms crossed, the polar of Byron. He is short and skinny, in that skinny-fat kind of way reminiscent of overcooked noodles. His potbelly pushes through his unbuttoned sports coat, supporting an uneven tie the color of unconcern.

"This shouldn't have happened." Quinton pushes a palm against his temple, fingers sprawled through his salt and pepper hair. "These monsters keep waking too soon. We can't have them trying to breathe this early, it starts the life cycle before development is finished and-"

Careful what you say about my children, the Eidolon grumbles a sandpaper voice into his ear.

"What if we reduce the amount of CO_2 in the chamber?" Jason suggests, eyebrows raised.

Idiot, Quinton sighs, *it's not a vacuum.* He ignores the suggestion and locks the tablet, then tucks it under his arm.

"I can't guarantee a return on my investment with this kind of failure." Comins snarks, shaking his head. The last word punches Quinton in the gut. *What an unappreciative weasel. This work is more than business. Creation is art. Even a failure is more than he could ever accomplish.*

"This looks promising, Quinton. Rob is merely a businessman. He's only coming at it from an investor's perspective." Byron gives him a knowing look. As his mentor, the old man knows him well. He was there through the struggles, the lows, the OCD cycles of seventy-two hours without sleep. People expect miracles to be instantaneous, then lose all sense of wonder when the process takes longer than desired.

"But I still need results that produce a revenue. Do you know how much it cost to run this one example? We've far outweighed our budget."

"Rob, we've talked about this." Byron puts up a halting hand and glances at Quinton. Quinton loosens his collar, the heat from his chest steaming up his chin.

"We're on the last step here. One more experiment and you will have your *investment*." Quinton says, withholding the sting in his jab only slightly.

"Give me something I can work with. A dead giant is as useful as a pen with no ink." Comins grunts, shifting his overly polished shoes on the granite floor.

Quinton takes in a breath, ready to retaliate, but is interrupted by Byron stepping forward. "Alright, alright. Good things are happening. Let's not lose focus. The experiment isn't over, and despite what the numbers might say," Byron casts a warning eye at Comins, "We are not over budget. We have some new and promising investors who are very excited about the project."

"Get back to me when you have it figured out." Comin's soft chin sinks into his neck in a look of lazy conceit. He glances at the tablet under Quinton's arm, then turns to Byron. "If you'll excuse me, I have to make some phone calls."

The door shuts behind Comins, leaving an opaque shudder of an echo behind. Byron shakes his head, a look of mixed concern settling on his high cheekbones. The man has seen too much sun in his life. How many trips to the Bahamas can one person handle? Byron takes so many vacations it's a surprise to find him at the lab.

Quinton hands the tablet to Jason. "Recharge the collider. I'll need it charged up before Peru."

"Peru? Isn't that in three days?"

"Is there a problem, Campbell?"

"No sir. I'll start right away. Have you considered the Gibo machine? It's charged and ready."

He grits his teeth. "You just worry about Marlene. Nothing else." He holds Jason's gaze until the tech looks away. Nothing more needs to be said.

"You know Comin's is only talking." Byron sighs and looks through the glass at the dead giant. "Despite the outcome, this is the greatest creation since, well, creation itself."

"Don't tell me you believe in that garbage." Quinton slows his breathing. Exhale the negative. Inhale the positive. Dark out, light in. Combinations are always malleable. Finding them is the key.

"I'm not here to discuss religion with you. It's a compliment. Take it, will you?"

"Are you coming to Peru with me?" Quinton knows the answer but has to ask anyway.

"Haven't decided. The wife hasn't moved back in yet. Still not over… you know."

"I'm sorry to hear that."

"Ah, don't be." Byron waves the notion off and walks to the door. "The trip is important, I know. And I know you'd like to have me there. But I believe in you Quinton. You don't need me anymore."

"That's not true." Quinton knows he's right but has a responsibility to the old man.

"You know it is." Byron puts a hand on the doorknob. "I'll call the clean-up crew. You just keep doing what you do best. Impress me." He opens the door and starts to walk through but stops short. "And you're a terrible liar, by the way."

The door closes behind him. The old man is right. Quinton doesn't need him anymore, however much he likes the man. If the Eidolon says its time, then its time. Kelim Tekhnologies is in for a big surprise, and if Comins wants the project, he can have it, and all its *failures*.

Jason gives Quinton a shrug and sets the tablet down on the table. He watches Jason stroll out of the door. The kid is too arrogant. He'll be good bait in Peru. Quinton left enough breadcrumbs behind for him to follow, sure that his overconfidence would lead him right where Quinton wants him. In every culture, from the ancient times to the modern, the rite of passage is accomplished with a sacrifice. This one requires blood.

The Navel of the world. Where life is said to have started. And yet, so much chaos is coming with him. How poetic. If only Byron knew what he was really doing with the colliders.

He stands at the chamber, squinting dark eyes at the dead giant. The machine idles, cooling off, clicking now and then as the inner tube settles against its coils.

You'll never have to watch your children die, like I have. The Eidolon whispers, its energy uncomfortably close to his side.

"You're not talking about this, are you?" He responds, his low voice camouflaged by the humming of the machine.

I'll show you when you get here. The voice penetrates Quinton's skin, settling deep inside his chest. He shakes off the feeling of needles in his skin and turns quickly, hoping to catch a glimpse of the Eidolon.

Nothing stares back at him.

He is alone.

On his way out, he stops to pick up the tablet out of habit, then decides against it. Another breadcrumb. He won't need it where he's going anyway.

He leaves the stark room and walks to the lobby, checking his watch. Most personnel should be clocking out by now. Kelim Tekhnologies always runs a small crew, for the sake of confidentiality. Only techs and security.

These days, he hardly notices the paintings that blemish the otherwise gaunt hallway, even though they were his choice. The imaginations of Gustav Klimt captivate him in a way that breathes life into his tepid routine. The art pieces reach out to him, beckoning one last appraisal from their master, as he passes by each canvas. For a moment, one small and perhaps last moment, he stops to admire his favorite, *Mother and Child.* The earthy hues and tender cast render him vulnerable in a way that he appreciates and fears, all at the same time. Next to it hangs the *Tree of Life,* its branches swirling in delicate acceptance of all who come near to partake of the offering. If only its fruit - eternity, as he interprets - were attainable by any other means.

God has abandoned us, his father grumbles in his head, *therefore, it is up to us to create our own heaven.*

He shoves down the memory and forces his heels to turn away from the painting.

At the end of the hallway, he turns in to the security room. A wall of monitors greets him with a blast of blue light, in stark contrast to the pale guards who sit vegetative beneath the screens.

"What is the status of credential log-out?" he inquires, standing at the threshold.

"Like usual around this time, man." The guard wheels his chair around, unsurprised at the interruption. "Ninety-two percent logged out. Still have the techs cleaning up in the Marlene room, security, and you." He holds his hands out, nothing more to say.

"Byron is gone already?" Quinton gives the security a reason for his checking in.

"Just left right before you got here." The guard replies.

Quinton nods his head and glances up at the screens. The clean-up crew wheels out a massive body-bag, on their way to the incinerator. They've done the hard work already, which means the rest should be fast. Fifteen minutes, at most. The process was made to be quick and easy for a reason.

On a different screen, he catches a glimpse of a guard walking past the front door on routine patrol. He points to the screen, "Tell the new guy to cut his hair. He should have never gotten away with that in the first place." He turns away and walks out the door, but before shutting the guard back in his post, mentions one last thing. "I'll be working late today."

The guard nods his head.

He heads back to his office, taking his time. Inside the quaint cube of exact proportions is a standing desk with an oversized monitor. It is placed adjacent to a window that overlooks a nearby golf course. The skeletons of maples stretch their barren arms into the cold Georgia sky, praising the glory of hibernation. Instead of snow, the hills roll with a blanket of decaying leaves, knitted with brown and orange. Not another building is in sight from his view, save for a lonely golf clubhouse.

On the opposite wall of the computer sits a Japanese export table of modest size with intricate carvings of flora and scrolling clouds, held up by legs comprised of rising dragons. The table was a piece from the Meiji period, a time not too long ago when Japan moved from the ancient belief system to a more modern and realistic era, but without sacrificing culture or tradition. His father passed, leaving the table to him. Culture was important to the family, and this was one of few pieces left from the migration to America. His father tried hard to balance the families' Japanese heritage while still accommodating American values. He didn't appreciate the effort growing up, and now, since his father's passing, the importance has become clear to him. To him, the table represents his life and work. Reinventing the old with a new approach, without cutting the roots. Creating something out of something, because there is no such thing as nothing. Not yet.

Atop the table sits a bonsai Juniper, standing merely a foot tall, gnarled and perfectly pruned to resemble a castle dotted with miniature trees. Old, leafless trunks tower above the greenery, carved naturally enough to camouflage years of meticulous control. The tree was a gift from Byron, an unassuming stereotype given under the premise of innocence. When Quinton first saw the tree, he bit back a dagger meant to remind Byron of his bumbling American-ness. Ironically, he had grown to like the dumb thing over the few years spent at Kelim Tekhnologies, despite his initial adverse reaction. Byron genuinely didn't know any better of it, and likely spent a good penny.

The clock on the wall reads 5:57, more than fifteen minutes since the cleanup crew finished up their process.

He walks to the table and picks up a tiny pair of pruning clips and snips a few rogue leaves that have escaped their form. The difference is minute. Only an experienced eye would have noticed, and few would have bothered scrutinizing.

You're ready now. Everyone is gone. The Eidolon hovers to his side, a dark flit persistently escaping through his peripheral vision. Quinton nods, takes a deep breath, and calms his shaking hand.

He replaces the clippers gently, an act that demands ritual for such a particular process. As though a stage of the ritual, he kneels onto his knees, closes his eyes, and whispers, "*Akuji mi ni tomaru.*"

He reaches his hand underneath the table and procures a Smith and Wesson model 500 with a ten-and-a-half-inch barrel, pulls back the hammer, places the muzzle against his temple, and pulls the trigger.

The wall shimmers with a dark red the likes to make Jackson Pollock jealous, while an iPhone vibrates to the rhythm of Marimba on the stand-up desk and flickers a bright light in tandem with the upbeat.

1.

*"**The wife sprang up**, with her hair standing out from her head like flames of fire. 'Then I will go out too,' she said, 'and see if it will lighten my misery, for I feel as if the world were coming to an end.'"* Everett closes the book, heaves a sigh, and kicks his leg off the side of the bed. "And they all lived happily ever after."

"Daddy! That's not the end. You always skip the scary parts." Julianna smacks Everett on the leg, her black curls wiggling from the impact.

"Sure, it is," Everett grimaces beneath the shade of overgrown dirty blond hair. Two months overdue, he reminds himself. Tomorrow, he'll go to the barber. "That's it. There was no gift for the stepmother because she was mean and the story ends. Just like that."

"No, it's not. She gets smashed by a big rock." Julianna frowns, genuinely upset about the loss of story, and snuggles deeper into the comforter as though the conversation turned boring.

"Hey, how do you know that?"

"You also skipped the part where she cuts off the boy's head."

"Whoa, whoa now! That's not this story. What story are you talking about?"

"I thought you said it was bad to lie, Daddy." She picks up a stuffed princess and marionettes the arms in a soft dance. She's always

singing, and when she isn't singing aloud, she has
a song in her head.

"You're right honey. I shouldn't lie. And
you," Everett noogies her head, a little too hard.
"shouldn't know the scary parts of the story.
Especially right before bed."

"Ow, that hurt." She rubs her head.

"Sorry." He pokes her in the stomach,
guaranteed giggle on command. "But really. Who
read the other parts of the story to you?" He gives
her a playful lazy eye, trying hard not to make her
feel uncomfortable so she'll actually spill the
beans rather than pretend to not know.

"Bastion." She mumbles shyly. "But only
'cause I annoyed him lots!"

"Well, that's good for you to look out for
your brother, but he shouldn't have done it. And
you shouldn't be bothering him either." He gives
her the more serious eyebrow raise to emphasize.

"Okay."

"You going to be okay going to sleep?"

"Ugh," she groans, "I'm four and a half
years old Dad. I can handle a little scary."

"You're way too mature for four years
old. Don't think about it too much. Last time you
woke me up in the middle of the night after
saying the same thing."

"That was when I was only four and a
quarter!"

"Alright, but no more." Everett pulls the
sheets up to her chin and tucks it around her
shoulders. "Goodnight, lovebug."

"Leave the nightlight on?" She gives him the puppy eyes, glossy with anticipation of the dark.

"Always." Of course. He'll be roused in a few hours to talk her out of it. Just like last week. Bastion is getting a more serious talk this time. Being a book worm can't always get him off the hook. Perhaps, Everett thinks, he'll just make Bastion wake up in the middle of the night to tend to her as his punishment.

He hustles down the stairs where his wife is laid back on the couch, her face lit up by the screen saver on the T.V. vacillating over a fake picture of the earth. With how busy life is these days, movie night is a rarity. At least, movie night that travels outside the spectrum of the Family genre.

Olivia pops an eyebrow at him, breaking her trance from social media. "Well, how do you feel about your first week on the new job so far?"

"Glamorized cardio. I haven't been that bored since active duty." Everett drops onto the couch and heaves a big sigh.

"Did you get written up for that hair?" Olivia points up and down his head and smirks.

"No one even noticed." Everett looks away. "No one important, anyway. But I'll get it cut. Tomorrow."

"Uh huh." Olivia turns back to her phone, closes the screen out, and tosses it on the couch between them. "You can't be getting that shaggy with your size, babe. You look like a cyclops with two eyes. Gon' get yourself fired, like last time."

Everett drops his head back. "Having a six-foot-five caveman roaming the place is a bonus for them as far as I'm concerned. And that last job was different."

"And the one before that?"

"Liv," Everett cranks his neck back her direction. Her dark eyes search his face, as thick shelled as eggs on the outside but behind the hardened exterior, he can see the soft concern. "It's different this time. This job has potential, and I don't think I'm going anywhere, locks or not. Of course, I'll still get it cut, but I'm not worried about it. They like me."

"This job is as reliable as active duty but with a shiny cherry on top. Sometimes, I think you miss it." Olivia crosses her leg over and picks up an unsuspecting glass of wine. "But I'm glad you like it."

"I'm tellin' ya babe. You gotta trust me. And I don't miss the army."

Olivia responds by taking a sip of the wine. A long, quiet sip.

"I'll cut the hair myself before work in the morning if I have to."

"Oh, dear God, please don't do that." Olivia's mouth contorts, revealing stark white teeth masked with burgundy. "I swear if I find your nappy locks in my bathroom sink," she pauses, unsure of to what degree to threaten him.

Everett smiles, lips glossed with the proverbial excrement bliss.

"Just don't." Olivia sighs and shakes her head, looking to the side.

Everett kicks his legs up on the recliner and releases a victorious sigh. "Brooklyn 99 or The Office?"

"Actually," she pauses for effect, picking up the remote. "I was thinking something completely different."

"Oooh, is it a home video?" He grabs a handful of popcorn and jams it into his mouth, deliberately smashing butter on his face to emphasize the suggestion.

"Ha! In your dreams buddy."

"Oh, come on. I'd pay eight dollars a month for that, no questions asked." Maybe not the best joke, in retrospect.

"Really? Isn't that a bit steep compared to your deployment budget?"

"Oh ho, ho. Right. Let's go back there again huh. Not exactly the sweaty night I was thinking of."

She laughs. She always had the best sense of humor. Though he could tell the joke did sting a little. In no way did he mean it to call her cheap. *This is why you think before you speak, Everett Bailey.*

"The hooker PTSD is that bad, huh?"

"Oh, terrible. Too much hair. And they had dirt in their-"

"Okay too far There's a line. I'm not one of your squad buddies, remember? There's a reason I didn't sign up."

"Some of them even had beards. Just… horrible." He grins at her, even though she's completely turned her attention away and ignores him.

"Babe, I need something serious. I'm tired of jokes. Everything is a joke to you."

"Huh," He stiffens his back and frowns, nodding his head. "Sorry for trying to make life a little more jovial. I guess."

"I didn't mean it like that." She sighs and turns on the T.V. "I just meant I want to watch something different. I'm just in a different mood is all."

"Hey, I mean, do what you want." He says, "I've had my fill of intense, but I understand. No big deal. I handled Afghanistan. I can handle bad T.V."

She glares at him and ignores the dig, to his relief, "Just this once is all I'm asking. I can't handle Jake Peralta's idiot grin right now."

"Better watch what you say about my boy," He teases, "Sorry. Habit. You're right. Let's switch it up."

"I mean like, serious-serious. I miss Black Mirror."

He laughs. "You know, Liv, if the only thing we ever fight about is what to watch, I'm okay with that. Queue it up." He smiles and squeezes her leg. "Whatever we do, it doesn't matter. As long as I get to do it with you."

She raises an eyebrow and bites her lip. "We'll save that for later."

"Oh, now you got jokes? That's not fair." He scoots a little closer, carefully pulling the popcorn over with him. "Where did we leave off? It's been a while."

...

Everett lays back on the couch, his head cocked back just enough to rest but not so much as to look as though he's in full sleep mode. The darkness closes in around his eyes as he struggles to keep them open. Two episodes in and already they are both too exhausted to make it for a third. Hashtag parent life.

He rolls his head to the side and peeks at Olivia curled up against the arm of the couch, her feet situated strategically underneath his leg for warmth. The wine has done its duty for the day, ahead of schedule as made clear by the remaining liquid still in the glass.

The show lulls out of one episode to the next, more quickly than they used to. That's how they get the hook in. Not enough time between shows to decide if it's worth one more. He leans his head back again. Let it play. Perhaps it will help him sleep.

...

Gun chambers rack in Everett's head. Is it from the show or a dream? A voice mumbles in the background, *We gotta take them out if humankind is gonna carry on in this world.*

The sound of dress shoes clanking against tile taps in his head. A different voice rolls out, separate from the previous one as though an alternate dimension shimmered into view. *Was it successful?*

That voice. Everett knows that voice like he knows his own father's.

If there's such thing as too successful, sir, then this is it.

Good. And he'll be activated when we need him?

He cracks open an eye, but is it in real life or the dream? Is there a difference between the two? Through blurry vision he sees the coiled line of a drip system leading from his arm. He twitches his finger against the tube, curious.

The clacking shoes get louder as they approach his bedside. *I assume he's in full stasis at the moment?*

At the moment. This is, sir, an unpredictable experiment. I recommend another dose of the tranquilizer at the top of the hour.

I recommend you shut up and leave now, doctor. Everett opens his eye a little more, enough to see a pair of black, glossy shoes duck-toed at the foot of his bed. One of them turns to him as the sound of a door closing muffles in his ear. The other shoe follows. Is there a man attached to the shoes?

The scratching of a chair sliding over tile abuses his sensitive ears. He hears a voice, the same man's voice, but not in the same way. The words trickle into his brain like a worm slithered in through his ear canal, *What an amazing specimen. My friend, you will set me free.*

The man sits and folds his hands between his legs. Everett pulls his neck up in an attempt to raise his head and see the man's face but drops back down under the pressure on his brain.

The man speaks, *You like the shoes?* He taps a foot and gestures at his shoes with his hands. *I see you checking them out. Cole Haan. I'd offer to buy you a pair, but they don't produce this style anymore. Did I do a good shine on them, soldier?* The man laughs.

Everett engages his throat to speak but only a crackle comes out. Then, a sweet rumble of noise on chords like oil on hinges, *I can hear your thoughts,* he says, pointing a lazy finger upward to nothing.

The man laughs again. *Well then, I've got big plans for you, son.* The man twists a ring on his finger, silver with a black stone.

The other dimension interrupts with screaming and gunfire. Everett snaps out of the dream and onto his feet, pulling at his side for the gun that isn't there. Ugly white faces with rat-sharp teeth taunt him from the T.V. screen, creatures that look like Michael Myers mated with a possum and produced a whole litter of demons.

"What!" Olivia gasps behind him, her voice swallowed by the gunfire coming from the show. "Is everything okay?" She jumps to her feet, shuffling a blanket off.

"Yeah, yeah. Just," He closes his eyes and puts a hand to his head. "Having a dream."

"Not again." Olivia touches his arm and looks at the T.V. She grabs the remote and turns it off, then steps in between Everett and the screen. "I'm so sorry."

"You didn't know. It happens."

"It wouldn't have," She reaches around his waist and looks up at him, her eyes pained with regret.

"Don't worry about it. Let's just go to bed." He smiles and wipes her face, then kisses her.

...

A yellow light flickers. Gibo sits alone, unsupervised. She shudders and moans, her cylindrical frame warming up in tandem with the timer counting down.

3:26:59.

She is twenty point three meters long by two point zero three meters in diameter, lined by thirteen oscillating silver mirrored superconducting magnets. The magnets start the spin at a slow pace, gradually increasing to 343 miles per second, the exact speed of sound.

24

Common misconception had the assumption that the faster the collider spun, the better the chances. In reality, it wasn't about speed. It was about accuracy.

Accuracy in quantities.

Sizes.

Air quality control.

Hope.

No, not hope.

Faith.

2:03:11.

Frost begins to form on the metallic surface of Gibo. She is an ouroboros, the snake with her head in the physical and her tail in…

No one knows.

No one, but Quinton.

On the other side of Gibo sits a glass chamber custom made to contain the largest of land mammals. With each new experiment came a new requirement of size. Up the ante.

However, this particular experiment took no consideration of size. Rather, value.

A very precise value.

Activists would have the world think that all biological life is equally valuable, but the reptilian brain, when challenged, says otherwise.

In the center of the chamber, a pinkish-red swirl of a worm forms midair. The worm takes on flesh and multiplies, branching out like rogue grapevines attempting to attach to the nearest object, of which there are none. Ends split upon ends splitting and take the form of a human, as though a medical textbook had come to life, revealing the sensitive underlining of a nervous system.

Tendons stretch between the places where joints continue expansion, both quickly becoming covered in red tissue, followed by the milky layers of skin upon skin until an epidermis is accomplished. Hair and fingernails sprout.

The chest expands and holds in an eternity of spiritual expeditions, of which only the dead are familiar, then releases the secret in the form of intangible carbons like a scattered jigsaw puzzle that spills out and spreads like a cancer cell experiencing rapid, disconnected meiosis.

Controlled pandemic metastasis.

Quinton opens his eyes.

00:00:00.

2.

Everett and Olivia lie on the early morning sheets, yin-yanged together after a wake-up call meant to make up for the previous night's misfortune.

A phone vibrates on the nightstand, startling Everett.

Blocked call.

"Tell me they don't want you in early today." Oliva noses over lazily, her coarse black hair stuck to the side of her face.

"I don't know about this one babe." His tone is dry. "Something doesn't feel normal."

She cocks her head and glares.

"I have to." He sighs, and she holds her breath.

He clicks accept. "Bailey."

"Are you alone?" Major Viggo's voice rattles on the other end.

"Yes, sir." Everett sits up straight and pulls on his boxers. He keeps his eyes off Olivia but can feel the heat emanating from her body in waves.

"Your mission has changed. Get something to write with. Not your phone."

He shoots up, running to his desk to scramble for a pen and paper. Behind him, Olivia groans.

The voice on the other line continues, "Travel northbound only. Avoid all potential personnel contact. Your DTG is 170500 Romeo

Foxtrot Echo Bravo Mike Oscar November 20 do you need me to repeat?"

"No sir." He finishes scribbling out the code.

"Very good. Coordinates to follow." The line goes dead.

He tosses the phone on the desk and decodes the time, already knowing subconsciously the result. "Tomorrow." He mumbles, shaking his head. "They're changing up the mission that soon. I just got this job."

"What was that?" Olivia slings bare legs over the edge of the bed and pulls a shirt over her head.

"New mission."

"Is this how it's going to be?" She fluffs her hair out over her shoulder and sighs. "A new job every other day?"

"I don't know, too soon to tell. But I have to-" The phone vibrates again. Blocked caller. She raises her eyebrow, and he puts up a gentle hand, "One minute."

She grunts and walks to the bathroom. "Whatever."

He picks up the phone, not bothering with a greeting. A mechanical voice reads off a series of numbers, "34 POINT 622001 DASH 84 POINT 105342." Pause, repeat, end.

For a minute, he sits at the desk, unscrambling the message between the pen and the maps app. With a sigh, he tears off the paper and folds it into a small square then jams it in his wallet.

"When I hear the word *mission* I hear *long, overseas trip*." Olivia mumbles from the bathroom.

"That's not what it is. They promised."

"Uh huh." She grunts, touching up her makeup in the mirror. "It's six thirty, and the kids need breakfast. You know they'll be up soon."

He walks to the threshold between him and the bathroom and leans on the wall. "I'm sure it's just a different aspect of the same job. This is one of those covert places that does some weird stuff."

"Are you supposed to be telling me that?" She glances at him, pausing the brush stroke on her cheek, then resumes the routine. "All you've ever wanted since you got discharged was to get back in. I think you're sabotaging, if I'm being honest. What's so wrong with being home? With us? With me?" She drops her hands and shakes her head at the mirror, then pulls out a nearby tissue and wipes her eyes. "Really? I just put that on."

"I just don't know what to do with myself. I've been government property the second I stepped out of high school." He grabs a pair of jeans steps into them.

"I hate it when you say that."

"It's true."

"No, it's not. That's in your head. You are no one's property." She snaps.

"Except yours." He winks, pulling on a shirt.

Olivia smiles, then bites it back, struggling to hold it in. "Don't try to charm me, mister. I'm immune."

"Sometimes." He grumbles without thinking.

"You're a real piece of work." Olivia's smile disappears for real, and she stomps off to the closet.

You had her, and then you lost her with that dumb mouth. Everett sighs. "Why is this such a problem? I make good money. *Really* good money, doing this."

"You think it's about the money?" Olivia's muffled voice thumps from the walk-in closet.

"You know what I mean."

"No, I don't." She walks out and brushes past him to the room. "Enlighten me."

"I *do* want to be home. Of course. I just feel…" He pauses, looking for the right word, "useless."

She flops down on the edge of the bed and frowns. "You're not. I know you don't see that, and I know this is important. I just wish it were different. I want to eat my cake and have it too."

He nods. "Me too. But I don't even know what my cake is."

"That's the strangest thing to say, even with context." She laughs and slaps the side of his leg, then stands back up. "I just don't feel right about it. There's something wrong. I don't trust them."

"But do you trust *me?*" He leans in closer.

She looks up into his eyes, her dark curls framing her face effortlessly, grimaces and says, "Not really."

…

A cell phone lights up the dark corner of a bed stand and rumbles in a rhythmic pattern. The vibration acts as a ringer on its own, causing Byron to crack open a ruddy eye and curse.

Bryon answers. "What is it." As for greetings, you get what you get at this hour.

His face turns grim and he curses again, swinging his feet out from the sheets. He slams the phone down and pulls on a pair of pants that had been strangled on the floor next to his boots.

A woman turns over and mumbles, "Everything okay?"

"I have to go to the office."

"Will you be back soon?"

He sighs and slides his wedding ring onto his finger. "No."

"Then I guess I'll see you at work."

He winces, "Don't say those kinds of things out loud."

"Not sure what difference it makes but okay." She rolls back over and is silent as he finishes dressing. He doesn't know what difference it makes either. It's almost as though saying it is confirming it. When he's with her, the actions feel different. Numb. Set apart. But words…

Those mean something.

Thirty minutes later he is standing in Quinton's office, the sun rising over the low hills, casting a speckled pattern of leaves on the walls. The shadow is interrupted by chaotic splashes of blood, darkened to a crispy brown after a night spent oxidizing.

"Has anyone else seen this?" Byron looks at Jason.

"I followed protocol exactly, sir."

"Good. Call in the clean-up crew." Oh, Quinton. What have you done? Or was it you? "The feds are onto us." Byron mumbles, more to himself than anything.

"Sure looks like it." Jason's voice startles Byron, but before he can say anything Jason is distracted with a voice on the other end of his phone. Doing as he's told.

Clean up on aisle nine. Protocol instigating dissociation. In this business, when friends die, they become evidence. Survival is always impersonal. Byron tries to shove the idea of the incinerator out of his head but nothing else can be done. It's just a body now. Maybe he's in shock. Maybe he's just a horrible person. But now isn't the time for a psychological reading.

"Jason," He grunts as the assistant hangs up the phone. "What brought you in so early?"

"I got an alert from Gibo. She was receiving some type of activity. I've yet to check in on her, due to, well, obvious reasons."

"Okay. Check all the archives for tampering. Notate anything that looks out of place. Report back to me ASAP. I'll check on Gibo. Then we're shutting this facility down until further notice. Clear out all personnel but security when clean-up is through."

Jason hesitates.

"Is there a problem, Campbell?" Byron bites his tongue.

"The tablet is missing, sir." Jason takes a sideways glance at the ground.

"What do you mean the tablet is missing? Didn't you have it last?"

"I left it with Quinton yesterday. Haven't seen it since."

"Well, you better find it! In the meantime, I'll have to check in manually. Find that tablet or we're all screwed."

"Will do." Jason rushes off on his mission.

Byron growls to himself and stalks down the stark hallway. The fluorescents flicker in their usual code, alien and ominous. He thinks for a moment that perhaps they are trying to tell him something. Leave this place. Go back to the Bahamas and never return. Of course, that could very well just be his own desires. Now that Quinton is gone, the job is up to him. Whether that's finding another engineer tech to teach the process or doing it himself, it's work all the same.

Exactly what he doesn't want. He curses himself for being more worried about vacation than the death of a friend, then waves it off, ascribing the selfish reaction to shock. *Yeah, shock. That's what this is.*

The tall double doors glimmer, reflecting his haggard face back to him in the silvery sheen. He pulls back a rogue strand of hair and sighs, then pushes his face against the scanner to let the laser molest his eye. Since utilizing that thing, he could swear his vision in that particular eye had been getting worse. Of course, that could just be normal aging. Paranoia comes with the territory.

The machine sits idle, it's lone eye peering at him like a fox through a patch of leaves. The massive cylinder spirals down the center of the tiled room, so clean it could be a mirror. Byron walks to the monitors and scans again, enters a unique passcode and overrides the firewall, attaining access to the SHIVA program. A golden sphere swirls on the main screen, an arachnid pair of arms unfurling on each side in a blurry motion that folds back into the sphere. The inner circle of the sphere fades into twelve angled separations, with a dark center. The gold turns to black as the sphere dissipates into the background and reveals the secrets hidden beneath.

Nothing has changed. Nothing has been touched.

Gibo oscillates, then purrs back to an idle.

He cocks his head curiously to the side and glares at the machine as though she were a student interrupting silent reading time.

"What the…" the words trail off as he abandons the monitor and walks cautiously to the machine. Slowly, he places a hand on the cylinder, fighting back the blood sugar shakes.

Already, he can feel the heat of the machine without even touching it. The metal should be cold, even at an idle. The insulation is state of the art, especially considering this particular art. His hand makes contact.

"Mr. Dempsey, I think you need to see this."

Byron twirls around, his face pale.

Jason mirrors Byron's startled image from the doorway.

He follows Jason out of the room and pauses one last second before exiting, his hand on the doorknob. Through his peripheral vision, he notices something out of place on the glass chamber connected to the collider.

He turns to look, his skin tingling. The chamber doors are open. Only two people have the clearance and authority to open those doors.

And he is one of them.

Everett steps out of his lifted red GMC 3500 and shifts his boots on the blacktop. The sun threatens his sensitive blue eyes but not his white-boy skin. Too cold for that. Olivia always teases him about burning so easy for such a beach bum. What's

worse is the lack of tan on the outset of the burn.
All that red skin for no reward, while Olivia sits
back with her perfect melanin-enhanced natural
sunblock and laughs. If only it were beach season
now.

He heaves the door shut and frowns.
Something is wrong.

The air on this property always had that
odd feel to it, like an ancient Native American
burial ground. The kind of place that might have a
sign posted, *You Don't Belong Here.* He thinks
of his days scouting neighborhoods to get
contracts for sales of windows and solar panels,
trudging right past the little gold-on-black *No
Soliciting* sign tacked compulsively on the top
stair, as though an angry garden gnome finally
had enough and thought, 'That'll tell 'em.' Then
huffed through a rathole into the house, hammer
slung over the shoulder.

Just play stupid, his boss would tell him.
Ignore the sign. Knock anyway.

He approaches the front door to Kelim
Tekhnologies and hesitates. What little dwarf will
he upset today? His morning surprises left him no
time for a barber. The boss already threatened
him yesterday right at the end of shift. But what
did it matter? Would he even be here tomorrow
anyway? What is this new assignment coming
down the pipeline? *Let him huff,* he thinks.

"Bailey," Edgar Cofield coughs from
behind the security scanner counter.

"Sir." Everett pulls out his badge and slings it around his neck as he walks to the security room.

"High alert today. Had some trouble last night." Cofield adjusts a setting on the scanner, his eyes still on the display screen.

"Oh yeah?" Everett opens the door to the security room and clocks in on the monitor.

"Yeah, apparently one of the bosses offed himself."

"Wow." Everett stops just short of grabbing his pistol. "I thought all the windows had that security seal on them for that reason."

"Ha, ha. You're a cold-hearted S.O.B. Bailey. The man shot himself."

Everett holsters the gun. "How did he get a gun in here?"

"Top dog. They do what they want." Cofield breaks his focus on the security display and lifts an eyebrow. "It gets weirder though. You've got military background, right?"

"Unfortunately."

"Check this out," Cofield looks up and motions Everett into the security room, then cracks his neck in a double-take. "You kiddin' me, Bailey? You trying to get me in trouble with that hair?"

"I had a family emergency." Everett lies, "I'll do it right after shift today."

Cofield shakes his head, "Doesn't matter much at the moment anyway. The boss that's been hounding me is the one who blew his brains out. I'm guessing he probably won't bug me about it anymore." He pulls up the review security monitor. "But do it anyway."

"Will do." Everett flops down in a rolling chair and waits.

"You do any of that secretive stuff in the service?" Cofield chews at a square brown mustache, his puffy cheeks warbling from the motion.

"Nah. I was a cook." Everett lies again, but this time with intention. No one needs to know what he did. Even he didn't want to.

"Lame. Well tell me what you think anyway. You *might* know more than me. The most experience I have is driving armored trucks for banks." Cofield puffs his chest a bit, a difficult gesture considering his extended abdomen. "Got shot at once." He glances at Everett for approval.

Everett nods in appeasement.

"We'll save that story for another time though. Look at this." Cofield points at the screen. Through blurry green, Everett watches with a frown on his face as a naked man walks out of a 'screening' room where the techs do their experiments. This is the first time he has been allowed to see this part of the operation, something that is supposedly above his pay grade, according to Cofield.

"If you're showing me this, does that mean I'm getting a promotion?"

Cofield furrows his eyebrows and points at the screen without looking at it, then speaks in broken iterations, "Naked man appears out of nowhere and you want a promotion?"

"It was a joke. I thought I wasn't high level enough to monitor the screening rooms…" He attempts the explanation to Cofield's incredulous face but gives up. "Never mind. Why is there a naked dude walking around? When was this?"

"Right after we had a power outage."

Everett cocks his head. "How long was the outage?"

"About three and a half hours. Started right after the last clock out."

"I thought we had security around the clock?" Everett leans forward and watches the screen switch from the hallway to the lobby as the man walks through.

"Normally we do. But every once in a while," Cofield looks around, then whispers, "the boss has a special request." Cofield rubs the fingers and thumb of one hand together, then winks.

Everett watches the man on the screen walk out the front doors and disappear into the night. *This is connected to the new mission. Has to be.*

"And get this. All the power went down, right? But the generators kicked in. Guess what room sucked up most of that energy?"

"I'm going to go out on a limb and say the one where the naked guy came from."

Cofield smacks his lips and nods. "Bingo."

"Did the security cameras go down with the power?"

"For about fifteen minutes."

"That's awfully long. Why didn't they come right back up? There should only be a few seconds of lull at most."

Cofield raises an eyebrow at Everett. "Just a cook, huh?"

"Where do you want me today?" Everett changes the subject, counting the doors on the screen in his head, coming to the number six.

"You've got no conclusions on all this?" Cofield says, pulling his chin into his second one.

"I told you, I was a cook. Your guess is as good as mine." Everett stands up and adjusts his belt.

Cofield shakes his head and sighs, "Well, it's going to be a weird day, that's for sure." He closes out the display. "Why don't you patrol inside today? I'll put Hofmann on outside when he gets here. I know you were just a cook, but we need all the experience in here that we can get. Just in case. And Hofmann, well, I think his previous job was loss prevention at Ross if you know what I mean. Not quite our caliber."

"Will do." Everett nods, biting his tongue, and walks out of the security room. For a second, he stares at the lobby, calculating the whereabouts of the office. "Where did you go, little dwarf?"

40

He mumbles to himself and walks down the hallway.

While the situation is certainly serious, Everett is sure the cops won't get too involved. Lots of hands in lots of pockets, and Kelim Tekhnologies will want to keep this on the DL for sure. Which means the cleanup crew likely already got to the room. But did they clear out or just mop up is the question.

He fidgets with his night stick as he nonchalantly stalks the hallway. *Interesting training program for the security at this place*, he thinks, *nothing like full immersion with no warning.*

Most security positions would come with at least a tour around the facility and a specified route. He wonders if the lack of planning is due to strategical spontaneity or poor management. He had never seen the former work in real life. Of course, that's what happens when you hire someone out of nepotism. *That'd be you, too, Bailey,* he reminds himself, *at least in a way.*

Olivia's uncle landed him this position, ultimately, lodging Everett between the CIA and Uncle Sam's misguided children program. While the government offered him assistance through a veiled program meant only for a select few, it didn't normally work out as well as this one had. Of course, that came with a price. The one he was looking at now. Immediate change without explanation. He had been lucky so far to stay in his hometown, and now he wasn't so sure it would stay that way. Olivia might be right. Something does feel wrong about this new mission. The same feeling in his gut that wrecked him the first deployment creeped in after that phone call.

The sixth door on the right comes into sight and he slows his pace, listening close. With one of two main bosses down for the count, that means about half the workforce is out of work and likely stayed home. At least.

He checks his six o'clock and tries the door handle. Locked, like any good secret warehouse.

With a swiftness, he pulls the master key card out of his pocket that he swiped from Cofield earlier and motions it over the lock, popping the door open. He swings narrow and slips through as quick as a mouse, unlocking his holster at the same time and missing his days in theater when his squad was by his side.

"Oh! Hey," A tech pops out from behind the desk and breaks a sweat immediately. "I uh, just tidying up some things and I'll be out of your way." He slides a pen into his breast pocket and Everett takes note of the name: *J. Campbell.*

"Not a problem," Everett feigns business as usual, keeping as close to the corner of the room as possible, directly underneath the security camera. Was Cofield not watching? The shmuck was probably looking at some questionable anime on his phone again. Everett had caught that over the shoulder a few times in the last couple days. The dude had it bad.

The man named Campbell smiles awkwardly, looks at the desk as though he wants something, decides the better for it and walks out avoiding eye contact.

The door closes and Everett breathes in. Despite his experience in the military, he is way out of bounds with this. Not only that, but he really doesn't know what he's trying to do. Something is just… wrong.

And it's in here.

He takes his cap off, swipes it upward and pops it over the camera from the side. Cofield will think Wi-Fi is down, and by the time anyone with brains looks at the footage, Everett will be long gone and this Campbell kid might take the fall. Still though, time is valuable.

Everett rushes over to the desk and pilfers through the drawers. Pens. USB storage devices. An old family photo. Odd. But even more odd, just below the photo, sits a conspicuous airline ticket receipt.

With today's departure date.

To Peru.

Check-in at 10:39 pm last night.

Now the question is, was that before, or after the man shot himself?

3.

Cambor Albright, the CEO and owner of *Fifth Helix*, walks across the stage at the Global Initiative 2030 Summit in Austin, Texas. He sports a rainbow colored tie and shoes that glimmer under the blue light like dancing stars in the night sky. He waves as he walks, feigned humility at the applause, a curve on the side of his mouth.

At the podium, Albright shakes hands with the previous speaker, or the "opener" as he likes to think of them. Of course, this is a show. These people are here for entertainment in the form of hope. A story of the future. Albright is the genie, and the stage is his lamp.

The previous speaker walks off the stage with a fangirl smile and Albright takes his place, quelling the applause with a hushing hand.

"Well, I haven't had quite a reception since last night." He pauses for laughter and pushes his glasses to the top of his nose. "No really, you people are lovely. *You* are the reason I'm here.

"Speaking of which, I have great news for you." More applause, and some cheering. "There was a time when I could say that not all news was good news, and that time has come to an end. You've all seen the lights in the skies."

The crowd hushes, a few gasps speckle the room with anticipation. "I'm here to tell you that is no accident. With our recent global operatives working diligently to unify representatives from each country on earth, we have finally come to the long-awaited era of peace. Not just peace from war, famine, pestilence, but a peace that the world has never known. Until now.

"I have been working with world governments on initial contact, which I'm sure you've all suspected was on the horizon. We have reached the peak of that mountain, and I can see the other side. Let me tell you, it's beautiful."

Violent applause erupts, and some stand to their feet while others wipe at their eyes, pretending not to. Albright continues, "Peace between our fellow humans. No more contention or division. Peace that gives you the comfort to let your children walk the streets unharmed, like we did when we were kids. Remember? Peace that destroys all strife with each other.

"For too long, we have seen the suffering of poverty. Poverty has been the driving force behind wars. Not just international wars, but personal ones as well. Division amongst political factions. Heartache at work. Domestic violence. Arguments over politics and football over the Thanksgiving turkey!"

Laughter ripples throughout the auditorium. Albright chuckles, "It is *Poverty* that causes all these evil things, not the human condition. We were not created with such hearts as we have seen for far too long. And yes, I say created.

"It is possible that many truths have come together to reveal the ultimate truth. All along, we have been fighting amongst drawn black lines, scratched on the surface, an invisible hand wedging walls like labyrinths between us. But that black line was merely a figment, an illusion. The curtain has been drawn back, and we are finally ready to step through to the other side.

"We have been talking to the Galactic Federation," He pauses, letting the words sink in. "Yes, it is *exactly* what you think it is. Until now, the general population has not been ready for First Contact, but we have been discussing global affairs and how to fix them with an advanced race called the *Eidolon*. Before your imaginations go too far, let me tell you they look like us. However, they are taller. Of which many of us will be jealous." More laughter.

"And they have been around since the beginning of time, watching us. Waiting for us to come to them. Waiting to help us settle our wars until the time was right. I know this sounds crazy, but you trust me, right?"

The crowd responds with a vigorous 'yes' and Albright nods. "This is the hope we have all felt for years! I know you want to know more, but as we adjust to cold waters, we must take it slow. The President has made plans to reveal the Eidolon's presence, but these things take time.

"In the meantime, know that wealth is in your future. Not just you individually, but humanity in its entirety. There is enough wealth on our own planet to provide for *every single* global citizen. Unending wealth. Unending happiness. Unending peace.

"We at Fifth Helix have been leading the way to this prosperity, and now it is *everyone's* turn. Follow us. The future is bright. The future is right now."

Albright walks off the stage to a thunderous applause. A man stands in the shadow of the curtain, waiting for him with an applause of his own. "They're going to want more information, and soon. That was only the appetizer." Albright mumbles to the man. "How was the flight over?"

"Fast. Stick to the plan, Cambor. One step at a time. It'll all come together in the right timing."

"Of course, of course. It only worries me that we might have a revolt on our hands if we withhold too much."

The man smirks and pats a hand on his potbelly. "With the kind of technology that the Eidolon have, I wouldn't be too worried even if it did come to that."

Cambor nods and glances at the crowd, still standing in ovation. "You've always been the logical one, Rob. Let's get to that after party. I can hear a Cosmo calling my name."

"Sorry buddy. The crew is ready to go and waiting at the strip. I hope you partied hard enough last night to make up for it." Rob nods and walks to the back door, pushing passed techies and other show-closers.

"But daddy," Cambor grins, "my friends are waiting." He frowns and droops puppy eyes, cocking his Bic-bald head to the side.

Rob sighs, checks his phone, and glares up at Cambor from across the stark room. "One drink."

Cambor smiles. "And a lap dance. Thanks pops. I can take it from here." He turns and walks away, loosening his tie.

"You've got one hour! Otherwise, I'll tell them to leave without you." Rob shakes his head and writes a text.

...

Everett pushes his palm against the steering wheel and maneuvers it to the left, barely noticing a crooked brown road sign that reads Cloverleaf Trail, inconspicuously tucking his truck into the thick of trees with a not so accidental harrumph from the engine. He pulls up into what appears to be private property, but seeing no warning signs, he continues to the most obvious place to park.

Three small storage units appear to his left, and he swings around, pulling the obnoxious truck approximately two car spaces away from the idling jet-black Suburban.

He takes his time shutting off the engine, unplugs his phone from the cord, thinks better of taking it with him and tosses it into the cup holder.

The door cranks open and he hops out, adjusting his jeans unnecessarily. He scans the scenery, more for show than awareness.

The rear passenger window of the Suburban rolls to three-quarter length, and a female voice grunts with a practiced force, "Take a walk."

He sticks his hands in his pockets, glances around, and notices a trail leading north into the

48

thick part of the woods. He nods, "Up that-a-way?"

The window rolls up.

"Typical." He snorts and strolls toward the trail, trying not to look too much at the storage units. Something about them feels familiar, like déjà vu.

The sound of running water comes slowly into the foreground. Around the soft corner he sees the pool of a small waterfall, and next to it the light silhouette of a man sitting on a large stone. His elbows rest on his knees and he is dressed casually, jeans and a rough wooly sweatshirt with rolled up sleeves. His boots are caked with mud, but he appears to be otherwise strikingly clean.

"Beautiful day for a walk." He says, squinting as though anticipating a camera flash.

"Sure is. Nothing like that crisp 0-500 air. Add in a little humidity and you got an almost uncomfortable early morning adventure." He grins stupidly and pulls a chunk of hair behind his ear.

"You talk a lot."

"Only when I'm annoyed."

"You're going to need to stop that." The man puts a grizzly cigar in his mouth and inhales. Everett remembers that it was Major Viggo who called him last night, which means the chances that this man is either the same rank or lower is very unlikely. Couldn't be the same man, the voice is too different.

"Sir, I mean no disrespect, but I'm not active anymore. I've been discharged for over two years. I've been under special placement in my hometown for my duties and also been promised to keep it at that. I'd like to keep my current situation unless another local opportunity comes up." But why did that Quinton fellow buy a ticket to Peru and then kill himself? Everett shakes the thought away.

The man squints hard enough to blind himself, and takes another long drag from the cigar, nodding his head. He lets out the smoke, scratches his barren chin, and croaks, "Well, that's all fine and dandy son. But I'm sorry to say, it's not that simple. You're a smart one, I always figured that. But you're going overseas."

Everett's heartbeat speeds up and he takes in a deep breath through the diaphragm, holding the oxygen in his head for a moment before letting it out. Little forms of meditation, he learned, help him through the PTSD. This is nothing short of similar.

"I hope you have success with your mission, sir, but I won't be on it." He turns on a heel and walks away, doing his best to keep his fists unclenched.

"I saw the property that was flown out. It's not dead."

Everett stops in his tracks, heel lifted off the ground. It's not possible. The man is lying to keep his attention.

"If you'll excuse me, sir," he looks back, but not at the man, "I have a lot to get done. Have a fine day." He continues his walk. How could that be?

As he walks, his feet slow down. A smell fills his nostrils, the musky smell of rotting skunks. He shakes it off and squeezes his eyes. The image of private Daniels skewered on a spike flashes in front of his eyes. A horrendous roar fills his ears, meshed with the sound of frantic gunfire.

He covers his ears and restrains a scream, growling with the pressure.

"Listen son," the man stands behind him, careful not to touch him. "This ain't the usual routine. We're breaking some rules here and it's for a good reason. You want that thing, and others like it, comin' over here and causin' a raucous?"

Others like it? He had assumed there was only one, and that it was dead.

The man continues, "You can bet one thing," Everett turns to see him blowing out another cloud of smoke. "If we're breaking the rules already, ain't nothing stopping us from breaking some more to make sure we do what we have to do. You understand?"

"Good luck on your mission, sir." Everett salutes the man lazily, which might have been a bad idea in retrospect, and walks solidly to the truck.

The engine turns and he backs out, wheeling the rear end in the general direction of the trail. The man stands in the same spot, watching him drive away.

At the house, he quietly opens the door. Olivia sits at the counter, sipping on orange juice and staring at the wall. Breakfast plates dot the table, wiped mostly clean. Normally, those would be in the drainer by now.

"Liv?" he cautiously breaks her trance.

She doesn't budge, and mumbles robotically, "When do you leave?"

He heaves a sigh. The poor girl has been convinced he was going since the ominous phone call. Has she even slept?

"Honey, I told you. I'm not going anywhere. And you were right. They do want me overseas." He sets his keys down on the counter and sits.

Olivia nods, biting her lower lip, and pulls back a strand of hair. She blinks rapidly and sniffs, then puts her face in her hands and groans, her chest convulsing to the offbeat of her sobs.

He puts his arm around her shoulder and squeezes her tight.

"I was sure," she whimpers, "so sure you were as good as gone again. I don't know why. I know it's not logical. I haven't even completely gotten over what happened last time you were gone for so long," She shakes her head and looks up at him, guilt seeping from her eyes into the day-old mascara blurred across her cheekbone. "I could *feel* it, Everett. Just like last time. I don't want you to go back."

"Me neither. And last time was completely different. There was an element of stress that was unexpected. We managed. We got through it." He rubs her back, and she cringes. "And I'm here now." He pulls her chin up and wipes the mascara. The act does nothing but bring comfort and extend the damage of makeup. He smiles, kisses her forehead, and puts a hand down on the counter.

"I'd ask how it went, but if that's the final answer, I don't want to know."

"Oh, that's the final answer. And I even still have my current job." *As far as I know.* He opens the refrigerator door and scans for breakfast. "Bastion leave already?" He mumbles.

"Yeah, I made him walk this morning. I couldn't get myself together to make the drive. Julianna is still in bed. Want me to scramble you a few eggs?"

"Nah. Turns out I'm not that hungry yet. Think I'll take advantage of my sick day and play some Black Ops until I'm hungry enough for leftovers." He glances at Olivia, hoping for at least a small show of humor, but she is still in a cloud.

She picks up her phone and scrolls through some form of social media, another attempt at comfort. The phone vibrates in her hand, and she answers.

"Hello?" She sniffles and pulls the phone away for a second, clearing her throat. "He's what?"

Everett shuts the refrigerator door and looks at her face.

She laughs nervously, "Well it's only ten minutes. He walked today so maybe it's taking him a little longer."

The voice on the other line goes for a short moment and she responds with a shaky voice, "Okay, yeah. Please let me know. Thank you."

She puts the phone down and shoots him a dagger, thankfully not meant for him. "Bastion hasn't showed up yet. He's ten minutes passed the bell."

Everett's heart drops to his stomach. It's only ten minutes, he tells himself. That's not that much.

He nods and takes a deep breath.

"Is there something more you need to tell me?" She reads the look on his face. "Everett?"

He is frozen.

She raises her voice, "What happened Everett! What did they tell you?"

"I don't know." He grabs the keys and rushes to the front door.

"What's going on!" She yells in the background.

"Mommy?" A little voice bounces down the stairs.

"Tell me!" She screams, losing control of her emotions.

"It's probably nothing!" he yells back. Olivia stares at the floor, a hand to her nose, sniffling. Everett takes in a breath and puts a hand on her shoulder. "But I need to check. Did he take the usual route?"

"Yes," she stammers, "yes, he did. At least he should have."

"Okay," he points at her from the front door, holding the door halfway open. "You stay here. I'm sure it's nothing. I'll be back soon, okay?"

She stands at the threshold between the living room and kitchen, tears running down her face.

"Mommy, is everything okay?" Julianna stands at the top of the stairs.

"Just fine honey," she nods and forces a smile at her daughter, then turns back to Everett. "Go!"

In the truck, Everett slams the key into ignition nearly breaking the cheap metal and slings the seatbelt over his shoulder in tandem with the swing of the truck backing out of the driveway.

His phone vibrates.

Blocked call.

"What." He answers abruptly.

"Your son is safe." Major Viggo sighs.

Anxiety mixes with adrenaline through his veins, ripping his nervous system in two. Stars ripple around the edges of his eyes, and he pulls over, slamming the truck into park.

The voice continues, "He is in good hands. We have to do what we have to do. Major

General Stockard would like to speak with you again, same place. Asap.”

“You've crossed the line, Major! This is grounds to take you all to court, I don't care how high up any of you are. I'll-”

The line is silent. Everett slams the phone against the steering wheel, barking the horn sporadically. Tears threaten the corners of his red eyes. He rolls down the window and takes a deep breath of the fresh air and opens the phone. He clicks on *Olivia* in the contacts section, puts the truck into drive, and heads northbound, away from the house.

No answer.

...

I didn't really believe it at first when I saw it, because of, well, you know.” Jason looks at the floor as though Quinton's dead body was still there, emanating judgement from a leftover stain. “But check this out. Going through the logs, everything is normal. Checkout times for all personnel ranging around the six o'clock mark. What you'd expect. Even Quinton's, six on the dot. Then there's this.” He points to a particular line on the timeclock log.

“Quinton logs back in at, what, eleven last night?” *To come in and shoot himself?* Byron states the fact flatly, like it wasn't that impressive. The man was a workaholic. No news there. But suicide?

"No. That's another log *out*. No log back in in-between." Jason raises his eyebrows, waiting for a reply.

"That's not possible. Our security is way too tight for even the best covert agents to manipulate."

"I asked security if they ever saw Quinton come back in after logging out at six, and they said no. No Quinton. No strangers. No suspicious break-in type of behavior. The only unusual thing was Comin's leaving a little later than expected, but no red flags. I have them going through the cam-logs now." Jason straightens and takes a deep breath. "All I know is that something is wrong. There's more."

Jason pulls open another window on the monitor, the SHIVA program. He navigates to the collider records.

Byron holds his breath.

Gibo had already behaved strangely, while he was in the room with it, standing in front of the only access to the program. He had convinced himself he was imagining things, but that collider was acting as though it was still going through the routine cooling pulsations from recent usage.

"Marlene has been perfectly normal. No errors or disruptions to report. But Gibo," he pauses for effect, casting a sideways glance at Byron. *Get on with it, man.*

"She's been misbehaving. Look at this. Activity instigated at 6:06, like a regular experiment. Inactivity logged exactly at 9:33. Do you recognize that math?" Jason gestures a hand at the computer.

"Enlighten me." Byron rubs his face, condemning the early morning calculation. All he can calculate at the moment is the inevitable rise in legal fees and those numbers were beginning to outrun his abilities.

"That's the exact time we decoded would take to transmutate a human body."

Byron's heart drops to his knees.

"But we concluded that's not possible. We've never had a successful run." Byron whispers, his hands shaking as he places them on the table for stability.

"Someone disagrees." Jason points at the screen, "because this was recorded as a successful diffusion."

"By who?" Byron knows the answer but doesn't want to verify it to the universe himself by giving it audible recognition.

Jason looks him in the eye, then looks at the blood stain on the floor.

4.

Major General Stockard stands in the same spot Everett left him, a grim look on his face. He doesn't like this any more than Everett does. But it's not his kid that's been, for all intents and purposes, kidnapped.

Everett slams the door and puts his hands up. Amazing. No one steps out of the Suburban. Stockard must either be crazy or overly secure. He has half a mind to rip the man's throat out.

"Too much, too far." Everett barks, walking toward Stockard.

"Operation WhiskerChew." Stockard mutters in response.

Everett stops. *WhiskerChew? Why is that so familiar?* The storage units hover in his peripheral, emanating an energy that makes his chest tighten.

He picks up walking again.

"You were ordered, soldier, to forget. And you did. Well done." Stockard spits to the side, stoic and impassive. "But you didn't forget everything."

"I completed my mission and went home. Nothing more. And I would like my son back now." *I will murder everyone to get him, including you.*

"I'm commanding you to remember the rest. We need the rest of the story. Something happened there, solider, something important." Stockard chews his tongue and watches Everett carefully, hands on his hips like a hot summer day seeking air in all the crevices, nothing more. Nothing less.

"I don't know what you're talking about. But you're going to give my son back to me."

"Daniels isn't dead."

Everett's vision blurs and a headache drills from his brain into his spine as though struck by lightning.

Gunshots.

Screaming.

Bursting eardrums.

Everything is heavy.

Water in the mouth. He's breathing water. Sputtering.

'What happened in theater!'

'Ambush! We were ambushed.'

More water.

'What happened in theater!'

'Nothing! Nothing happened.'

'Who is Daniels?' Blurred faces look over him, no expression.

'Never heard of him!'

'Him?'

Upside down. More water.

'There is no Daniels.'

'What happened in theater!'

More water. Too much blood to the brain. Upside down figures.

'Routine assessment. Nothing reportable.'

Voices echo adjacent. Mission accomplished.

Everett comes back to reality to find himself spitting up blood onto the dirt in front of his face. Another dry heave, a pathetic attempt at a yell, crackling through the lurch.

"The property is in stasis. *You did that.* We need to know how." Stockard's boots sit within arm's reach.

"Why," Everett croaks, "why are you doing this? And why now? Why not then?" he pleads, holding on to the fragments still left unbroken in his mind.

"I told you, son," Stockard grunts empathetically, "it's not that simple. Wish to God it were."

An oil-stained hand appears in front of his face, palm open. A gesture of peace.

Everett places his palms on the dirt and squares his shoulders back, crawls to his feet, and straightens his back. "I wish I could help you, but I blacked out. I don't know what happened."

Stockard squints an eye and cocks his head to the side. "You were informed of the potential of unlikely chances. You agreed."

Everett nods his head. He never told Liv that part. Perhaps he took "unlikely chances" too much at face value.

"Report to base immediately. I had more time set aside for you before, but we've wasted it now on this misunderstanding. Civilian dress. One carry-on. You know the specs."

"Yes, sir." Everett clears his throat. "What about the job?" *Why do you care, Bailey? Why are you going with this? FIGHT IT!*

Stockard nods his head and looks at the ground. His eyes generate a minuscule degree of moisture, hardly enough to notice. The man doesn't like this job. "It's taken care of. You know that."

"Sir," Everett pauses. *Tell him about Peru.* Stockard waits. Everett opens his palms and studies them. *These were made for killing.* "What about my family?"

Stockard strides toward the Suburban and stops, turning slightly, "Bailey,"

"Yes sir." Everett rubs his eyes.

"I haven't lied about a thing. But it ain't what you think either. Don't go making presumptions. That's more than I should have said. Y'understand?" Stockard keeps his eyes on the vehicle with head turned Everett's direction.

"But what about my family?" Everett stares into the distance, his mind fighting between a PTSD stun and reality. His body is robotic, disconnected, a phantom limb dangling off a cadaver.

The Suburban door pops open and Stockard disappears inside. The vehicle remains motionless but has lurched into gear. The window rolls down.

Stockard sighs heavily, "Bailey,"

"Yes, sir."

"We're keeping them all for collateral." The Suburban moves forward, "In a safe place, of course. And all the agencies are aware, so don't go causing a scene, y'understand?"

Everett feels the heat in his face swell to a blister as he holds back a scream.

The Suburban blazes off, leaving a ghostly trail of smoke behind.

5.

Olivia's ears perk up to the sound of
mufflers rolling into the driveway. Her shoulders
drop and she mumbles, "Thank God." With
Everett coming home so soon, the news must be
good. Now the question is, how much of an earful
did he give to Bastion for running late?

The trucks' door shuts, and Olivia rushes
to greet Everett, her hands shaking with the
quelling of adrenaline. On the kitchen counter her
phone vibrates, the gushy pet name "Hubby"
glowing with a trapped anxiety that she would
feel if only she were present.

Another door outside shuts.

Olivia stops in her tracks, a hand on the
couch. Footsteps clack against the concrete
driveway outside, the marker of dress shoes, not
work boots. More than one pair.

"Julianna, go upstairs." Olivia turns back
toward the kitchen.

"Mommy, did you see my princess?"
Julianna looks up from the kitchen table, a crayon
in her hand.

"Upstairs! Now!" Olivia hisses, keeping
her voice low. Her heart sinks as the smile from
her daughter wrinkles into a frown. The girl
thinks she did something wrong. A tear works its
way out of the corner of Julianna's eye and
streaks down her cheek as she swings a leg out
from the chair.

"Sorry, Mommy." She whimpers, leaving her artwork behind.

Olivia kneels and pulls her in tightly, her heart bruising the inside of her chest. "No, I'm sorry baby. You're not in trouble. Mommy just needs you go upstairs for a while, okay?"

Julianna nods in return, gripping the crayon in her hand still.

"Now," Olivia continues, interrupted by the ring of the doorbell, "I want you to go into my closet. Do you know the part where I keep all my long coats? The place I always tell you that you can't use as a hiding spot for hide and seek?"

"Mhm." Julianna mumbles.

The doorbell rings again, this time followed by a cop-knock.

"I want you to stay there until I tell you it's okay to come out. Don't come out unless *I say*, do you understand?"

"Is something wrong?"

"Everything is fine." Olivia runs a finger across Julianna's temple, pulling her hair behind her ear, and cups her chin in her palm. She clenches her teeth in hopes that it holds the tears back. "But you *have to* do exactly as I said, okay?"

"Okay Mommy."

"And be absolutely silent. Not a peep, do you understand?" Olivia holds her daughter by the shoulders and squeezes.

"Mrs. Bailey, we need a moment of your time." A woman's muffled voice barrels through the front door. Everett had always told Olivia that if the government ever came knocking, to simply not answer the door. They couldn't legally pursue anything without a warrant, and they would never have a reason for one. Of course, he always said it with a slight of jest, that paranoid former military mindset geared up for the apocalypse. Either way, she had an escape plan, albeit a haphazard one. If she could just call Everett and get her Glock without causing too much stress on Julianna, it would work out perfect. Whoever these suits are would never guess they had a fire escape upstairs.

"Okay baby, go ahead. I will be there in just a minute." Olivia forces a reassuring smile and guides Julianna to the stairs.

The front door handle jiggles. *This can't be real*, she tells herself. She rushes to her phone and jams in the passcode. *Try Again*, the phone vibrates the keypad.

The handle on the front door clicks a few times, then pops open.

"No!" Olivia shakes her phone and enters the passcode again. Footsteps rap down the hallway. *They can't be serious! Breaking and entering? Something is terribly wrong.*

"Mrs. Bailey," Now a man's voice, searching down the hallway. "You have five minutes to pack a bag of essentials for you and one for each of your children."

Olivia flips to 'recents', clicks on Everett, and slams the phone against her ear. Maybe if

Everett is close by, with enough warning, he can settle this.

The agents step into the kitchen.

The phone rings on the other end once before it is wrangled out of her grip.

"No!" She screams, wrestling up against the stranger. "Get out of my house! What are you doing? This isn't legal!" Tears glisten across her face, more out of anger than fear. If there was ever a difference between the two, she couldn't recognize it in this moment. Mama Bear had come out to protect her children, but she felt more like a teddy bear in the grip of the stranger.

"If there were options, we would give them to you." The man grunts, now exerting control over the situation through his words and not just brute force. "I'm going to let you go, but I have to inform you, my partner has a Taser at the ready and she *will not hesitate* to use it."

Olivia punches the man in the chest for good measure and drops her shoulders. "Where is my husband?" She sobs, pushing her hand under her nose.

"You'll get to talk to him soon enough, *after* you pack your things and come with us."

Olivia nods, still plotting the fire escape route in the hopes that these suits stay downstairs.

"Your son is in the car waiting." The woman says, her arms in a relaxed aiming pose with the Taser.

Olivia sighs. How could such good news be so terrible at the same time? If only she had just driven him to school that morning. Instead, she had to sit around and sulk. She had never been one to let fear run her life, but she had also never been one to fool around. Ever since the last deployment, she had been hiding under a rock, afraid of making terrible mistakes. Parenthood came as a surprise, more to Everett than her. With it came life changes she couldn't have ever known existed. Paranoia was a foreign word until Bastion first opened his eyes. Nothing mattered more than family, and it was now being torn apart, after so many years of finally getting it put back together.

"Time to pack." The man says, his jaw clenched. Either this guy has done this too many times or he has some serious problems at home.

"Piss off. I'm not going anywhere and you're going to bring my son in here and leave. What you're doing is illegal no matter who you are. Now give me my phone." She holds out a hand.

The man shakes his head and looks at the floor. With a grimace and a sudden jolt of his arm, he clenches her shoulder by the shirt and drags her toward the stairs forcing her to either abandon the shirt or obey.

"Hey!" She screams, "Get your hands off of me!"

"We could have done this the easy way. Remember I told you about your options?" He raises an eyebrow at her as he pulls her up the stairs, his dark eyes hollow with the echo of experience. "There aren't any." He finishes the statement with a shove into the upstairs foyer.

Olivia glances at the rip in her shirt from the manhandling and gives him an evil eye. In response, he cracks his neck, folds his hands, and nods at the bedroom door. "You don't want me to help you."

"You think I'm some sort of brat child?" Olivia brushes at the rip, knowing it won't do anything.

"Keep proving me right. Get your bags, or I'll get them for you."

"You don't even know where they are." At least there can be one more small act of defiance.

"I'm sure Julianna does." The man states, taking a step forward.

"Don't you dare!" Olivia backs toward her bedroom door, arms up to block it.

"So she's in there? Let me guess, closet?" The man decreases the gap between, a freight train versus a parked sedan.

"No!" Olivia takes a swing, only to be turned around into a tight hold by the arm. "Don't you touch her!"

The sound of crying trickles out from inside the room as the man drags Olivia in and throws her on the bed. "Maybe this will convince you to move a little faster." He walks toward the closet and Olivia jumps back up, twisting on the sheets, ready to pounce. Around the corner, a

Taser gun appears, the other agent trailing behind it.

"Don't move." The woman puts her finger on the trigger. "It won't kill you, but I doubt your daughter will ever forget the sight of her mother twitching on the floor."

Olivia puts her hands up, breathing heavy. "Okay, just don't let him hurt her."

"You're the only person hurting anyone here, miss." The woman remarks, ignoring the irony.

The sound of hangers sliding across a pole alerts Olivia to the closet.

"Hello, Julianna. Your mother would like to see you." The man rumbles a gentle voice.

Olivia's face turns red and she bites her lip. "Our suitcases are under the bed."

"I'm sure they are," the man steps out from the closet, holding a crying Julianna by the hand. He kneels, looks her in the face, and says, "Honey, would you be a darling and fetch those suitcases for us? Your mother isn't feeling well enough to do it herself."

Olivia shakes her head, gritting her teeth, but changes the look as soon as Julianna looks to her for approval. "It's okay baby, do as the man says."

Julianna nods, looks at the crayon in her hand and gives it to the man. He smiles, holds it up and looks at Olivia as the girl walks toward the bed. "Forest Green. Hmm, I really like that color." The man smiles at the crayon, tucks it in his breast pocket, and stands up.

Olivia keeps her eyes on her daughter, ignoring the man. "They're just right there honey." She points toward the foot of the bed.

"Why do we need suitcases, Mommy?" Julianna's voice quivers.

Before Olivia forms a thought to respond, the man interjects. "We're all going to go on a little trip." Then smiles at Olivia. "Aren't children wonderful?"

Everett sits across the aisle from a team of strangers with various backgrounds, some of which are unrelated to military operations. The C130 Hercules hums a tune, reminiscent of a more exciting time when he actually wanted to travel the world and fight battles.

Stockard's voice haunts his numb mind with the infuriatingly powerless message. *Your family is safe and en route to an undisclosed location. Upon arrival at your mission barracks, contact will be coordinated and implemented at your commanding officer's discretion. Due to the nature of this mission, I'm sorry to say that contact will be akin to theater. If I could make a promise, I would. The sooner the mission is over, soldier, the sooner you go home.*

"*Will home be the same, or a different location this time?*"

Everett's elbows dig into his knees, his hair spilling over his shoulders and onto a backpack on his lap, cuddled like a comfort blanket. He stares at the opposite wall just to the side of two obnoxiously chatty recruits, pretending he's back at home with his family. Wishing he could have said goodbye. Someone is going to pay for this, when the time is right. More than a few someone's.

A boy, no more than twenty-five at best, fiddles with a laptop while throwing some embarrassing game at the girl next to him. If only he knew it was embarrassing. She reciprocates to a degree, but the look on her face suggests she can tell what he's up to. She likes the attention, performing the usual pre-mating rituals of throwing back her straight black hair and playing with the back of her neck. A little bite of the lower lip here and there, and she has this poor sucker in her web. She'll eat him up and toss him out, if she wants.

The boy is strangely good looking for an obvious nerd. Rectangular wire rimmed glasses perch midway atop the bridge of his nose, giving him a reason to push them up like a sophisticate. He has a thick black tribal tattoo plastered on his right forearm which looks out of place on his small frame. His hair is a high fade, folded to the side, a wave in a 1950's rock 'n' roll style that should have died with its era. He is clean shaven and white toothed, James Dean prototype.

Everett tries his best to ignore his pretentious rambling. The kid's smart, he can tell, but perhaps too smart too young. The girl giggles abruptly and covers her mouth in phony shame, cutesy and irresistible to her pandering dupe. She says something in Spanish that sounds flirtatious, and the boy responds with his best translation.

The doors of the front cabin slide open, and a tall man walks out, dressed in combat boots, pressed Wranglers, and a plaid button up. He is bald and has a short cropped black beard with touches of gray. He puts his hands on his hips and looks around, causing the crew to silence.

"My apologies for making y'all wait. We've had quite a few complications." A touch of Texan lingers around his speech, a blend of Hispanic and redneck camouflaged underneath the dapper presentation of an Army Major. "Your patience is appreciated." He nods, almost as though he's unsure of what to say next. "If you don't know by now, I am Major Viggo. But for this mission, you all will drop the major part, understood?" He scans the room for recognition. All heads nod. Half of the crew, the more-than-likely former military half, respond with a "Yessir".

He continues, "I know this looks like a ragtag group and it won't make much sense at first, but Uncle Sam knows best." He pauses. His speech is slow, methodical. "You have all been selected based upon a required and very particular mission. Each one of you has a background and training that befits the country's needs. I know that sounds like a lofty compliment, but don't take it as one."

A hand goes up.

Viggo furrows his eyebrows, irked at the interruption. With his slow speech, perhaps the motion counts as such. He nods, giving permission.

"Sir, what sort of clearance are we all working under here?" The man has an air of confidence, the student that knows the answer but wants the teacher to recognize the validity of the question for the rest of the class.

"Were you not briefed, soldier?" Viggo's soft words puncture like a Chinese drip torture.

"Yes, sir. I understand my own clearance. My question is, how free am I to speak about the mission considering present company?"

Viggo sighs. "Same clearance as you, O'Connor. You may speak freely when I am done doing so myself."

O'Connor smiles shyly and retreats into the wall behind him.

"Speaking a' which, y'all need to get to know each other a little better. This is a tight mission. I expect you'll be best friends by tomorrow. I know this is, whaddya call, *unconventional*, but like I said. Strange nature to the mission. Think of it like summer camp, and it'll be less awkward I promise ya."

O'Connor puts his hand up, then back down, scratching his forehead on the way, and stares into his lap.

"Anderson!" Viggo grunts, an impressively medium intonation for such a powerful blast.

"Yessir." A woman stands, black curly hair descending down her wide shoulders. Her voice is velvet, controlled. She is dressed modestly.

"State your title, would ya please darlin', for the sake of breakin' some ice here."

"Historian." Sweet and simple. Everett hm's at the purpose.

Viggo barks again, "Willard."

"IT. Friends call me Squirrel." Of course. The nerdy looking kid.

"Jimenez."

"CS. Combat Support, for the uninitiated." The Hispanic girl Squirrel was hitting on. She smirks his direction. He doesn't have a chance.

"Jones."

One of the quiet ones stands up. Former army from a mile away. "Medic." He scratches an overgrown beard and glances to the side, nervous about speaking, then sits down abruptly as though he hoped no one noticed him standing in the first place.

"O'Connor."

"CS." Now it gets interesting. With at least half of these recruits bearing military background and now two, if not more, having the

sole duty of combat, they must be expecting
something.

"Bailey."

Everett stands up. "Sergeant." He tries to
soften up the title but it still pulls some raised
eyebrows.

The list goes on until the last, and perhaps
most interesting to Everett. The old man with
stark blue eyes, who had been staring at him the
entire ride, by the name of Samuel Crane.

Title: Chaplain.

In the back of the car, squeezed between
her polar children, Olivia's swollen face quivers
as though stung by bees. She hates to let her
children see her like this, but in reality, she
wouldn't have been able to hide the danger
regardless. Her babies were a solid mess from the
get-go. Even Bastion, at twelve, can't stop the
rivers from flowing. At least she's with them, she
reassures herself.

"When do I get to talk to my husband?"

"When you're settled at your new home. If
he's available." The man says, stoic.

"And where is that?"

"We have a country location just outside
Leesburg set up and ready for your move in. It's a
long drive but shouldn't take more than a day."

"Leesburg? Why so far away? I'm sure
there's got to be something closer to Georgia.
How is that going to work just snatching me out

of my life here? This doesn't make any sense how you can get away with it." Olivia puts a hand to her head, trying to take it all in.

The woman continues the response from the passenger seat, "The move should be temporary, depending on the success of your husband's mission. You have to be in an unassuming place. Too close to home, and too close to potential problems that are likely to arise with the kind of mission your husband is on. You will get new names, temporary social security numbers, and will be provided with food and curriculum."

"Curriculum?" Olivia's tongue fumbles over the word, followed by a frown.

"You have recently taken serious consideration of homeschooling, Mrs. Bailey. Nothing could be safer for your children." The woman turns enough to catch her profile for a second as she nods, then back to the road.

"Great." Olivia shakes her head. This is really happening. "I thought this kind of thing only happened in the movies." She grumbles rhetorically.

The woman chuckles, "Where do you think they got all that from, hun?"

Olivia notices the man smile as he shakes his head, hands robotically gripping the steering wheel. She squeezes her sniffling children tight, rubs their shoulders, and closes her eyes.

6.

"I thought you were coming with me?" Albright frowns emphatically on the runway. He sports a blue suit with a purple button-up underneath, loose to the third button down, exposing a proud sprawl of circling hair. He holds a carryon satchel in one hand and a cocktail in the other, replete with umbrella and straw.

"I told you, Cambor. I have a huge thing coming up and I can't get around it this time."

"This project has you by the balls, my friend." Albright points with his cocktail hand and takes a sip.

"You really never have worked for the government before, have you?"

"Nope. But I sure have taken a lot of their money."

Rob shakes his head. *I'm in the wrong business. But maybe not for long.* "Your research has treated you well. But, there comes a time when we all have to roll up our sleeves and do the crap no one else wants to do."

Albright smirks, "You trying to say I don't know what hard work is?"

"You know I'm not saying that. This is your deal, not mine. Which is why I have to go attend to some other business. It's all coming down. We'll meet up on the other end of this when the technology catches up."

"Oh, the tech is *there*. It just needs a Master." Albright winks and turns to the

Gulfstream G-550 jet. "I'd love to stay and chat, but 'G' is waiting for me sweetie. Need to get my pamper on before I have to *roll up my sleeves*." Albright raises an eyebrow and walks away.

"Tell Miguel I said hi. Enjoy the trip." Rob yells after Albright who returns the adieu with a raised, nearly empty Cosmo glass.

Rob turns toward the airport and pulls out his government issue phone to schedule a ride. Take off one face, put on another.

The life of a CIA agent. What a confusing mess.

"Why do you think we need a historian?" Squirrel plops down comfortably next to Everett. He is smacking on a Cliff bar and scrolling through something on his phone. Must be a book or PDF since reception is gone.

Everett ignores him.

"Listen, I don't have a military background so I'm not sure if I'm supposed to salute you or something. From the looks the ex-military-"

"Former." Everett grunts.

"I'm sorry, former what?"

"Former military. The only ex-military are dishonorably discharged." Everett gives him a hard look to emphasize, "Never assume that, soldier."

"Oh." Squirrel pushes his glasses onto his nose, "Did I mention I'm not former military?

Not a soldier. No offense." He laughs, grinning at the thought.

"You are now."

"Sticking feathers up your butt does not make you a chicken."

"Don't quote movies at me," Everett responds, eyes fixed on the floorboard. "Especially if you're going to botch them."

Squirrel sighs. "Listen man, I don't want to be here either. Just trying to make friends. And since you appear to be the boss, I figure we should get to know each other."

Everett shakes his head. He had always hated elbow rubbing, but at least this guy was making his intentions clear rather than trying to be manipulative.

"So, why are you here?" Squirrel says, changing the mood.

"To complete the mission." Everett sighs.

"Right, but I mean, *why* are you here? From what I've gathered, none of us are technically volunteers. Volunteers in the government's definition of the word I guess, but not Webster." He chuckles at his joke.

"Why are *you* here, being a non-former military contract?" Everett points his look up and down the boy, letting him know he sees just how civilian he really is.

"I uh, well I don't wanna brag,"

Of course you do. Everett raises his eyebrows.

Squirrel continues, "but I got an early release deal from the BOP via the CIA in exchange for my special set of skills."

Everett takes the bait, admittedly curious at how ironic the claim is. "And what did you do to end up in federal prison? Embezzlement?"

"Why does everyone think that?"

"Likely because you look like a coffee shop hipster who could use a little extra funds diverted to your suffering bank account. Just a thought, at a glance." Everett chuckles and refocuses his attention on the opposing wall.

Squirrel's cheeks flush, but he otherwise pretends it doesn't bother him. "Yeah, yeah. The hipster accusation. But no. I hacked the FBI website and doxed corrupt agents to the public."

"So you're an activist." It was not a question or a compliment.

Squirrel shook his head; another label he'd heard before by the look in his eyes. "I don't work for PETA, if that's what you mean. I just hate to see people get away with dishonest practices."

"Or, practices that *you* think are dishonest. Disclosure of private information is not a game."

"I'm aware. And trust me, I paid the price."

Everett laughed, "Some of it."

"Oh, what," Squirrel snarked, "like this is a vacation? We're going to ANTARCTICA. Not Jamaica, mon." Even Squirrel grimaced at that joke but moved on quickly. "And I don't even know what they want me to do there. If there's a more technologically outdated continent, I can't think of one."

He makes a good point. Everett lifts his chin and peeks out the closest window. A flat horizon reveals a stark separation of blue and white.

"Speaking of which, I'd suggest you buckle up soldier. Land, ho."

"You can stop calling me that." Squirrel pulls the five-point harness over his shoulders and fumbles with the clips. Nodding to the Chaplain, he mumbles, "By the way, why is that guy staring at you so much?"

Olivia glares at the back of the agent's head as the suburban pulls into a gas station. "My kids and I need to use the restroom."

"Of course you do." The man chortles. "After I'm done pumping gas, I'll take the boy in and in the meantime my partner here will take you girls."

"What do you think we're going to do? Run away?" Olivia throws her hands up.

"You'd be surprised at the stupid sh-" the man catches himself, glancing at Julianna, "stuff that some people do."

"How many people have you kidnapped before?" Bastion retorts.

"Don't talk to them, Bastion. I told you that."

The man glances in the rearview mirror and smiles wide. A sad smile, but wide nonetheless. Olivia glares back and rubs the hair back down on her arms. "Could you get a move on? I'm going to pee my pants."

"Anything for you, dear." The man laughs and opens the door. The woman agent sneaks a sideways glance, poker face.

"Is he always like this?" Olivia tries to break some ice.

"No, actually. I think he likes you." She holds back a smile at the corners of her mouth.

So she is human after all, Olivia grinds her teeth. "Great way to show it."

Hours later, as the sun sets behind a hill, the suburban pulls up to a modest house with a long white porch and a swinging bench, the kind of place Olivia might like to settle in someday. That is, if she ever gets over the shock of her current situation. Under any other circumstance, even difficult ones, she would be excited about this kind of adventure. Perhaps even if she had never had children, this exact thing might not be so bad. She likes adventure, but not at the cost of her children's security and emotions. They thought life was complicated before.

Olivia waits for a smart remark from one of the agents as the driver puts the car into park and feels slightly deceived by the lack of one. The agents, in practiced and habitual tandem, unbuckle and open the doors. The back doors open, and they motion Olivia and the kids out as though she should be grateful for such red-carpet treatment.

"What do we do?" Olivia mutters, staring at the house.

"You live." The man says, grabbing the luggage and heading to the house.

"Come inside and we'll explain the rules." The woman gestures with a nod, picking up the last suitcase.

Inside the house is cozy but barren with a stark lack of warmth, otherwise known as decor. The furniture is simple and only exactly what is needed, nothing more. Olivia notes a television and sighs, thanking God and everything else in the universe for the babysitter.

The agents set the luggage down against a wall and split two different directions. The man to the window, hand behind his breast pocket and eyes roaming. The woman to the couch, but without sitting.

Olivia flops her hands in the air and frowns, Julianna strapped to her leg like a monkey.

"You're not to leave the house after curfew. No visitors of any kind, including family. Food will be provided until further notice so you don't have to go to the store." The woman reaches down and picks up a blue folder. "Everything you need to know is in this packet. You're going to have a simple life for a while."

"How long?" Olivia lets her eyes settle to the floor, too tired to lift them.

"Like I said, it depends on the success of the mission. It could be three months, maybe more."

"Three months?" Olivia jerks her head up, the number alerting her like headlights to a deer in the road.

"Don't get your hopes up." The woman sets the folder back down on the coffee table.

"What's that supposed to mean?" Olivia says, putting a hand on Bastion's shoulder. The boy is shut down, staring off into space.

The man turns his chiseled face and responds, "It means you know too much already. Read the files. We'll be back to check on you tomorrow." He opens the door and steps through without waiting, then walks out.

"When is my husband coming?" Olivia puts a hand toward the woman, stopping her short. "Or is that in the folder too?"

The woman sighs. "He's not." She looks out the door as the man gets into the car, then into Olivia's eyes. "This isn't the first time I've confiscated a family for covert missions. If you're husband comes home, *that* will be a first."

7.

As the tailgate descends, the passengers
gasp at the shocking cold. Despite being decked
in harsh, cold weather gear (military grade) the
sudden contrast is shocking. One of the
passengers coughs a dry heave, then scrambles for
an inhaler only to find that it can no longer propel
the needed albuterol into the lungs.

"This is the hell I deserve." Squirrel
mumbles under his breath.

Everett glances back toward him, already
knowing who it is but satisfying that carnal nature
to quench one's ego and confirm accuracy.

"Isn't she beautiful?" A gruff voice
expands slowly through the air next to him, as
though the cold even slows down the speed of
sound. Slowly, the stench of sour coffee and
sickly-sweet diabetes reaches his nostrils and he
pulls his balaclava back up over his nose.

"That's a word for it, I suppose." Even
through the polarized, photochromic lenses of his
goggles he has to squint at the snow glare. After a
quiet moment, he pulls the balaclava back down,
that never ending struggle between a cold chin
and fogged vision causing him to lose his mind.

"By the way, name is Crane. My apologies
for not properly introducing myself earlier." The
man puts out a hand.

"Bailey." Everett returns the gesture,
unsure of how to end a handshake turned
awkward due to the sole fact that neither party

can naturally feel the others pressure or contact through the clumsy swollen fabric. Everett sighs, "Why do we need a Chaplain, Mr. Crane?" The question is more rhetorical than anything. Why do any of them need to be here at all? When do they get their debriefing? Will they?

"Security." Crane replies, the skin on his cheekbones wrinkling into the aftereffects of a wide smile hidden by the foliage green fabric over his mouth.

Not the answer Everett was hoping for. Not that he knew what to expect.

Major Viggo appears in the haze of frozen noon, rippled by the optical illusion of heat waves on snow. He yells over the hum of the Hercules, "Your temporary quarters are South," he points, "Chow Hall this way, follow me." He motions.

The crew readjusts packs in tandem as they force their feet through the powder. Bringing up the rear are the CS's hauling their own packs as well as large foliage green trunks.

Squirrel catches up to the pair and whistles, "Man! It's colder than a-"

"Witches tit?" Everett interrupts him. "Or were you going to say something else?" He smiles proudly to himself.

"Well, I was gonna say-"

"A brass toilet seat in the Yukon?" Crane suggests drily.

"Oh, oh, maybe, 'A polar bear after a Brazilian wax?'" Everett continues.

"Colder than an Alaskan funeral." Crane retorts once more.

Squirrel throws up his hands and curses. "I was going to say witches tit but-"

"In a brass bra doing pushups on the shady side of an iceberg!" Jimenez yells as she catches up, jog walking.

"Better than I got." Everett looks at Crane, who nods in agreement.

"I can't win." Squirrel gives up, rubbing his hands together.

A sound of ascension wobbles behind them, causing Squirrel to turn around. "Hey, uh, how long are we supposed to be here?"

"Don't worry, they'll be back." Everett reassures him.

"Yeah, but when?"

"When the mission is complete."

Squirrel quips a short laugh, "Is there a timeline for anything?"

"No." Everett responds, "Welcome to military scheduling."

"Get used to it, Chica." Jimenez finishes the conversation, slaps something onto Squirrels chest, and jogs toward quarters.

Squirrel examines the item closely, curses, then throws it on the ground.

A tampon.

"Making friends was never this hard in college." Squirrel mumbles to himself, watching the rest of the crew disappear into the chow hall.

"I know you all have a lot of questions," Major Viggo announces, standing in front of an oversized woodstove. "And I'm going to do my best to answer all of them. But first, you have to know, if you haven't already figured out, that this is a very unusual mission. In fact, we've never had one quite like it before it's humble beginnings. There's a reason for that."

The crew sits or stands quietly, seeking only the solace of warmth as the cold draws the energy translated as heat out of their bodies.

Viggo continues, "What you're about to encounter is something we have never seen, studied, or experienced before. This is not your common 'eradicate the enemy' assignment. In fact, we don't even know if this is a foe or friend. However," he pauses, clears his throat, and looks each of the crew of twelve directly in the eye in one quick glance, "well, you're just going to have to see it to believe it."

The air in the room thins out as the fear of the unknown trickles in. Everyone knows the military, government, etc. is full of secrets. It's easy to assume aliens. Hollywood has done its job conditioning the public to believe that well enough, so why does Major Viggo look so pale? Hands shift in pockets. Feet tap on the floor nervously.

Viggo shakes his head, "Unfortunately, I cannot debrief you with words for what you're about to witness. Just know that each of you has been chosen for a specific reason for this assignment, and that you are relevant, even if you think you're not. But," he hesitates again, looking unsure, "We will get to that after you experience the Trance."

Someone clears their throat, the equivalent of a scream erupting in the middle of a quiet, moonless night.

"Sir," O'Connor speaks up, "This might be a dumb question, but what is *the Trance?*" Dumb or not, everyone is glad he asked, though no one will admit it.

Major Viggo stares back, a story playing behind his eyes. One he is apparently not happy to tell.

Luck would have it that Everett is sitting by Squirrel again, this time in the Sno-Cat as the beast of a machine rolls solidly over tufts of powdered snow. The groundskeeper, who goes by the name of "Hare" for his ability to weave imperceptibly through the snow drifts like a rabbit, calls it Gossamer, named after the big orange monster from an old cartoon, in either irony or providence.

The horizon is a stoic grin, warping with the contrast of nothing on nothing, causing a feeling of endlessness. Everett was never one to pander to any sort of fear, but in this place, he decided agoraphobia was within the realm of possibilities. When exposed to extremes, the human condition is to react with extremes.

"So why do you think we need a historian?" Squirrel brings up the question again, almost as though he was developing a Pavlovian response to being travel buddies.

"Probably in the same way we need a computer geek."

"Ouch." Squirrel nods, giving up for the moment. He scratches his thin beard and looks around at the other passengers. "You know," he yells, combatting the hum of the Sno-Cat, "I think I like you. Like, not in a bromantic kind of way though. Even though you belittle me. Maybe it's psychological. Like how an abused wife doesn't want her husband to go to jail."

"Can you shut up?"

"Not sure really. Talking is kind of like a comfort blanket for me. And if there's any place I need a blanky, well, it's this God forsaken land for sure. You think that's where we're heading?" He points in a general southward direction.

A mountain rears up in defense against their approach, giving Everett the feeling that he's trespassing. As though a large vampiric tooth, the anomaly is supernaturally pointed and aggressive. Its smooth sides speak of ancient design versus the assumed wild culmination of weather.

"Eventually." Everett croaks, eyes scanning the whole scene for signs of potential intimidation, then nods at a campsite on the other side of the Sno-Cat.

As the company approaches the site, split into two separate groups by vehicle limitation, the sun tap dances on the horizon, playing with the dusk. For the time being, not setting completely, but keeping an eye on the company like a mythical guardian standing between humanity and eternity.

Gossamer and Jack'O (not to be left out, the other Sno-Cat, predictably named by the Halloween obsessed groundskeeper who doesn't speak) crest the small camp's borders, uncomfortably close to the mountain. The teams unload, every head turned awkwardly to the ominous formation as they work.

A south wind picks up, brushing with the kind of chill that can only be described in terms of cutlery.

"You can load up in here." Major Viggo directs the company toward a handful of gray polar shelters, arranged in git'r done fashion. In the center of the camp sits the remnants of a firepit. Nothing else decorates the bleak campsite.

"Welcome home." Viggo grins, throwing out a hand in a luscious introduction.

"Who goes where?" Squirrel pipes up, trying hard not to eyeball Jimenez.

"When your counselors get here, they'll call you by name. After that, we'll play a rousing game of capture the flag and then we'll all break up into groups to discuss what we've learned about our day's activities." Viggo drops his hand to his side, as well as the grin. "The shelters house three each. You're all adults. Figure it out. Chow in thirty, at the main shelter here." He points toward a large polar shelter, one that looks a bit more permanent. Smoke rises out of a chimney, the only sign of life outside the company for miles.

Squirrel looks around, glancing at Jimenez, who gives him a wink. She then immediately averts her attention to the two other women in the company and they band together quicker than a pack after prey, shuffling off to one of the shelters.

Squirrel looks at Everett, a toothy grin spreading across his face and a raised eyebrow.

8.

"So, what do you think it is?" Squirrel shovels a spoon up to his mouth and slurps.

"Looks man-made to me." Everett glances to the side, catching a peak through the small filmy window.

"You've seen it already? When did that happen?" Squirrel stops, spoon mid-mouth, confused.

"I thought we were talking about-"

"Gentlemen," Crane scoots back a chair next to Everett and sets his bowl on the table. "I see you've encountered the problem I've been fearing." He looks at the bowls, still mostly full even after plenty of time to have finished the meal.

"It's not that bad." Squirrel suggests and crumbles another packet of Saltines into the mush.

Crane grunts. He pushes back his chair a little more to make way for his rotund shape. Not necessarily obese, but *insulated,* as Crane would say. However, despite his extra weight, he appears to keep up just as well as anyone.

"So, how did you get tangled into this?" Everett plays the polite card, mostly to keep Squirrel from talking.

"You think it's odd that a preacher would be on a government assignment in the covert fringe territory of the most mysterious place on earth?" Crane chuckles, the spitting image of

Santa Clause's awkward cousin, only emphasized by the location. "Well, let me tell ya' something right now. If there's anyone who knows a little something about the unknown, it's a believer."

"A who?" Squirrel opens another Saltine packet.

"Believer. In God." Everett offers.

"It's not my favorite term, but it gets the message across." Crane tries out the soup, dons a look of cartoonish surprise, and goes in for more.

"Oh." Squirrel responds, almost begrudgingly. "I've always been more of a mother earth type, you know. Like, there's a god, but she's probably not interested in what I'm doing as long as I keep her clean." He stops for a second, considering the unspoken Freudian concept he may have just accidentally revealed about himself.

Crane harrumphs indifferently and busies himself with emptying his bowl. "Not too bad." He proclaims, excusing himself for seconds.

"Did you ask him why he keeps giving you the evil eye?" Squirrel emulates the look, dumbing it down with his unthreatening demeanor.

"He was probably just spacing out."

"Or he's like a dog and can see that you're demon possessed." Squirrel reconsiders the joke internally, opens his mouth to amend it, then closes again, having come to no resolve.

Everett shakes his head lightly and ignores him, figuring it was the most mercy he could bestow at the moment.

"We head to the site at daybreak tomorrow. It's been a long day. I think sleep is in order."

"Kinda hard to sleep with that crazy sun still out, doing whatever it's doing." Squirrel squints at the window and rubs his eyes for effect.

"Hey, it only takes a few days in combat to discover you can sleep just about anywhere, anytime."

Squirrel looks back at him as though he doesn't want to tell him he's full of it, but keeps his mouth shut. For once.

The stark clacking of hardened leather penetrates the hallway like a hammer on a stubborn nail. Byron runs tired hands through his unkempt hair, a telling contrast considering the time of day as the noon light spills in through vapid windows that speckle the hallway like an afterthought. While the machinery in the facility is decades in advance of even the government's toys, the building itself was never intended to be quite so modern. The project is, you could say, pushing the boundaries, which requires a sort of camouflage.

Which is why surveillance is so important.

The physical layout and condition of the building suggests general warehouse operations, doomed to self-destruction via poor funding and management. Low key. High stakes.

"What do you mean Quinton walked out the front doors?" Byron looks over his shoulders at a passing tech.

"Naked." Jason responds, pointing a pen at an invisible target in front of the path.

"Right, yeah. I understand that. What time?"

"Around midnight."

"Do we know why security didn't stop him? Ask any questions?" Byron asks.

"Security on duty have no recollection. It's not like this is a normal situation either, someone would have remembered that. I can stipulate a stress analysis exam for the officers on shift."

"No, no. I don't want a lot of attention on this," Byron waves it off, "and the security cameras show him…"

"Shooting himself in his office at 6pm, on the dot."

Byron sighs. "This is crazy."

"You know what he did."

"It can't be done. We tried that." Byron pushes through the door. It cracks with an empty announcement that echoes through the stark foyer.

"Have you gone to his place yet?" Jason waves to the security and smiles wide, as though they were just discussing the recent victory of a mutually praised sports team.

"Giving it time. I don't want too many suspicious connections."

The gray sun harasses Byron's peripheral through a grid of swollen contrails, a haphazard catcall that makes him feel chemically abused. The pair walk towards his car, a silver BMW coupe with lusty curves and a vanity license plate that only he can decode, a now lamented decision that he tries to ignore.

"There may be something valuable to us. Something to lead us to solving this mystery." Jason drops his arms to his side. So, the pupil has become the teacher.

Byron groans, thoughts of retirement fleeing his grip with every new discovery in this mysterious drama. He can feel his future shifting dynamics right before his eyes, like mercury sliding over his palm. Resistant to form. Untamed. Unpredictable. Dissipating into his skin, poisoning him slowly.

And to think, he was almost there. If only he were by some miracle still in the Bahamas when all this happened. Responsibility is much easier to shirk with great distance and opportunity.

Byron plops into the BMW and shuts the door, staring into his lap.

"Think about it. The sooner the better. You're the only one who knows where he lives, or I'd do it myself."

"Yeah," Byron fiddles with the keys, "He was always the withdrawn genius type, wasn't he?"

Jason just smiles and walks away, tapping his pen on his glasses. The poor shmuck. Such a smart kid to be getting wrapped up in all this. Not quite the genius Quinton was (is?) but close behind. Good looking kid, too. Should be married by now but with all the work required recently, not likely to happen anytime soon. He hopes Jason has a secret social life, for his own sake.

He sighs, slides the key into the ignition with ease just like every time. When you're in a BMW as nice as this one, you have to take your time and enjoy every second.

The engine turns. A millisecond after ignition, a small click is heard. He cocks his head to the side.

The vehicle and its sole occupant ignite in a miniature Hiroshima, obliterating everything within a twenty-foot radius. The heat is so immediate that Byron's glasses plaster to his face, exposing them for the cheap plastic they really are. Not that it matters. The two become one, then become something different entirely. The kind of charcoal that could never be pressured into diamonds.

Jason would always wonder what Byron's last thoughts were as debris and flames consumed the unlucky soul. Or was it good luck after all? Perspective is anything but universal, an angle only to be duplicated by the genetic zero-gap zygosity of identical twins and even still, only to a certain degree.

Jason would also wonder if that artificial blackened grin was merely the aftereffects of extreme heat exposure peeling Byron's lips back or the last comical sigh of blissful abdication. Maybe Byron thought of Quinton, affixing a barbaric bomb in his birthday suit, straddled beneath the engine in vulnerable display.

Or maybe he thought of his wife, finally ready to give it another shot, waiting for him at their condo until that ominous phone call breaks the silence. A tragedy is still a tragedy, whether the tears burn for one reason or another.

What Jason may have not suspected was that perhaps, deep down, Byron had only time enough to think, *Thank God.*

9.

Cambor picks his teeth and stares at the walls of his new office. So strange, to be stuck in such a stark and dreary land, but to have his own little world plopped amongst the wild nothing. The room came pre-decorated, according to his taste. He was easy. Palm trees. Bright colors. Happy things.

"He mentioned Daniels." The voice from the computer interrupts Cambor's daydreaming.

"Oh, he did, did he? What else did he talk about in his stupor?" Cambor knew the flippant statement would set the Major General off, but he didn't care. The military wasn't in control anymore. The new guard has replaced the old and thank you Uncle Sam for all you've done for the world but your shift is over now.

"Listen, Albright,"

"I believe you mean, *sir,* Major General Stockard." Cambor interrupts.

Stockard stutters for a second and his face turns red. "I will not be talked down to. A certain amount of respect is due for the country that put you in the position you currently hold. What we are doing isn't right, and I don't like it one bit."

Cambor studies the tip of his fingernail and re-crosses his legs on the desk.

"This man has a family. He served for twelve years, more of those years spent in theater than most can say after retirement. He deserves to be cut loose and I plan to do that at the end of this mission."

Cambor sighs and glances at the wall again, imagining what the warm breeze on the Florida beaches might feel like right at this moment. "Why are you complaining to me about something that you've already accomplished?" Cambor keeps his eyes on the picture.

"Excuse me?" Stockard is off his guard today. He's normally a bit more direct and thought out.

"We all have our duties. We all have to spend time in the trenches. Some of us more than others. No matter how high our post, how decorated our chest. This isn't just about America anymore. It's about prosperity for the planet." Cambor turns his head and looks out the eastern window across the barren white landscape that splits the horizon with a sharp, straight line, and smiles at the irony.

"No," Stockard grunts, "it's about control. Yours."

Cambor drops his feet to the ground and leans into the computer, close enough so that Stockard can see his eyes but not so close that it looks comical. "Listen to me you knuckledragger," he says calmly, as though asking for the weather, "you've already done your duty. I don't even know why we're having this conversation. The man is here, and the mission is underway, whether you like it or not. And unless you plan on flying over here yourself to start a war with my project and *my* soldiers, I'd recommend shutting your mouth and moving on with business as usual."

Stockard cringes at the emphasis and shakes his head. "It won't last. You're playing with fire."

"He's not taking my advice." Cambor says to the room.

"And you're going to get burned." Stockard growls.

"Didn't see that coming." Cambor rolls his eyes.

"We're having this conversation because I like to tell a man face to face when I quit a job, and this is as good as that is going to get."

Cambor shrugs his shoulders. "You were done anyway. The Galactic Federation thanks you for your service. May you live a prosperous and peaceful life. Good day, soldier." Cambor reaches over to shut the conversation off and squints at the computer. New technology always takes a minute to navigate, even if you created it. Habits.

"One more thing." Stockard chews his lower lip. Cambor pretends to not hear and continues searching for the exit. "He's more than what you think he is. I'd be careful if I were you. But I know you won't. Good luck. You're going to need it."

Cambor finds the exit, takes one last glance at the screen, winks, and closes out the window.

"Well," Cambor leans back into his chair and looks across the room. "He was certainly full of clichés today, wasn't he?"

Across the room stands a massive soldier, silent and bulked out with gear. His head is partly shaven, a thick scar encircling his skull causing the hair to grow in odd patterns. He sports a full beard and stands over eight feet tall, balanced out with an excess of muscle and a severe lack of fat, skin patterned with ugly stretch marks. He clenches and unclenches his fists but makes no other move. An electric blue tattoo sprawls across the surface of his right hand in intricate patterns unique to his DNA. Light moves through the lines like blood through veins, pulsing with information.

Cambor lifts his chin and studies the soldier. "Take off your shirt, Daniels. I want to see what a hybrid man looks like."

Everett knows it's not going to last long, but he finally has a reprieve from Squirrel's mouth. Bumping along in the backend of Gossamer, Everett finds himself dazing into daydream land, his heart getting heavier by the minute at the fuzzy images of his family running through his head. He wonders if they are comfortable. Protected, for sure, and likely in some safehouse somewhere. But what kind of emotional rollercoaster has it been for them? He didn't even get to say goodbye. What if he doesn't come back?

That thing he skirmished with in Afghanistan was no walk in the park. It's amazing the squad got out with only one casualty. He credits the advice to keep the guns pointed high for that.

"You got someone at home waiting on ya, don't you?" Crane smacks and squints his eyes. He's not an elder by any means, but he's been around the block a few times. The male pattern baldness has only settled in a little on his upper forehead, accentuated by the taught pull of a thin gray ponytail to the back. He rubs his short beard, spotted with black and gray like a sheepdog, and speaks again, "Can see it. You're a family man. What are you doing out here?"

"Unfortunately, the government still thinks they own me. And they have collateral."

"Really?" Cranes eyebrows raise higher than physically expected, "That serious, huh? Well, I've got good juju for you pal. You'll come home to 'em soon." He nods, confidence unwavering.

"Sure hope so." Everett averts his eyes to the destination as it closes in. The mountain is blurry in the haze of snow flurries. There is no falling snow or blizzard, but when the wind picks up, feels like the same difference.

"Hey," Everett pipes up and looks back at Crane, "I mean no offense, and forgive me if I'm mistaken, but why were you staring at me on the flight over?"

Crane's face is unchanged except for the tiniest thought that flutters across his eyes, "Praying for ya. Very direct, concise praying. Takes focus." He doesn't move.

Chills rattle through Everett's spine. For a moment, he holds his gaze, then nods as though the answer was perfectly normal.

Gossamer stops. The latch opens. Cold air blasts through the cabin like an EOD through a window.

"Aim high! Aim high!" He hears his own voice screaming but doesn't remember thinking to say the words.

The ground shakes. Tucker screams, the blast of automated rounds competing with his voice. Noise everywhere. The stench.

Dear God, the foul stench.

It moves too fast for its size. Daniels moves in closer. Everett moves toward a boulder for cover.

"Daniels!" He screams but is overpowered by the guttural charge of the beast.

The sound... a ripping thunk of wood on flesh, buried between layers of what was once nearly impenetrable armor. Like a crack of a watermelon, the smack of puncture through rind and the squash of sensitive flesh inside.

Everett notices the girth of the spear, as thick as his arm, raising Daniels into the air.

More gunfire. More. More.

The stench is only getting worse.

"That bad, huh?" Crane breaks Everett's daze and leans over, "You'll be home soon, soldier. Stay vigilant." Crane pats him on the shoulder lightly, trying not to interfere too much in the obvious flashback. He gives a half smile, nods, and eases out the door.

The wind is a flurry of ice papers cutting his face to shreds, at least the exposed parts. As for the rest of his body, he tries to shuffle images of hanging meat stock away, out of his head. This isn't merely a struggle against the cold. This is a threat of death.

Through the flurry he sees Major Viggo motion the team forward, toward the mouth of the mountain. At this distance, all he can see is the darkness of an opening. Whatever it is, he wants in it and out of this blizzard. His body knows it is close to shelter and shivers at the thought of impending relief, accentuating the disparity of the potential state of being versus the current one in the same way the bladder begins to bulge when a restroom is nearby.

Thankfully, the trek is a short one, even though vision is constricted by the whiteout. Within a very long moment, the team is inside the opening, shuddering and focused solely on regaining the dramatic loss of body heat, ignoring the atmosphere.

"That wind kicked up out of nowhere." Hare apologizes, taking responsibility for the weather. He's usually a little better at predicting a coming western wind and is taking the miscalculation hard.

"Looks like we'll be here until it passes." Viggo frowns, not with disappointment but rather realism, "How long before then?"

Hare shrugs, hesitant to make another misstep. "Could be a few days. We'll likely have to dig out of here too. Darn it, I'm sorry boss. That's gotta be the first time…" he interrupts himself to silence, unsure of how to finish the apology and looks at the ground.

"Nothin' we can't handle, Navigator. Not like you mislead on purpose. That's why," Viggo reaches to the wall next to him and slaps a large switch, "you always prepare."

The hum of generators rumbles from somewhere deep in the ground, large ones. Viggo hits another switch, and the sound increases. He walks further down the hallway and hits another switch, this time a smaller one, lighting up the vestibule. It is as stark as a refrigerator, and just as cold, which sadly is warm in comparison to what is building up outside.

"It ain't much," Viggo walks down the wide corridor and turns around, "but we have for ourselves here a little campout. Follow me down this hall to the dorm and we'll warm up for a moment before the descent."

Viggo leads the crew to a connected anterior where they gladly shed packs in exchange for a quick switch into dry coats.

In moments, the crew is descending inside a single deck cage down a drum winding shaft, into the dark. With a loud bang and series of clicks, the cage comes to a halt. Viggo unlatches the caution-yellow tram sliders and exits the cage, followed by a hesitant but curious entourage.

The surrounding walls are exposed cave, glistening with cold moisture, black with the stain of ancient burial. A lonely stretch of galvanized steel plank grading reaches into a soft glow that appears more distant than it is in reality. Within the delicate orb of conserved light sits a modest arrangement of monitors befuddled with an idiolect foreign to Everett despite its common root of the English lexicon.

Beyond the monitors, where cords and cables run rodent paths into the dark, something unseen watches them.

Something Everett intrinsically understands with a familiarity uncannily rogue yet intimate.

Bailey... a voice not his own warbles inside his head.

Aim high.

10.

Despite his destination, the Hawaiian shirt fits him nicely, in both senses of the word. Slim Fit, the tag underscored. Bright red Hibiscus blossoms express an aggressive cordiality amidst the pointed pinup legs of Americanized aborigines, that tendency to self-aggregate a distinct culture into a misleading iteration disconnected from reality. First it was Jesus, now it is merely habit.

Luggage in the overhead bin space. One case, metallic blue. Price tag: Ross clearance special. Sunglasses slumped one leg on the chest, one leg tucked beneath, situated amidst the above-mentioned patterned legs in similar fashion. Lenses still branded with the negative space of irksome label placement, molested by fingerprints.

"If you haven't already done so, please stow your carry-on luggage underneath…" the words trail off into oblivion, the only resuscitation in the history of instruction forever garbled amongst the clamor of need and importance to be reduced to such a miserable obligation. Any objective and uninitiated onlooker would be perplexed at such a flippant dismissal.

No laptop. No business. No after hour work special.

Just one Bloody Mary, please, and a moist towelette.

Quinton folds his hands on his lap and looks out the window as the runway blurs by, smiles, and reclines his chair, ignoring the protest of the preceding occupant.

"What is this?" Everett barks, startled at the voice inside his head that was not his own.

"This is the Chamber. Some of you may already be feeling the effects of the Trance, and that's perfectly normal." Viggo responds, starting a steady walk down the steel plank toward the light.

"No, no Trance. I mean, what *is the meaning of this?* Why are we here? We haven't been given any instruction. Most of us are here against our will. You've put us in a foreign land and expected us to learn the language by immersion." Everett lets his tongue slip a little more than normal. Viggo notices, cocks a soft eyebrow, and responds with words that were not in his head.

"This is no walk in the park, you're right, Sergeant." The title comes with a little punch, reminding Everett of his position. One that needs to be controlled and calm, not stressed and questioning.

"My apologies, sir. I don't want to make excuses, but I feel as though I speak for the team when I say that I'm tired and concerned about our mission." Not concerned. Confused. But a Sergeant can't show weakness.

"Understood." Viggo nods, "As I said earlier, what you're about to experience is not something that can be explained in words. However, I owe you all a warning. One that could not come before gathering you here."

Viggo's expression turns dark, the kind of look Everett knows well enough when being told an inescapable mission may well be his last one. He closes his eyes and thinks of his family back home, his most powerful anchor. Here it comes.

"Excuse me sir," Jones interrupts, the medic on duty. "Can I ask for an elaboration on what exactly the Trance is, sir?" He looks to the side, as though he expects the Trance to be a creature that might rush out at him any moment.

"Follow me." Viggo responds and continues the walk across the plank to the platform where the monitors sit buzzing. "The Trance," he emphasizes the word with an intentional mystery, as though he's not entirely positive what it may be himself, "is basically what you think it is. Where it comes from and how it happens is the question, but we have our suspicions. Unfortunately, we've never been able to acquire a complete psycho analysis of anyone who's experienced the Trance, or I would have a better answer for you. However, you'll notice-" he points to the ground in the distance, just where the edge of the yellow light dissipates into the vacuumed blackness, "there's a red line. Do not cross it. It is exactly what you would assume it is on the other side."

"Danger zone." Jimenez whispers, eyes glazed, affixed to the barrier marking.

O'Connor snorts and spits, a smirk on his face. He gives Everett a mocking look and smiles, thumbs in his belt loops, then looks at the red line the way an MMA fighter sizes up his opponent.

Viggo turns the attention adjacent with a four finger point to a nearby cubicle, "This is Omerta. She is the most advanced of computer systems in the military. You've never seen her before. You never will again. You all have now exceeded Top Security clearance as well as SCI, which is better known as Q. You have entered a clearance level that hasn't even been labeled due to the necessity of covert operations deemed of the utmost importance for concealment so much so that we cannot label it for fear of exposing it. This is not a compliment." Viggo turns a harsh eye at the group. "You've done nothing special to achieve this obligation. It is not an honor. Quite frankly," and here, the weariness in his eyes shows through to a small degree, "it is a burden. But it is a very important burden. The security, survival, and longevity of our great country and the world depends on your ability to maintain this anonymous clearance. Your own longevity depends on it as well." The weariness is quickly replaced with a promise.

O'Connor clears his throat, breaking the awkward air, nods with a flat grin and looks away.

"Willard," Viggo barks, "I know your dying inside. What's your question?"

Squirrel rubs his hands together, a grin on his face that he simply cannot physically retract. "Do – am I – is that-" he clears his throat and starts again, "May I look at her please?" He is a toddler in a toy shop with a promise of limitless excursion.

"We have a problem," Viggo strolls to Omerta, "and I need you to be extra cautious about this Willard. This isn't a game. You understand?"

"Yes, sir, of course." Squirrel puts on his best adult face.

"Our last tech opted out."

Everett scans Squirrels face, looking to see if he thoroughly understands the implications of the statement. His expression fiddles from assumed comprehension through questioning and finally lands on mostly confident, but with questions.

"Yes sir. I don't believe I will do that."

"I trust that you have every intention of that. However, you must be prepared. If there was a training for this, trust me, you would have received it. This is a learning experience for us all."

"Sir?" Jimenez speaks up, holding a hand up and staring off into the darkness. "Why are we all here? I mean no disrespect, but this appears to be a mission for IT and other related geeky things, not combat." She puts the hand back down, her eyes still locked in on the darkness.

Viggo takes in a deep breath. "My intentions were not to drag this on. And in that, we come to our purpose. You were not all brought here just for Omerta." Viggo steps into the control room and places his hand on a switch. Everett runs his eyes from the electrical box behind the switch, down the cord and across the ground to the other end where a series of dormant spotlights stand erect, all pointed to one particular area in the dark. Beyond the danger zone.

Viggo lets out his breath, looks directly at Everett, and mumbles the words, "Full immersion." He flips the switch and the spotlights blast on, exploding a brilliant white light into the darkness that blinds at first.

Everett puts up his hands, guarding from the blast. After a moment, his eyes adjust, and he follows a line of cords across the danger zone and zig-zagged up a slight incline.

They are attached to a large, clear capsule that radiates in the same fashion as a diamond, with a light blue tint. The capsule is roughly shaped like a downward pointed triangle, the size of a Cessna airplane.

Inside the capsule, a man is suspended with arms stretched to the side.

No, not a man. This creature fills the large capsule.

A giant.

11.

Rob Comins folds a dinner napkin sloppily and lays it on his lap. What once was a masterpiece of prime rib and steamed vegetables has been whipped into an unrecognizable goulash of impish whim. He lifts a hand and flicks his fingers, eyes fixed on the handheld screen decorating the end of his other delicate extremity.

A server stops by and fills his water glass.

"Check." Comins mumbles, never taking his eyes off the screen. He absent-mindedly wipes his free hand on the cobalt blue button up stretched torturously over his stomach, leaving behind a smudge of grease.

Moments later, he scribbles on a receipt, folds two one-dollar bills neatly and tucks them underneath the water glass and leaves, slipping the phone into his coat pocket.

The brisk air outside feels colder with the background noise of Dallas, in comparison to the deep green of Georgia. That dirty hole. Why anyone would want to live there was a mystery to him. However, he could see the draw for the kind of operation that pathetic company was undertaking. *Was.*

You can't cover up something as dramatic as a car bomb explosion and expect the local authorities not to notice.

Investor. Comins snarls at the thought. Who would want that job? Giving other people your own money to do a bunch of risky experiments? Not the risk-taking kind of guy, Comins always made sure his next move, his next dozen moves, were guaranteed. What they call 3D chess. And that tablet just pushed him a dozen moves in advance. Going back in for it was a risk, but one worth the potential consequences.

Comins puts out a hand, hailing a taxi. Once inside, he pulls out his phone again. Kelim had a strict no phone policy, how clandestine of them. For such a technologically advanced program, one would think they would screen for phone cameras. Perhaps they didn't think of an *investor* as a threat. Perhaps they just got lazy. Either way, none of it mattered now. The company is tanking by the second. Just like a corrupt governor destroys his own state in order to diminish its value, buys everything up at a steal, then raises it all up again, so Comin's is hoping for Kelim. Time will tell.

Comins scrolls through pictures of the Gibo machine, studying them. He had no idea what they really were or what they did. Just another mission he wasn't given enough details on. Just like every other. And like always, he manipulated the situation to his benefit.

Maybe it was his failing physical attributes that gave him such camouflage. Certainly, an Operations Officer from the CIA would be a Jack Ryan replica. Square jawed, uber-muscled, always packing, legs spring loaded just waiting and ready for a roundhouse kick any moment.

Those days were over. Not that Comins ever really was the dapper James Bond type of agent. He had always relied on his brains more than his brawn to get the job done. Though he wasn't weak by any means. He simply discovered he didn't need to powerhouse kick his way through every door to get to where he needed to go. Most doors just swing wide open if you jiggle the handle the right way. Or long enough.

"Airport." He grunts to the driver, realizing the man is waiting patiently. The driver nods and pulls into traffic.

"You look like a man headed for vacation." The driver smirks, attempting a joke.

Comins looks up and smiles at the reverse face in the mirror, then back down to the screen. Now what exactly would the government want to do with one of these little bad boys? Of course, he knew what Cambor was doing with this project But we have nukes. Who cares about the perfect super soldier? Seems as though they were always wanting to do that. There must be more with the kind of keen interest they seemed to have taken into this project. Perhaps that was just the launching pad. Or a cover. Every government loves a good decoy.

One thing Comins learned long ago was that everything is connected. There are no coincidences. It's just a matter of drawing a line between dots. Eventually, you come up with a logical picture, no matter how chaotic it may appear at first. Kindergarten wasn't far off with those little worksheets. So simple, yet so effective.

So how did this connect?

"Hawaii? Europe? Which way you going? Everyone's getting' outta here this time of year. Must be someplace warm." The driver shivers in his coat. Comins notices the air control dials are turned all the way to hot, all the way up, and producing no such suggested effect. Must be broken. If the man thinks this is cold, he should try a few states north.

"Montana. To visit family." Comins throws out the most boring place he can think of to hopefully curb the driver's inclination to continue talking.

"Is that right? I got family in Montana! What city, eh?"

Of course. "The one with all the trees. How much further to the airport?"

"From here, you're talking a good thirty minutes."

"That's just enough time for a nap. If you don't mind." Comins forces a grin and leans his head back.

"Sure, sure." The driver grunts, a bit of disappointment touching his voice.

Comins' phone rings. The number is blocked.

He sighs and answers.

"Uncle?" A woman's voice shakes on the other end.

"Yes?" Comins cocks an eyebrow, the unexpected voice catching him off guard. "Is everything okay? What's going on?"

"I'm fine, everything's okay. Well, sorta. I know I'm only supposed to call this number when there's a serious emergency, but I feel like this call counts as something you don't want recorded."

What in the world does that mean? Comins turns to the side, muffling his mouth away from the driver. "Are you calling from a secure line then?" Safety first, niceties later.

"As secure as I know. Track phone."

"Okay. Are the kids safe?"

"Yes, yes, they are. I just needed some advice. I'm in kind of a strange position and you're the only person I can think of who would understand."

A strange position that only *a CIA agent* would understand, that is.

"Of course." Comins always had a soft spot for his niece, never having had kids of his own. She was the only little one in the family, which made her worse than an only child, but he didn't care. She never took advantage. Was always a sweet girl, responsible, did the right things.

"I'm in a safe house." The words sounded foreign. Why in all the world would this lovely little girl end up in a safe house?

"You're not supposed to tell me that." He didn't have to ask to know. If he didn't know already, he wasn't supposed to.

"I know. I'm not supposed to tell anyone. But I'm scared uncle. They've done some questionable things to put me here and I don't trust them."

"What about your husband? Is it something to do with him? Did he screw up that job at Kelim?" *I knew it was a bad idea to get him in there. Cutting it too close this time, Rob. Your projects need more space apart.*

"That's why I'm here. It's Everett. They took Everett, and I don't know where they sent him."

Comins drops the phone in his lap. Of course. Another dot to connect. Why was he not informed of this?

"What is that?" O'Connor barks, spitting chew out of his mouth.

"That's not possible," Anderson takes a step forward, dark brown eyes entranced. "We proved time and time again that these were just exaggerations. Miscalculated measurements. Pure mythology. Is this some sick joke? Or a government experiment gone terribly wrong?"

"Gene manipulation, probably. This is some serious Dr. Moreau BS." O'Connor snorts.

"If y'all would stop yappin' for longer than point five seconds, I'll tell you what's going on here." Viggo interrupts, stepping in between the company and the monster. "We did not create this. We found this."

"Just like Kandahar." Everett grumbles. "I was told there was only one." He shakes his head, pressing the memories out with his thumbs.

"You've seen one of these things before?" O'Connor spits and grimaces, challenging the suggestion.

"You were also likely told before you went into theater that there was no such thing at all. From childhood. Government doesn't always tell the whole truth son, unfortunately." Viggo chews his inner lip.

"Then how do we know you're telling us the truth now?" Jimenez nods her head upward and licks her lips.

"That's why I chose to show instead of tell. It wasn't for dramatic effect." Viggo responds.

Jimenez nods, accepting the answer. Anderson takes another step closer, holding her fingers out as though she was close enough to touch the thing.

"Don't forget about that red line," Viggo warns, "and since we're on the subject, let's talk about the Trance. Some of you may be experiencing it minimally, even now." He glances at Anderson another moment, her ebony face blending into the dark shrouding her. "Little John here has a nasty trick he's pulled on too many people already."

"Little John?" Squirrel squeaks out from the Omerta booth, amazingly distracted by the display of technology. Somehow, Everett's not surprised.

Viggo points to the giant. Everett leans over and whispers to Squirrel, "Robin Hood."

"Oh…" Squirrel responds, still lost.

"This great beast has the ability to trap you in a trance, draw you in, and, pardon the simple gore, explode your brains inside your skull. Hence the red line. You cross that line, stir fry brains." He points to the line and gestures its girth. "He's trapped some certain individuals in such a trance that they've willingly walked right over the line, knowing the consequences, having seen others do it before, but still going."

"That's scary man." Jimenez shakes her head and shrugs the heebie jeebies off her shoulders.

"All of you have been chosen based on your character and your abilities." Viggo paces the line, keeping a safe distance. "We scrutinized your every detail before choosing you out. We had to be certain of the kind of individuals who would have a better chance at handling this type of pressure. Now, that doesn't mean you're all invincible. It simply means that our psychologists and other professionals deemed you most fit, given the options."

"Sir?" Jones speaks up, his voice crackling from rarely speaking the whole time, "How many have come before us?"

"We've been in official operation for just over ten years in this particular unit, and in that time frame we have had four separate teams of a dozen each." Viggo nods, thinking over the numbers in his head.

"May I ask how many crossed the line?"

Viggo stops for a minute, considering, knuckles to his chin. "An average of eighty percent. The rest have been decommissioned and are currently in memory reconstructive therapy."

12.

Jason Campbell slams a handful of shirts into his suitcase and rushes into the bathroom. "Toothpaste! What did I do with my toothpaste?" He bangs the bathroom drawers closed so hard that they bounce back out.

"Did you leave it at my place?" A girl sits on the edge of the bed, bare legs crossed, smoking a cigarette.

"Would you put that crap out?" Jason swings by and snags the cancer stick out of her hand, then smashes it into the bathroom sink.

"I would'a done it myself but no," she rolls her eyes and crosses her legs the other way, then eyeballs the pack of cigarettes on the nightstand lustfully.

"Underwear, chapstick, phone charger, laptop..." Jason presses his palms to his head and grits his teeth, "It'll have to do. If I forgot something, I'll just buy it." Suitcase flap flies shut, zips up, and hops onto the ground with a rattle. "Remember, you have no idea where I went or what I'm doing."

"Right. Which is annoyingly true." The girl wraps her hair in a bun and grabs the remote.

"You can't stay here." Jason gestures a hand at the dirty apartment, squinching his eyebrows.

"Why not?"

"It's my apartment. It doesn't look good." He steps in front of the television, as though mediating a hostage situation.

"Listen, I don't know what kind of dramatic crap you're making a big deal out of, but me being here isn't gonna change a thing. Plus, you have Netflix and I have lame roommates. Duh." She bobs her head as though she's made the most obvious point of the century.

"Fine. Your funeral. You keep on thinking this is no big deal and you'll end up somewhere you don't want to be. Trust me, you don't want to be connected to this." He rolls the suitcase away, toward the door.

"Whatever you say, Mr. Bourne. Just come back and save me, if you find the time." She clicks on the television and smacks. Jason sighs, shaking his head, and pulls the door open. He hates it when she calls him that.

"What, no goodbye?" She gives him the puppy eyes. He sighs again and leans over, kisses her on the mouth, and straightens out. "Let me know when your done with your vacation. I'll probably be here. And no STI escapades, I seriously can't go through that again. If you're in need, just text me baby." She winks, a strand of hair popping out as she bobbles her head again.

"I will."

The door closes behind him and he immediately pulls out his phone, removes the SIM card, snaps it in half, and throws one half over the hedge while throwing the other half down a gutter. As he walks to his car, he pulls out a Ziplock bag from his pocket and fills it with water from a bottle. Carefully, he drops the phone inside the Ziplock, seals it tight so that the entire phone is submerged and sidesteps toward the dumpster. Tomorrow happens to be dump day. This thing will be history in no time.

On his way to the airport, he stops by the local Walmart and picks up a track phone, a bag of jerky, and a tube of toothpaste.

It's going to be a long flight to Peru.

Everett walks through the barracks, still trying to decide whether his brain is in shock or not, a glaze in his eyes. The groundskeeper, Hare, sits alone at a small, square card table staring at what appears to be a picture. He glances up, sees Everett, and quickly puts the photo away.

"I miss mine too." Everett nods and invites himself to sit down.

Hare just nods in return, scratching an unkempt black beard. His eyes are hollow, like he's been looking at the snow for too long.

"I don't know how it works down here but seems very military. You on a time restricted mission? Doing your time then back home to family?"

"Nope." Hare shakes his head, holding slightly shaking hands together, knees on his lap. He avoids eye contact. "Here for the time being. No rush to get home."

"That's quite the commitment. Do they have family barracks in this facility?"

"Nope." Hare shakes his head and looks away. Everett takes the hint. Though he could swear he saw what looked like a woman and two little girls in the picture, he didn't want to push the man. The mysterious story seemed to resemble too closely that of some sort of tragedy.

Squirrel slams down a deck of cards out of nowhere. "Gentlemen. I believe this is a card table. And I believe I'm the best poker player in this joint."

Neither of the other men respond, out of mutual respect for the recently unspoken.

Squirrel leans over the table, raises his eyebrows, and whispers, "That was a pretty hard challenge I feel like. Neither of you seem the kind of guys to take that lightly." He prods a little further.

"You've only just scratched the surface." Hare mumbles, still staring off into the distance.

"Now that's the spirit!" Squirrel dons a huge grin and pulls the cards out of the case. "Five card? Texas?"

"There's more below. Literally, you just scratched the surface. Viggo hasn't told you yet." Hare glances at Everett, who leans over in deep interest.

"More what, Hare?" Everett folds his hands, replicating Hare's position.

"Twenty dollar buy-in sound good?" Squirrel pops his head up from an intense session of a deck shuffle struggle.

"More of those giants?" Everett scoots in a little closer, but not too close.

"Fifty? Wait, what?" Squirrel leans over, only just now hearing what was actually being said.

"Not just that. Other worldly creatures. I don't know what they are, but they scare the hell outta me. Some look like aliens, but I know they're not." Hare directs a look into Everett's eyes and glances away again, rubbing his hands together.

"Ahhh you got us. Well, you got me." Squirrel goes back to wrestling the cards together, with little success.

Hare glances at Squirrel, then back to the floor, "If I had to do it all over again, I'd never come to this place." He coughs, then cracks out, "Whatever you do," he looks into Everett's eyes, "especially as a family man, make whatever excuse you can and get out of here." With that, he stands abruptly and walks briskly away, sniffling as he walks, looking from side to side.

"What was that?" Squirrel holds the deck of cards split in half in each hand, raised in WTF pose.

"That was a warning, Squirrel. Something I'm sure you're used to ignoring." Everett stands up and walks away.

"Everyone's so freaking miserable around here. It's just a giant. Probably fake too. I bet we're on candid camera." Squirrel looks around searching for cameras, more paranoid about being made the fool than anything in reality.

"**Major, may I** speak with you?" Everett finds Major Viggo walking down a long and unfamiliar corridor.

"Of course, Sergeant." Viggo continues his walk without slowing.

"Pardon my lack of tact, sir, but I have to ask. What else is in this facility?"

"Generators, a chow hall, another barracks for family placement but that hasn't been used in years. Not quite the family atmosphere, if you know what I mean."

Everett squints, then shakes off the apparent lie of Hare's. "Other than that, sir? If you don't mind my asking?"

Viggo chuckles. "You been chattin' up the ole groundskeeper, I imagine." Viggo checks his watch.

Everett nods, unsure of how to respond without giving the man away.

"Now listen," Viggo continues his pace, keeping his eyes straight ahead. "I'll tell you this much. There are more teams on the premises, all routine work, nothing of interest to you and your squadron. As for anything you may hear from some of the locals, we'll call em, it's all ghost

130

stories." He glances at Everett, then continues, "I understand that's hard to believe, considering the circumstances with the giant and whatnot, but it's simple truth of the matter son. You pen up even the most reasonable of fellas and they crack at some point. Our friend Hare needs a vacation, and I'll be sure to make that happen. Anyway, You'll do best to keep to your mission. The sooner we figure this creature out; the sooner you go home to your family." He looks at Everett again, this time for longer. "Which I'm sure you're most interested in anyway."

The pair reach a set of doors that stand unmarked, decorated only by a print reader. Viggo turns to Everett and nods. This is where they part ways.

"Thank you, sir." Everett nods, "One last question."

Viggo waits patiently but emits obvious time constriction vibes and nods curtly.

"What really is our purpose here?"

"Security. For most of you. Research and technical support for the rest. We'll talk more in the morning, Sergeant. Get some downtime and rest. Your squadron is more emotionally exhausted than they may think." He squints his eyes, "You're not exempt."

Everett salutes and turns back down the hallway, fighting the urge to continuously glance over his shoulder. He can nearly feel Viggo's eyes on his back, like a tick crawling around looking for a place to burrow in.

As if there weren't enough questions
before the grand display of that cursed giant.

13.

Comins rushes from security to his gate, trench coat flapping behind, battling with the carry-on sized rolling case. What's he going to do about Olivia? Right in the middle of the biggest technological investigation of his lifetime? This is it, his chance to climb another rung. Provide something truly useful to the powers that be. With the top two dogs out of the picture (thank God that Quinton character offed himself, he was going to be tricky) he's got a whole project of great interest to hand over. That little two-and-a-half-acre lot is going to turn into a three hundred acre closed base in no time. Maybe he'll even get a placard on the wall.

What'll likely happen is that he'll get a pat on the back and Hughes will take all the credit as though he actually did something for once in his career. Either way, a climb is a climb whether or not it's universally recognized as such.

The smell of fresh baked bread picks up his nose, trailing from a generic bakery that may or may not have been titled something stereotypically Italian like, "Gino's Almost Fresh Baked Carb Sticks". He picks his way through the bustling crowd, checking his watch. Should be enough time for a quick purchase, and he didn't have much hope for the chicken cordon bleu and "steamed" veggies on the plane.

Shuffling his ticket in one hand and his wallet in the other, a man bumps into his shoulder and disappears into the crowd.

"Hey!" Comins yelps in reaction, fumbling a few credit cards out of his wallet that splatter on the ground. The man glances back, his square jaw grimacing over the top of a rigid collar decorated with God-awful patterns of fake Hawaiian girls and red Hibiscus flowers. What a tourist.

The face turns back into the crowd and disappears, recognition slowly creeping up Comin's spine like a bad Shiatsu massage. He drops to his knees and quickly picks up the credit cards, jamming them into his wallet as he rushes after the man.

That face. Stoically Japanese. Black hair perfectly cut and slicked back in a Keanu Reeves fashion, the right physical stature…

Quinton. That's it. But it's not possible.

Comins picks up his pace, rushing the opposite way of his gate. An alarm rings off in the back of his head, *You don't have much time, Rob. Six minutes and counting.*

For such an obnoxious shirt, it sure blends in well with the crowd. Further and further down he barely spots the red flowers, disappearing further out of reach.

Four minutes. No more pastry for you.

He picks up another notch on his pace, weaving into positions of clearer vision.

Three minutes. You have to pee now, Rob. Turn around.

He throws up his hands, no longer able to see the man at all. Perhaps it was just a mirage. Quinton's doppelganger. The man's style certainly didn't seem like anything Quinton would be caught dead in. He was more of a slacks and overpriced gray V-neck kind of guy.

That must be it. His doppelganger.

There's no such thing as coincidence.

Comins shakes his head as he turns into the nearest restroom, cursing under his breath.

The sound of generators descends to a low hum, then dissipates altogether. The lights flicker, then blink out and into darkness.

Everett lifts his head and rubs his eyes after a too-short nap and looks around. Too many questions. Not enough answers. No real explanations of anything. And now this.

Power outage.

"Great." Jimenez officiates the problem with the first recognition of it.

"Hey, where's Anderson?" O'Connor spurts, his silhouette moving back and forth in search.

"Is that a race joke? Seriously man?" Jimenez responds.

"No, I'm serious. I just now noticed she's gone. I thought we were all supposed to hang tight here till Major Viggo returned?" He throws his hands up, genuinely frustrated at the accusation. "If I'm gonna make a race joke, it would at least be funny and original."

"Sure it would." Jimenez retorts.

I can take you back to your family. A voice whispers inside Everett's head. With a gasp, he shoots up out bed, skimming his head on the upper bunk with a thunk.

"Ah!" He rubs his head, trying to erase the pain.

"You alright?" Squirrel's head pops down from the upper bunk, fumbling glasses onto his nose. The poor kid has been following Everett around and doing just about everything he was doing. Or poor Everett, either way.

"Did you say something?" Everett gives him an eye, even though he can't see it.

"Yeah," Squirrel throws some attitude, but the admission gives Everett some relief, "I asked if you were alright." Squirrel throws his legs over the bunk.

"You didn't say anything else?" Everett plays the words over again in his head, trying to make sense of them. Some dumb joke from Squirrel again? A weird form of encouragement?

"Dude, I just woke up and heard you bash your head. That's all. You okay man?" the timbre of his voice travels from irritation to concern as Everett walks away, rubbing his head.

"Yeah, yeah. I'm fine."

Crane sits on the edge of his bed, fingers in between a now useless-in-the-dark book that looks like a Bible. "Is there a protocol for this?" He grunts to no one in particular.

"Would we know if there was?" O'Connor complains, pulling up a chair and flopping down in defeat.

"Just sit tight. This is normal for an area like this. Generators go out all the time. They'll be back on soon." Everett winces from the now throbbing headache pushing against the inner backsides of his eyes.

You just have to let me out.

The voice again. Everett shakes it away. Must be remnants of a weird dream, floating around in his head.

The double doors swing open, emitting the silhouette of what appears to be Viggo. "Routine outage. My apologies for not warning y'all." Viggo walks into the room, a calm demeanor emanating from his walk. Everett forces himself to relax and tells himself the man is being truthful. *Ghost stories.* Right. Viggo continues, "Everyone accounted for, Sergeant?"

"Sir, we are missing Anderson. We just discovered this right before you entered."

"Did you try calling her on the radio?" Viggo's voice holds back some but not all of his annoyance.

Everett pulls the radio to his face mechanically, "Anderson, location. Respond immediately. Out."

Seconds pass.

Everett repeats the command.

Nothing.

Viggo curses. "Did she talk to anyone before she left?"

Silence.

"Any clues? Hints?" Viggo struts to the doors and pauses one more moment.

"I don't believe any of us are aware of her intentions, sir." Everett responds, just to fill the air with something.

"I need all CS immediately." Viggo barks, motioning them onward. "Ah, and you too Crane. Everyone else, stay put. And I mean it!" Viggo blasts through the doors, assuming the appropriate persons follow, unaware that the term "everyone else" quite literally meant just Squirrel, since Hare was also nowhere to be found due to having freedom to roam, being a local.

Jones grabs his medic bag and tails along at the end, a somber look on his face. The man has hardly said more than two sentences the entire time but looks determined. Crane waddles in the middle, doing his best not to huff at the pace. Squirrel sits at the card table shaking his head, "Really? In the dark? Alone? Great. Just fantastic." Everett feels for the guy but can't change the situation and gives a sympathetic smirk that he likely can't see anyway as he closes the doors behind him.

The corridor looks different in the dark, small battery powered lights glowing along the footpath to keep them in line. The team moves through without a word, at a near-march, eyes and mind alert as though on mission in theater.

Everett falls back to line up with Crane and slows his pace. He keeps his voice low so the others can't hear. "Hey, uh, question for you."

"What's up?" Crane grunts through his nose.

"I know this is going to sound crazy, but I figure in light of the current scenario, it could be meaningful. But uh, I had a voice in my head earlier that wasn't mine. I thought you might have some sort of Godly insight on that."

Crane nods and takes the information in, thinking about his response. "Perfectly normal, actually."

Everett drops his shoulders after realizing he had been holding them up, tense. The response is comforting but alarming at the same time.

Crane continues, "The trick is knowing whose voice it is. One of the oldest conundrums. Is it you? God? The devil?"

Everett nods like he knows what the preacher means. "How do you know?"

"Ahh, you see, that's the real question. Took me years to figure that one out. What it comes down to is you'll know it's God when it agrees with the Word. If it goes against the Word..." he gestures the suggestion.

"It's either me or the devil." Everett doesn't know whether to believe it, but he follows the logic.

"Right-o."

"And by 'Word' you mean the Bible, right?"

Crane nods. "Hey, someone paid at least a little bit of attention in Sunday school."

Everett laughs, "It's been a minute."

"So now," Crane picks back up, "the process only works if you know the Word. So study up, and you'll have the filter you need."

Everett sighs, then refocuses back on the mission. The destination comes into view, down and to the right, then a steep descent down a short staircase. In the dark, the steel double doors that stand between the team and the Cave, as they've taken to calling it, gleam with a blackened reflection from the corridor's emergency lights.

In the foyer is a collection of different lockers, camouflaged up against the gray walls, unmarked. Viggo presses his thumbprint in a reader on the side of one and pulls the door open. Inside is a rack decked with military issue semi-automatic rifles. Viggo pulls one out and hands it to Everett.

"What the?" Everett accepts the gun but with reservations.

O'Connor steps forward, hand out, and says, "You saw that monster in there. Seems appropriate to me." He takes the gun from Viggo, who only nods in consternation.

"Like a kid in a candy store." Jimenez chuckles, accepting her gun.

"What about armor?" Jones grumbles, almost too low to hear. He pushes circular glasses up his nose and looks to the side as though spotting a scurrying critter.

"Useless for this threat." Viggo sighs and turns away for a moment, tucking himself into a corner to make a call over the radio. The words are audible but incoherent from the distance and low volume. He turns around, shaking his head like a tired dad who has to go into the kid's room one more time to apply an overdue behavioral correction. "Aim high. If engaged by anything, and I mean *anything*, do not hesitate. This includes Anderson."

"Sir, are you issuing orders to exterminate personnel?" Everett replies.

"We are dealing with the supernatural here, Sergeant. This ain't a Disneyland ride. If engaged with aggression, shoot to kill."

"Understood."

Viggo nods and takes another deep breath. He presses a thumb into the reader and the doors unlock.

The crew all look at each other, an unusual kind of anticipation evenly distributed through each soldier's eyes. Everett notices Jimenez tremble for a split second, then regain confidence, if only minimally.

The doors open.

An other-worldly screech pierces their ears and drops each soldier to their knees, hanging on to rifles for balance.

The stench. Oh God, the stench.

14.

Jason Campbell taps nervously on the pull-down table from the seat in front of him and slides his laptop onto it, looking around as though someone might be paying him too much attention.

If someone is watching you, you're giving yourself away.

He sighs and lets his shoulders droop a second, working out the tension by rolling them back a few times. No work. No clues. Just… entertainment. Think of it as an overdue vacation. Blend in. He plugs in his headphones and pulls up a document folder packed with illegal torrents he downloaded while on vacation in Europe three years ago. With his high rate of distraction, he has a hard time settling on a movie mood but finally lands on a budget Armenian documentary about the supposed escape of Hitler to South America. Subtitled in English. The weird subject might take his mind of his even weirder circumstance. Having to read it might make it easier to disassociate from reality by having to redirect his focus. Hashtag nerd problems.

Hours later, he is hustling through customs, trying his hardest not to look over his shoulder. He leaves his earplugs in as a show of tourism but there is no audio distracting him. *Clever boy, Jason. Keep it up.*

Whatever Quinton wanted to do down here, he kept secret. Of course, there was always the promise of exposing this clandestine mission of his, but Jason never got the "in" on that information. He was pretty sure no one did. Did Quinton himself even know what he was doing down here? It seemed odd. What would Peru have to do with a particle collider?

Outside, Jason walks to the nearest hotel. Four years of high school Spanish was finally doing him some good, even if it wasn't the exact dialect he learned.

He drops his bag on the hotel counter and frowns at the cardboard quality bed. Best to budget. There was no telling how long he'd have to be here and despite his cunning con skills, the money would eventually run out. Not that he couldn't swindle anything out of some unsuspecting internet idiot somewhere in the online Poker world, but that was last resort. Raise no flags.

"Okay. If I were Quinton, where would I go in Peru?" *A nice restaurant. Sushi.* "What does Peru have to offer?" He picks out a travel brochure sticking out of his parcel and flips through. The usual. Visit the Amazon. Machu Picchu. Wrestle a crocodile. Nothing helpful.

What makes Peru special? Not their technological advancements. Got to think outside the Kelim box. What was Quinton interested in?

Well, that was a helluva question. Jason squeezes his temples. Perhaps this was a bad idea. Or maybe the only bad idea was to come unprepared. What were the options? Surely prison was awaiting him at home. His job wasn't exactly

144

legal, yet. Of course, they were always working on it but that was a carrot dangled in front of the cart. And he wasn't exactly powerful enough to stay out of the spotlight. Shoot, even Byron wasn't immune. They're going to blame everything on Jason for sure. If anyone's the fall guy, he's the perfect candidate.

Maybe a night out without responsibility would open up his mind. Clear the stress, calm the anxiety. It's not like anyone knows he's here. The paranoia is all in his head.

The sun is just starting to set as he steps out, hoping his apparent American attire won't give him away too much, one way or the other. There's a balance. Blue jeans. Knockoff all black high-tops. Generic polo. At this hour, all the clothing shops would be closed so it'll have to do.

At the bar, he orders a Pisco Sour, awkwardly saluting the bartender with a shrug and a "When in Rome" statement that didn't translate that well into Spanish. He nervously taps his foot and looks around, waiting for the paranoia to clear out of his brain any second.

A young girl, all toothpick limbs, slides into the stool next to him and glances at him before ordering a drink. He smiles back and evaluates her quickly. Too young. Why is she at the bar?

"Eres un Americano, no eres?" She says, her eyes looking him over.

He laughs. "Sí. Cómo pudiste decir?"

She pokes his shirt and giggles. "Come on, did you really think you'd fit in like that?"

The girl is flat chested but flaunts it like she's got it. Jason takes a deep breath and a long drink, raising his eyebrows in guilty admission as he sets the glass back down.

"Didn't exactly have a lot of options." He forces a closed mouth smile.

"What are you doing here, pata? You look stressed." She raises a bony shoulder to her cheek and crosses her legs. He looks up her bare arm and furrows his eyebrows. Her structure looks a little more masculine than he originally thought, but perhaps that was just the alcohol making suggestions.

"Vacation. Why else would a dumb American come to Peru?" He takes another long sip.

"For fun." Her drink slides over, the bartender's hand leaving it hesitantly. She takes a tiny sip and sets it back down gingerly.

"Isn't that the same thing?" He clears his throat. His subconscious tells him he knows where this is going, but his primal brain reminds him of how long it's been since he was last intimate with anyone. The result of long workdays recently plus a girlfriend that was almost certainly cheating on him added up to a twisted form of celibacy.

"Pe, no se´… there are different kinds of fun in Peru that aren't, how do you say, *legal* in the states." She winks and takes another tiny sip.

146

"Ah," he swallows the last bit of his drink and figures, *why not? Maybe THAT will help clear my mind. What's another illegal activity on top of it all?* "I'm here for all the fun I can't have back home."

She uncrosses her legs deliberately in front of him and walks a slow waltz out. The bartender gives him a hard look, then looks at their glasses. "Ah, what does it matter?" He slaps down enough *sol* to cover both drinks, and follows her outside.

Chaos.

Shrapnel spiraling in slow motion around his head.

Bursts of electricity arching from one end of the cave to the other.

Screams from his comrades.

Gunfire.

Something large moving fast. Too fast to sight in on.

Aim high.

Aim high.

For God's sake, aim high and just pull the trigger.

The sound of ocean waves pulls him into an immediate lull. He's laying back on a beach chair, watching the sweat bead down the brown glimmer of a lager stuck cockeyed in the cup holder.

Just beyond the tips of his sand covered toes he can see Julianna flipping sand out of a hole, splattering onto Bastion's castle. For now, Bastion isn't noticing, so Everett says nothing and enjoys the peaceful moment.

Liv reaches over and taps Everett's shoulder. Through oversized purple hued sunglasses, he sees her eyes smile.

"Check this one out," she says, turning her phone toward his face.

He tips his sunglasses and leans over, making a silent bet that he's already seen the meme that she's likely about to show him. He tucks his head down below the wide rim of her hat to get a better view and smirks preemptively.

Bastion has finally found out that Julianna is covering up part of his castle with her digging and starts protesting.

Everett does his best to ignore it, but Bastion raises his voice.

"Jules! Knock it off! You're destroying my castle!"

"Sorry!" She says in return, but she's not sorry. She continues to dig and throw.

"Seriously!"

Everett sighs and looks down at Liv's phone.

The GIF shows a man's large, square face. He is sporting a thick red beard and long red hair. His smirk jitters into a smile, like a GIF does when in poor reception. As he bares his teeth, blood seeps through the cracks and he laughs.

Then the GIF starts over.

"Liv, what in the world is that?"

Liv screams as though she just realized what was on her phone.

Bastion screams at Julianna.

Liv turns and looks at Everett, now silent, and pulls her glasses off her face. Her eyes are green and bloodshot. *What happened to the brown?*

"I can bring you back here," the GIF on the phone in her lap continues its eerie revolution, "Just let me out."

Bastion and Julianna stand erect, shovels in hand, staring at him with a smile on their faces.

Liv suddenly grabs his hand forcefully and pulls it toward her.

Everett snaps his head out of the vision and back into focus just in time to watch O'Connor blast off a flurry of bullets at the giant, right before the thing reaches over and wrenches his head off. O'Connor's body slumps to the floor on top of his rifle, spilling like a tipped glass of juice.

As though the beast was eating popcorn, the giant crams the head into his mouth and bites down, splattering blood all over his mouth. His body jolts from the hits of lead perforating his flesh, but he ignores it.

Everett watches, stunned at the quickness to which the wounds heal up after puncturing the skin.

The giant stops for a second, gloating over his escape and his predictably victorious skirmish. Jimenez screams and runs at him, gun blazing, and Everett watches in horror as the giant slaps her to the side, flinging her across the cave.

Everett takes a quick inventory of whoever remains of the crew and sees Viggo's lifeless body, folded against the natural bend in an A frame draped over a table. Crane lies motionless at the doorway. Jones leans up against a wall, frantically reloading his rifle, reminding Everett to check his. How long did he black out? Did he fire off even one round?

The giant shakes the ground with one stomp that bridges the gap between the danger zone and the walkway plank. Everett checks his chamber. Full.

Jones lifts his rifle into the air and fires at the giant's chest, who grunts in return and reaches out a hairy hand.

"Aim high!" Everett lifts his rifle and sights in on the giant's head as it moves forward, toward Jones. Just as he squeezes the trigger, the giant lunges forward with a speed too fast for any human eye to follow.

Everett pulls away from the scope to recalibrate the whereabouts of the giant, and watches as the beast pulls the rifle out of Jones' hands, grabs him by the shoulders, and skewers him with the burning hot metal. Everett shakes out the flashback of Daniels in his head. *But Daniels isn't dead...*

Jones screams, the sound stopping only by the abrupt collision with the ground as his body is dropped forcefully like a spoiled leftover flung into the trash bin.

The giant turns, bearing a wide, bloody mouth at Everett in the shape of a grin. His green eyes smile, framed by a tattered red mane. A barreling sound comes from his chest in the form of a grunt, and the giant rolls his tongue around his mouth. With words that sound like boulders rolling downhill, the giant speaks, *"Dia dhiut, deartháir."*

Everett drops his gun, pushes his hands against his temples, and braces for the pain. His head explodes with a buzzing sound, and he screams, but he can't hear it.

Suddenly, the buzzing stops.

The giant cocks his blocky head and frowns, curiosity spilling over his face. He takes a cautious step forward and stops, his arm halfway elevated as though uncertain about what to do with it.

Everett pulls his hands from his head, takes a deep breath, and remembers the disturbing vision that had him captivated at the onset of this slaughter.

"That was *you.*" Everett points a finger at the giant.

The giant turns his grimace into a smile and bellows a laugh that shakes the walls. His jagged, yellowed teeth clamp together in a flat line, and he rears his arms up into sprint-ready mode, engaging his entire body into the posture, a coiled gun ready for the flag to draw down and release permission to race.

Everett mimics the pose.

The giant barks a laugh, rears his head back, and charges.

15.

Comins stands impatiently in line, waiting for his section to be admitted to boarding, staring at his boarding pass. Back to Georgia.

He sorts through all the random memories floating around in his head, trying to pin a clearer face on Quinton. His job was to monitor the activity, not necessarily the individuals performing it. They were going to be replaced.

He shakes his head, trying to see through the one-way glass in his mind's eye to catch a likely faulty glimpse of Quinton's face.

"American Airlines would like to welcome section B on board." The voice drones over the intercom.

Campbell was there, but he's a nobody. The last he could recall was a conversation between him and Quinton. Something about firing up the other collider. He looks down at his phone at a picture of the chamber with hopes of generating some sort of hint.

"Not sure what you mean, sir…" Jason *looks confused.*

"Recharge the collider. I'll need it charged up before Peru." Quinton barks the command…

The memory fades quickly just as Quinton turns.

Wait a second… Comins holds up the line, transfixed on the image of the Gibo chamber on his phone.

"Excuse me, sir," a woman's voice peeps out from behind him.

"Shut up." He retorts, racking his brain. The woman blinks in shock and takes in a deep breath to say something.

Comins breaks his trance on the phone and rushes out of the line, heading to the nearest help desk.

"I need to change my flight to Lima, Peru." He slides his boarding pass to the attendant who gives an intrigued pursed lip response. This might be a bad idea, or it could be the best decision he's ever made.

Three days in the belly of the dragon. Three thousand years spent in awe. Three eternities a god, to come back to this cursed place.

Quinton wipes his hands on a napkin and spits. He remembers a day when street tacos brought him pleasure. The simple things. The corrupted things. All evil done clings to the body.

Not this body, though. They made a promise.

But so did he. And he meant to keep his end of the deal. Which meant a while of suffering, first. When he was just human, he would have succumbed to the philosophy that there is no pleasure without pain. After his trip into the god's realm, he couldn't possibly believe that garbage anymore. There *is* a reality without pain. Without labor. Without heartache. A world where

154

technology doesn't come from material goods, mined from the pits by the bones of abused children. It comes from *knowledge*. And knowledge comes from the spirit.

Unless the spirit is trapped in the material world. The things Quinton could do in Tarturia aren't possible in this archaic domain. There are rules. But the rules change depending on location. That is, dimensional location. Or, one could even say, spiritual location. But those things he knew of were quickly fading in the darkness of this world, which means he needs to act quicky before getting lost again.

Quinton watches from the corner of his eye as Jason Campbell walks into the San Francisco Church Museum. The poor kid doesn't even know what he's in for. So dumb for being so smart. He should have never come to this place.

Fortunately, for Quinton, this works out quite nicely. Knowing Jason, and the inevitable disaster that would turn *Kelim Tekhnologies* into a government carnival popup tent, he had no question the boy would get scared and run. It's what happens when you have just enough information to be dangerous. When Quinton was merely human, he felt sorry about setting Jason up. Leaving clues behind to Peru. Flight plans. Open calendars. Browsing histories.

He knew that Jason was smart enough to look for all those things once the "suicide" happened, but also too young and naïve to see the setup. The plan worked almost too perfectly.

He walks away from the taco stand, tossing the leftover half where it belongs, in a nearby receptacle. His tourist attire camouflages him nicely, but Jason will still recognize him. He subconsciously scratches the new growth of a beard, still in shock at the amount of gray that popped through once he finally let the beast out of its cage. If he had known he could grow a beard this well, he might have considered it a long time ago. His current shell may be an improvement on the former one but limited to organic matter even still. *This is only a transitional stage,* he reminds himself.

Saint Francis of Assisi peers down at him from the upper crust of the archway's dome, the second level of heaven where the gods rule. He stops, amusing himself with the simplicity of the depiction of that immortal realm. Soon, the two will become one, and he will reign as one of the high for the rest of eternity. But first, there is business to take care of. Get the dirty work done.

Inside the church, he takes a thorough overview to locate Jason's whereabouts. He lurks through rooms and exhibitions, careful to walk that balance between tourist and stalker, hoping only the former shows. His eyes land on the painting of *The Last Supper*, with its infamously blasphemous guinea pig providing the main course for a group of Hebrews. He laughs at the dig, causing a nearby family of tourists to glance his direction and scowl. *What a joke,* he humors himself, and moves on.

After a few moments of confirming Jason's absence, he deduces that the boy must have gone into the catacombs by now. Time to act quick.

He ducks into the tunnel, a hand in his pocket popping the picklock set loose. Over the last few days, he spent his spare time waiting and watching for Jason as well as practicing his picking skills.

The catacomb twists and turns, revealing wrought iron gates around every corner, blocking different kinds of rooms. Some with the bones of Peru's ancient commoners, others with the darkness of mystery beyond with no further description, not even a "keep out" sign. The tunnels look different from this dimensional perspective, but he spent an eternity memorizing the path to the correct gateway. His feet guide him without question, passed the morbid display of mass graves, bones encircling each other in a particular pattern, each tomb reminiscent of the ancient spiral, the portal to the realm of the gods.

Quinton had something right about his work. The problem was that science and technology, by human hands, could only take him so far. Creating the colliders was like standing on the dark side of one-way glass, beckoning onlookers to come in. He could see that there was another realm, could hear the muffled communications through the door, but could never experience the other realm. That is, not until he sacrificed himself to it. That was when he learned that the colliders aren't transporters or biological duplicators at all.

They are altars.

Humans think they are so smart with their fancy, shiny toys, when all along, the ancients knew best.

The collision between dimensions doesn't need anything fancy or modern. All it needs is the right place and the right time. And blood.

16.

I know he said to stay put, but I don't like this at all." Olivia picks through her open suitcase, searching for a toothbrush.

"Your uncle probably knows best, hun. Have you heard from Everett yet?" Olivia's best friend Elle smacks on the other line.

"No, and I don't think I'm going to. The woman agent doesn't seem to think he's ever coming back."

"You know that's not true."

Olivia bites her lip and breathes in slowly, "I do. I know. But," her hand quivers, "I'm not taking chances."

"This is crazy, Liv. You need to do what the agents say. They're probably listening in on this call anyway."

"Which is why I can't tell you where I'm going. But it is a track phone, so I doubt it." Olivia breaks the news.

A long silence fills the other end of the line, and then, "I understand."

"You know I hate doing this." Olivia closes the suitcase and waits.

"I get it hun. Just you be safe. Let me know as soon as you can what's going on."

"Of course. I gotta go."

Olivia hangs up the phone and tosses it on the bed. "So do I call an Uber?" She says to the air around her. *This isn't going to be easy, but*

I've got to get to my dad. The safest place on earth. And that means I need a car.

Just a few more days pretending. Olivia pops the suitcase back open and digs underneath her clothes. One thing those agents didn't expect was that the gun they figured was under the bed was actually *in the suitcase.* Idiots. With a former military husband, especially one of Everett's caliber, they should have at least guessed there would be guns hidden all over that house, in clever places.

She pulls the gun out, then the clip, and marries the two. "I'll be safe, baby. Just you get done as soon as possible and come find me. You know where I'm at."

A circle of bones lays out like a dinner plate. Someone took the time to arrange human bones in a decorative fashion. *No, not decorative,* Jason thinks, *ceremonial.*

Quinton had left the trail of breadcrumbs almost too easy to follow. Hacking into the computer wasn't even the hardest of it. Those older generation Millennials, Gen X'ers, whatever he was, just don't know how to sweep up behind themselves. It's called *search history.* It's also delete-able.

Quinton's computer was riddled with obsession of the dead and the spirit world. The most frequented topic? San Francisco museum in Lima. Not surprising. At least not to Jason. The dude had weird taste in art. The pictures in the hallway at Kelim were proof enough of that.

He didn't have anything against Quinton. Mutual respect. The usual irksomeness of a rough-edged boss. But Quinton was never a complete jerk. Just had a sporadic temper is all. No hard feelings.

Jason moves further into the dungeon, half searching for clues and half reminiscing. Quinton certainly wouldn't be interested in this place for the art upstairs alone. There had to be something more. Maybe it isn't the end all, be all, but there has got to be something.

He passes by an elderly couple stunned at the morbidity of it all, pointing and gasping as they walk. Must be the only other people down here.

"Excuse me," Jason clears his throat quietly. The place is like a library. "Do you know if the catacomb goes deeper?"

"You mean, uh, *lower?*" The old man gestures to the ground with a swirling motion.

"That too, yeah. More than just here."

"Sure, sure. Lower down, that-a-way." The man grins, his glossy cheekbone pushing up his oversized seeing glasses.

Where it's darker. Of course. "Thank you." He smiles and moves on, the sound of the couples chattering slowly dissipating behind and blending into the sound of their steps back up the stairs.

This is a dumb idea. He walks cautiously down the hallway, taking note of the decrease in light and glass exhibits.

Sandstone lines the walls in chunky bricks becoming more and more exposed as the museum portion fades into the neglected. If there's anything else here, it's got to be locked up.

Unless…

Maybe it's not important. Maybe no one ever comes this far because it's dark and incredibly scary and no one in their right mind would actually choose to walk deeper into a catacomb literally full of human bones when they can't see and don't know where they're going.

He pulls out his phone for light. It's not the greatest, but at least he might be able to see his feet and not stub his toe on a freakin' skull or something.

No data, of course, but never hurts to check. *How far did I walk down this thing in the dark?* He looks up from his phone and shines the light to check its reach. Not very far.

Something cracks behind him.

Shivers shoot up his spine and he freezes.

"Campbell." A familiar voice grumbles behind him.

He turns, backing further into the darkness, just in time to see a silhouette reach out.

The oxygen leaves his brain, and he is falling.

Only darkness now.

Light etches around the corners of his eyes as he struggles to open them. Something about his position feels eerily familiar. Not as though he's been here before as much as *who* is there with him.

"I shouldn't have let you go the first time around." A voice chuckles next to him. "Oh, Bailey, Bailey. Look at you!"

Everett manages to get an eye open. The face next to him is blurry, too blurry to recognize.

"I'm so proud." The man crosses his arms and seems to smile. He punches Everett on the shoulder, "My boy! This is just, well, it's beyond phenomenal. Is there such thing?" The man paces to the foot of Everett's bed. "I think so."

"Wha – what ha-" Everett crackles out an attempt at words.

"No, shh, shhhh. You don't have to talk yet. My God, it took an elephant tranq to take you down son! Just be still. No need for words. You need rest." The man nods and chuckles again.

What? What is this crazy guy talking about? Everett lets his head droop to the side and takes a deep breath. Then he sees it.

The shoes.

He points at the man's feet and grumbles, "'D'ya ever get me a pair?" His hand flops back down and he smiles, whispering a laugh. There must be something extra special in the drugs.

"Oh ho!" The man raises his abnormally high eyebrows, the edges of his face sharpening into normal vision. "Wow. You know, come to think of it, they like me so much over there at Cole Hann I bet they would make a special order just for me. Or, well, for you that is. I'll check into it." He laughs and walks back to the edge of the bed as though suddenly feeling exposed by the shoes.

"They look stupid anyway." Everett laughs again, then coughs and grabs his chest as an invisible dagger digs in.

"That's not very kind, darlin'. I was seriously considering it until you went and said something like that."

Everett clears his throat and squeezes his eyes. His vision returns nearly to normal, and he takes inventory of the room. Plexiglass chamber. Minimal medical equipment, the typical IVs, pumps, monitors. Security cameras. One door with scanning technology.

"Perhaps part of our problem is that we've never officially been introduced." The man steps over to the wall and taps on it, then motions with his finger at something behind Everett. "My name is Cambor Albright. I'm the man behind the mission."

"So you're the dirt bag that snatched my family from my home."

Cambor spreads his hands and grimaces, "I don't like it just as much as you don't."

Everett laughs and gives him the finger.

"Sergeant - may I call you Everett?" Cambor seconds.

"You're the boss."

"You can call me Cambor. My father had an affinity for planes and how they function. It got the you-know-what kicked out of me when I was little, but I've come to love the name now. Can't have quite as much of a charismatic power player without a dynamic name like that. And to think, I didn't even have to make mine up like so many do."

"I'm proud for you." Everett snorts.

"I'm going to be straightforward with you, son. You seem like a man who appreciates that."

Everett grunts.

"I need your blood. Or, well, I need some things *in it*. These bunch of stupid geeks think that technology is paving the way to a new future when the truth has been right there under their nose the whole time!" Cambor leans in and pinches his fingers together like a chef smelling fresh herbs. "You understand."

Everett keeps silent. A voice trickles into his head, but not like before as with the giant. This one is different.

I will rape the blood from your body and use it to make myself the new God. You have no idea what I can do with that kind of power.

"Do you," Everett clears his throat again. The drugs kick back up. His body sinks into the bed like a stone in mud. "Do you remember what I told you last time, Cambor?" His vision blurs again.

"Enlighten me." Cambor looks to the side and nods, then winks, presumably at a tech outside the chamber.

"I can hear your thoughts." Everett whispers as the blackness fades in.

Cambor leans in close and bites his upper lip, inches away from Everett's face. Then, with a slow drawl, he says, "Goooood."

17.

Orange splinters through the God forsaken open window next to seat 11A as the dumb snatch who thought it was good idea to keep it open lays her dumb face against the pane and drools. Rob sticks his head into the aisle and calculates the rate at which the flight attendant drags the drink cart down the narrow path.

Tired and hungry, but mostly in need of alcohol, Rob takes a chance and reaches over the empty seat next to him and across the woman to slide the shudder down. At least he scored with getting a spot next to a vacant seat, making the reach easier to accomplish. It bumps her face as it closes, startling her awake but not awake enough to know exactly what happened.

Perfect timing, he grins to himself as the attendant asks him what to drink. "Light beer. Whatever you pick up first is fine." He ignores the window lady staring at him as he graciously accepts the beer and settles it in to his lap table like pampering a tiny, exotic pet. Window lady asks drily for water and clears her throat. Rob picks up his plastic cup and raises it to her. "Cheers." He sips and smacks.

Window lady downs the water, crinkles the cup, slides it into the seat pouch and nestles back in but not before giving the closed shudder a mystified look.

"You don't look like a tourist." A different woman from across the aisle leans over. Her hair falls in blonde chunks across her cheekbones. Way too attractive to be talking to a guy like Rob Comins.

"I'll take that as a compliment."

"What are you doing, going to Peru?" She leans her elbow on the armrest and situates her position diagonally at him.

"Who said that was my final destination?" Rob retorts, playing the mysterious agent card. He knows he's not a bad looking dude, but this chick is certainly out of his league. She must be bored. Or trying to escape the body heat of Shrek squeezed in the next seat.

"You're on a flight to Lima. You're not going anywhere else. No one does that. That's not a thing."

"You caught me." Rob sips his beer and feigns indifference. Emphasis on the feigning.

"You're not answering my question." The girl teases.

Rob raises an eyebrow. *Is she hitting on me or am I overthinking this?* "You are correct."

"Ooh, the mystery. Most people are very open to talking about their vacation plans. Which means you must not be on vacation. Now, what kind of work would a man in a suit like yours be doing in a strange place like Lima?" She taps her chin in faux contemplation.

Rob shrugs, racking his brain for something unrelated but not so boring as to lose her attention. *Maybe the truth would be fun this time.*

"Just business. That's all. What about you?"

"Same." She shrugs like it's nothing.

"In that dress?" Rob bites his tongue as soon as the words come out. Amazingly, she doesn't skip a beat.

"This old thing? It's for travel. Comfy and cute." She pats her leg. "Hey, can I ask you a big favor?"

"Sure." Rob shrugs his shoulders.

She leans over closer and whispers, "Can I sit next to you? This is, uh, not my favorite." She gestures an eyebrow at Shrek.

"Uh, I mean," Rob glances at window lady, passed out and tucked in the corner. "Wouldn't bother me." *Not one bit.*

Without hesitating, the girl gets up, leaving Rob only time enough to push up the lap table and move his drink out of the way as she squeezes by. He averts his eyes and plays the gentleman but indulges in the peripheral snapshot, smiling awkwardly at Shrek.

"Thank God." She says as she sits.

"You can call me Rob." *No! Why! Not the dad joke…*

"I'd give you a courtesy laugh, but it's been a long day." She smirks. "It was funny what you did to her though." She thumbs toward window lady.

"You were watching?" Rob's face turns red.

She laughs, "The attendant saw it too, but she's a professional."

Rob shakes his head, "I was really trying to be discreet."

"Helen, by the way." She puts out a hand. They shake, and Rob returns to his beer.

"Nice to meet you. So, what kind of business are you in?" Rob strikes up some good ole fashioned small talk.

"I'm an independent contractor for the U.K. as a black-market operator in the quantum technology field seeking new and promising ventures for my anonymous representative."

The flight attendant interrupts with the drink cart again and offers a refill.

"Actually, I'll take a Jack and Coke this time. And whatever the lady wants."

He holds out his card to pay, trying to figure out if he should be cursing the gods or blessing them.

Gravel crunches underneath rubber as the Suburban rolls down the driveway at 0000 Nowhere Road, Leesburg VA. Olivia rushes to the front window, knowing well what view it will bring. Just the man agent this time, coming to check in. Great.

She sits on the couch and watches as he steps out and adjusts his glasses to the sunlight. He reaches into his breast pocket, pulls out a pack of Camels, and bites one out.

Olivia shakes her head. "Disgusting." She grumbles, glancing at her tech-zoned kids as they watch YouTube on their iPads. She waits for him to finish the cigarette before stepping out the front door.

"You can put that nasty thing in your ash tray instead of my driveway." She pushes her chin out, hands on her hips.

His face is stoic as he drops the butt and twists it out with his heel. "Who've you been talking to, Liv?" He puts a hand in his pocket and strides forward.

Olivia wrinkles her face and ignores the question. "You're a bastard."

The agent nods in agreement and puts a foot on the first step of the porch. "I might be. But what I am not, is stupid." He points. "And this is your opportunity to be honest."

Olivia shifts her weight in rebellion.

"I think we got off to a bad start." He takes his sunglasses off and slides them in his breast pocket.

"Ya think? Gee, I would have never thought manhandling someone would make a lifetime enemy out of them."

He nods again and purses his lips. "How about a proper introduction? I'm Gordon."

"Well then, screw you, Gordon. And thanks for giving me a proper noun to curse for the next time I stub my toe."

Gordon sighs and scans the horizon. "You know, I set up this place for you. Wanted to make sure you were safe and comfortable."

"You should kill yourself." Olivia searches for every button she can find to push.

"Your friend Elle won't be available anymore."

Olivia's skin flames up, a bead of sweat immediately forming down her back.

"Don't worry. I didn't go there myself. She'll forget all about it soon." Gordon sighs. "I could make your life miserable, Liv. I really could. But I don't want to do that. I'm just doing my job."

Olivia stares back, trying to quell the potential scenarios of Elle playing out in her head. "I've got lessons to teach my kids now that I'm suddenly a teacher so if you don't mind." She turns to walk away and stumbles on the wrinkled porch. "What a craphole." One way or another, she will find all of his buttons and push every single one.

"I'm sorry." Gordon stays still, unwavering.

Olivia slams the door behind her and stumbles to the couch, her nerves vibrating. Neither one of the kids look up from their devices, blue lights flashing on their faces. She peers out the window and watches as Gordon kicks at the dirt and walks toward the Suburban. He puts his glasses back on, takes one more look at the house, and opens the car door.

Olivia wrinkles her nose as burning hot tears stream down her face. One more day. Tomorrow, she'll do something about it. Regardless of how much of her conversation he heard, Gordon doesn't even know what's coming at him. If he thinks she's dumb enough to declare her intentions over a cell phone, he can guess again.

The general public has no idea what kind of graves are dug in the recesses of humanity. Day in and day out, they live their pitiful little lives, unaware of the calamity that could befall them at any moment. To the conspirators they say, *you don't exist.* And to the theorists they say, *you don't matter.* In the end, they become the food. The sacrifice. The blood upon the altar that drives the demons in their thirst.

You're one of them. Surface level, existing human. Refusing the right to knowledge and power. Ignoring the messages hidden in plain sight. Nothing is a secret. Everything is bare. "It is only the curious who have something to find." The ignorant – they become food.

History has shown the gods to have existed. Not only that, but mortal men have become gods. Quinton knows this. He's read a book or two. He knows that there is no such thing as myth or fable. That fact and fiction are merely concepts, not disparities. Consider Nebuchadnezzar. The number three and it's factors. Two thirds god; one third human. Perfection in organic material.

This is the justification. The act. The dagger raised in lady liberty pose. There is no perfection in organic material outside of the realm of the gods. Heracles was merely a prototype. But Quinton will be the Final Phase. All it takes is blood on the altar.

Of course, Quinton considers that his own blood was a sacrifice. However, sacrifice needs to be exact. What he did on the altar of his own humanity was merely a starting point and now, more blood was required to reach the next level.

Familiar blood.

His family was never close. His father passed leaving behind a legacy of critiques. As for his mother, she is a shell. Materialism engulfed his sisters and as for the rest, relocation to America was anathema. That leaves few options for a man like him when it comes to decision making.

The Eidolon said first born blood, but Quinton never married or had children. This boy, Jason Campbell, is the closest thing to a son he's ever had.

He pulls the cart, carrying a sleeping proverbial Isaac bound and clueless. Deeper into Abraham's bosom. There will be no ram for replacement in this story. No parable needed. Only abrasive, direct action, sans deception.

Ahead, a low light flickers around the corner. He remembers watching the movie

Stargate when it came out and laughing at the absurdity of the concept, but not anymore. Gibo and Marla are only the man-made versions of a phenomena that has already been around for centuries. Truth in fiction is a hard pill to swallow but at least for Quinton, his research lubricated the passage down.

He rounds the corner and curses the humanity still remaining in his given body as it recoils at the sight of the Eidolon. The being stands unnaturally tall, glowing a harsh white aura. Her cobalt eyes show no emotion as Quinton closes into the portal.

"He is not your blood." The Eidolon states.

"Forgive me. I have no children of my own and this boy is the closest human in that regard."

The Eidolon frowns and studies Jason's slumber. "It will work, but there will be a price to pay." The Eidolon turns toward the spiraling portal, flicking his hand upward. Jason's body lifts off the cart and floats as though bobbing in a river toward the portal.

Quinton takes the hint and follows close behind, disappearing into the portal.

18.

The chop of the Chinook boxes his ears and jams his eyes with dust. He turns his face and spits, a futile response to the desert dirt. At his feet, a beast of a man lies motionless- the Giant.

"Wrap it up!" the Sergeant on the Chinook swivels his fingers as a net drops down.

"You kiddin' me right now?" Gerald yells back, gesturing at the size of the giant.

The Sergeant hops out and grabs the net himself, laying it out for the beast. One by one, the soldiers follow suit, dragging the dead weight over.

After nearly an hour of heaving and lifting, the crew breathes in the stench of rotting skin for the sake of acquiring at least a survivable amount of oxygen.

"One more!" Everett holds up a finger in response to the Sergeant throwing up frustrated hands. He rushes over to Daniels' dead body and shakes his head. A gaping hole the size of a fist perforates his abdomen. Everett keeps his eyes off Daniels' face and picks the body up, grunting as he hauls it off.

"This isn't routine, soldier!" The Sergeant yells at Everett as one of his squad mates rushes to his aid, lifting Daniels' lifeless body into the cabin.

"I don't give a rip, Sergeant. He deserves a proper burial, and you know that won't happen out here!"

The Sergeant bites his tongue and motions them in. "Get back to base, ASAP. And don't say a word about this! You were ambushed by ragheads, ya hear? And you took them out. Nothing more. Routine response. Now go!"

The Chinook lifts off, wobbling from the awkward angles of the cliffside, with the cargo in tow. Everett wipes his face and shakes his head to adjust to the receding noise.

"This is crazy." Novak watches the Chinook disappear.

"I'm gonna blow this story up. Taking it all the way up too." Gerald walks down the hill, pulling out a pack of cigarettes.

"You'll do no such thing." Everett kicks up behind him.

"Did you not see what just happened?" Gerald turns back and gestures at the scene. "This is unreal. People need to know that these things exist."

"You're going to do what you're told, soldier, and nothing more." Everett barks back.

"And who made you General?"

"Listen, there's a different problem here," Novak interrupts. "No one's going to believe this. What are we to do? We get enough flack as it is, just being here. Add in a Giant? If you want that kind of ridicule, have at it."

"Daniels' family deserves to know." Gerald points at them. The squad nods in agreement.

"You're right." Everett taps the side of his gun, *"but timing is everything. We'll tell the story when it's right. Otherwise, we all end up in federal for something we didn't do as a cover to make this go away. You know how the government works. They aren't on our side."*

Cambor thumbs his chin as he stares through the Plexiglas at Everett's unconscious body. "Do you think the Giant rebooted his powers? God help me, I sound like one of those cliché marvel movies."

"That is my speculation." Dr. Hudson pushes round spectacles up the bridge of his nose and scribbles on a clipboard. His dark brown hair falls in two split waves down the side of his face, a constant curtain to his peripheral vision. Because of his tendency to over-analyze and hyper focus, the blockaded view doesn't bother him much. Tunnel vision was always an advantage in his mind. "And End Game was decent."

Cambor shakes his head. "You're my biggest mistake, Jeff. Never hire someone irreplaceable in case you want to fire them."

"You're too kind, Mr. Albright."

Cambor flinches, "You know I hate that."

"Tit for tat."

Everett's body twitches in the chamber, just enough to startle Cambor but not enough to know why. "What was that?"

"His vitals are good. Stable EEG. Probably a bad dream."

"Like a dog." Cambor muses.

"I don't follow."

Cambor shakes his head and moves on, "When will the serum be ready?"

"You know the answer to that." Dr. Hudson answers without looking. "Have you decided on a suitable lab rat?"

"I think so. I've poured over the records of the remaining crew. Not that I had a lot of options. That ugly thing was not supposed to get out."

Dr. Hudson sighs. "We know that Everett has the highest concentration of negative blood, among other factors. Family history, physical attributes, et cetera."

"I understand the qualifications. But we can't test on him first. CYA."

"Then why haven't you made a decision? The next in line of the surviving is obvious. Or should I say, limited."

Cambor squeezes his bald scalp and curses. "He's just qualified enough to meet the criteria! That O'Connor idiot was almost as qualified as Everett, but without the background. I can't have another experiment like Daniel's, which means I can't revive the dead. I need an already living being, otherwise we won't know for certain if it works."

Dr. Hudson looks up from his clipboard, glances at Everett, and then settles on Cambor.

"Your hands are tied, then. Unless you want to wait and bring in a new crew."

Cambor stares at Everett, rubbing his chin. "I suppose, since the original plan with the giant is squashed now that it's dead, we don't need an I.T. guy for the Omerta system. We've moved past that. Quickly." He turns to a pair of guards standing at the door. "Get Willard and take him to the ITU. Tell the nurse on deck to initiate the NABU protocol. Then bring him here and set him up in the next unit over."

"So I threw my cheeseburger at him, and if I didn't have the craziest luck," Helen holds her mouth as though it's helping to quell the volume of her laughter, "right on his mouth. And that's how I met Edgar. He's a great dude."

"Wow," Rob chuckles and takes another sip. Hour three has proven the trip to feel a lot shorter than he had anticipated. Of course, his new single serving friend is likely the sole cause of that. "I can't believe you know what Mr. E. looks like. I'm in the CIA and I still haven't seen his profile."

"Honestly, I think that's part of why he hired me. I already knew him. Easier to keep a secret that way. I'm no fan girl." Helen finishes off a swallow of wine and clears her throat. "But it's not like I see him much. He likes his privacy."

"Makes sense. When was the last time you saw him? If you don't mind me asking."

180

Helen brushes an imaginary crumb off her dress, "Oh, it's been years. We only communicate over tech. Which, from what I've heard, is pretty normal business in his realm. I don't even think he's married." She shrugs.

Rob grunts. "So even after that kind of history, he still hired you?"

"I mean, that was high school. He was over it for sure. He knows he was pompous, but he's different now. Still a know-it-all but at least with evidence. Also, I'm really good at what I do."

"And what is that?" he shakes the ice in his cup and peers at the watered-down whiskey pooled at the bottom. "I know you told me your basic title, but I really have no idea what that means."

She laughs, "I know. I say it that way to get a rise out of people. It's fun for me. Put simply, I'm a researcher at the end of the day. When I find a promising new tech venture, I pass that information along. If they want it, they get in on it."

He nods, "So, what exactly is it that you are doing in Peru then? Rumor has it, Mr. E. is a genius so it must be something exciting."

"You would think," she reports unenthusiastically, "but I'm actually going to check out some old museums and stuff. He wants history, for some reason. Genius he may be, but sometimes it feels more like I'm the Igor to his Frankenstein."

He scrunches his face, "That's odd. What would a tech giant want with obsolete social studies that he can't get from Google?"

"Great question." She turns her eyes down, "What about you? I mean, I understand that your employer would require a certain classification to divulge the really good stuff but I'd still like to hear about the boring stuff."

"Oh, you don't know how the government works then if you think I might be doing anything exciting." He pulls his collar down, releasing some heat. *What do I say? This isn't exactly stamped with approval...* "The reality is, all of it is boring. But you're right, still confidential."

"Lame." She nods, puppy dog face. "If you don't mind, I need to use the little girls room."

"Of course." He stands and situates out of the way.

As Helen stands up, she wobbles, then grabs her stomach. "Oh, for more reason than one. That's embarrassing."

"You okay?" He puts out a hand, offering stability to her obvious vertigo.

"No. Elevation. Alcohol." She wobbles and closes her eyes, then attempts to walk sideways and trips into Rob's seat, nearly pulling him down with her. "Oh no, I can't believe I did this."

"Hey, it's okay. Let me help you to the restroom." Robs face flushes in empathetic physiological response as he helps her up and into the aisle.

He can't help but think of a truncated, comical conga line. Not that any conga line is anything less than comical, but this one has the feeling that Wes Anderson directed it. Funny on screen, miserable in real life.

He reaches around her shoulder to pull open the restroom door while also playing the leaning post for her to grab onto as the plane rocks side to side. Even a gentle lull is enough to upset someone's entire world when inebriation is acquired.

Finally, he gets her into the stall and no sooner than the lid is up, she is puking into the tiny little blue bowl, splashing cleaner up the sides. Her hair falls into the bowl, creating a whirl of instability as she holds on with one hand and grabs at her hair with the other.

Rob shakes his head and curses under his breath, glancing behind him to see a multitude of people pretending like they're not watching. He reaches in and pulls her hair up and out of the way. "Hey, I gotcha. Just hold on."

Helen lurches again, "For Pete's sake, close the door."

"I can't fit in here with you." Mile High club is closed for business on this plane. Not that the timing was right anyway.

A Flight Attendant stops by and touches him on the shoulder, "Sir, is everything okay?"

"Yeah. I mean, well, she got sick and is having problems but that's all."

"You can't have the door open with someone in there, I'm sorry."

Rob huffs, "Well, do you have a hair tie by chance?"

The Attendant nods and reaches into her pocket, "Not the first time."

Thank God. He grabs the tie and pulls her hair up into a classic dad-style ponytail. "Hey, I have to close to door. You gonna be okay?"

Helen shoots out a thumbs up, and heaves again.

Rob closes the door, takes a deep breath, and turns around just as the cabin dwellers all suddenly avert their eyes. *Great first date.*

19.

Olivia sways on the front porch hanging swing, taking in deep breaths to calm her nerves. Down the driveway a cloud of dust boils up, hovering above the trees. *Are you ready for this?* She rolls her shoulders out, loosening up. *Need to look relaxed. Like nothing's up.*

The suburban pulls into view and Olivia exhales at the sight of only one occupant. Now that Gordon has seen her relaxing, she stands up and walks to the front column, hand on her hip.

Gordon keeps his eyes, or at least the direction of his face, locked tight on her as he parks and opens the door. "Good morning." He walks to the back of the SUV and opens the latch. Olivia ignores the greeting and watches closely.

Gordon leaves the latch open and the engine running, then walks toward Olivia with grocery bags in his hands, "I won't be long. Just dropping off some essentials and I'll be on my way." He nods as he ascends the steps. Olivia reaches over and opens the door for him, trying to control her shaking.

"There's one more in the back, but I can get that for you." Gordon walks in like he owns the place. His pace is comfortable, suggesting how often he's used this house for this purpose before.

Olivia glances at her kids on the couch. Bastion leans forward on the edge of his seat and stares at Gordon as he walks by, the faint sound of alt-rock fuzzing through his cheap earphones. Julianna is engulfed in a show on her tablet. As soon as Gordon rounds the corner to the kitchen, she nods at Bastion and whispers, *"Go."* Bastion reaches over and quickly but gently grabs Julianna up then carries her out the front door. Julianna bounces in his arms, blissfully unaware of the situation.

Olivia bites her lip and walks to the kitchen, hating herself for putting Bastion through this. Something in her drives her to keep forward though, a feeling that the safe-house setup is going to end badly. From what her uncle told her on the burner phone the other day, Everett's mission is one that leaves no trace behind, including family.

In the kitchen, Gordon raises his arms to set down the bags on the counter. "Right here okay?" He says, turning his face to meet Olivia's.

Olivia quivers, unable to speak to the man as she pulls a 9mm out from the backside of her jeans and aims it at Gordon. Like a machine, the man drops the groceries and reaches underneath his coat, moving quicker than Olivia imagined any human could but not quick enough before she unloads the clip into his chest, knocking him to the ground.

Her hand trembles like a bobble head as she draws the gun back in, working through a sense of shock that tremors throughout her body. Gordon's body lies motionless, his face against the ground where she can't see. Blood seeps beneath his torso, creating a pool that will burn in her memory the rest of her life. *Go, Liv. Go!*

She jams the gun back into her jeans and unlocks her knees, reminding herself to breath. As she turns to run, she notices something amongst the groceries spilled across the floor.

Coloring books and crayon boxes.

The incandescent hum of the room fills all five of Eric's senses with impending dread. Who knew that when the emergency switch was pulled, it would automatically lock down the barracks doors, essentially condemning the inhabitants to vulnerable mystery?

Or maybe the better tense is singular.

Eric sits on the edge of Everett's bed, not for any reason other than laziness and not wanting to climb up into his own. He heard the screams and the gunfire. Then: nothing. Paralyzing silence.

He sighs loudly, hoping that the sound will change the atmosphere. *Should I try to get out?* "I should probably try to get *completely* out." He grumbles to no one and looks around. The overhead lights have yet to turn on, but the battery powered lights at each doorway remain unconcerned, creating enough light to at least see his feet in front of him.

"This is so freakin' creepy." He looks behind his back. Nothing. "Stuck in the middle of a frozen wasteland, by myself, waiting to get my skull bashed in by some mythical giant that shouldn't exist. Not where I saw myself in five years, five years ago. Those stupid self-help books don't work, I'm tellin' ya'." He chuckles at himself.

A sound like doors slamming shut echoes down the hallway. The clomp of boots follows close behind.

Eric stands up and looks at the door, backing away slightly. *Where you gonna go, Squirrel? Ain't no tree to climb in here.*

The marching stops at the doorway. A beeping sound trickles through the cracks, followed by a click. Eric holds his breath.

The doors open, casting a muddled shadow of two soldiers Eric has never seen before. *Where did they come from?*

"Hey guys." Eric squeaks and waves an awkward hand.

"Come with us." One of the soldiers grunts, nodding toward the door.

"I think I'm cool in here." Eric's skin crawls. Something isn't right.

"It wasn't a question." The soldier keeps stoic, unmoved.

Eric grimaces, "I mean, I feel like I was pretty safe."

Before Eric can finish the sentence, the soldiers move with surprising speed toward him, marching faster than he can run.

Eric puts out a hand as though the motion is useful and stumbles backward. "I'm cool! No need to get physical!" he jumps around the back of the bed like a kid being chased by daddy for bedtime.

The soldiers catch up and grab him by the shoulder, with a little extra grip than necessary. "Ow! What is going on? What happened?"

"You don't have the clearance for that information." The other soldier harrumphs as they juggle him between them.

"What the - what in - I'm in the middle of Antarctica, tasked with troubleshooting one of the worlds most advanced computers, with a freakin' GIANT and that's above my clearance?"

The soldiers suppress a grin as they drag Eric out of the barracks, giving no response.

"I want my phone call!" Eric screams, still struggling against the soldier's grip. "I'm getting my lawyer involved! This is going viral!"

Samuel Crane groans and grabs his chest. His ribcage pushes on his lungs, making it hard to breathe. As his vision slowly creeps in, he shakes his head in a futile attempt to shoo away the stench.

He sits up and looks at the catastrophe. Blood everywhere. Mangled bodies. That foul smell.

"Dear Lord. Have mercy on them all." He grumbles, grunting as he pushes himself up the wall. He reaches over to a nearby gun and drags it to himself, checks the chamber, and stumbles to his feet.

"Well. That was unexpected."

Crane walks over to the first body and recoils at the headless corpse. Major Viggo. He reaches down and searches the pockets but finds nothing. With a grunt of frustration, he busts out a large pocketknife and whittles away in the dark, hovering over his task.

A groaning emits from the corner of the cave, startling Crane. He jumps to attention with the rifle and points the general direction of the sound in a militaristic fashion that exposes a previously hidden military background, a Pavlovian response that took years to subdue. With a life-threatening event comes a life-protecting reversion.

Samuel Crane had spent his first years out of high school as a Marine, mostly partying too hard and out-drinking even the saltiest of sailors. Out-fighting them too, when the time came. One dark night, in the throes of the usual drunken stupor, he looked at his bloody fists and made a life changing decision. Mama had always written letters with concern and love, and the last one had really penetrated his soul deep.

The letter broke hard news about his father passing. The man had always been good to Samuel, and Samuel gave him hell in return. The idea that he would never see the old man again to apologize, heal old wounds, and tell him he truly loved him, crushed Samuel to the point of despair. He knew better and decided that was not the man he would continue to be.

The next day, he inquired about becoming a Chaplain to which the Corporal laughed, of course. After a good stink-eye and a few threats, however, the man gave in and set Crane on a path of celibacy and abstinence, made easier by the help of distracting Theology school.

Now, those long-forgotten tactics came back in muscle memory, flooding his brain with memories he swore he'd never dwell on again.

A cough blubbers out from the corner where his rifle points and he sighs. Not the cough of a threat.

Crane lowers the rifle to his side, jams something in his pocket and jogs over, favoring his left leg for whatever happened to it. No time to inspect. This scene won't be quiet for long.

Jimenez sits propped up in the dark, blood pooling out of her side and trickling out of her mouth.

"Ah, preacher man, right? Come to give me the prayers?" Jimenez slurs the words, nodding her head.

"Its not your time." Crane lifts her jacket to inspect the wound and frowns in confirmation of a somewhat positive diagnosis. "You're fine. Let's get you out of here."

Crane reaches behind her back and pulls her up with surprising control and she groans.

"Ah! Hey man, just give me the prayers and let me go."

"Listen here, young lady. If all I do on this dismal continent is save you, then I've done my duty. Whatever it is that impaled you happened to miss any vital organs so let's get you out of here and in a bed, stitched and drugged up."

Jimenez laughs, then groans. "You don't sound like the preacher back home."

"I am all things to all people," Crane pulls her arm around his shoulder, "that I might by all means save some, even if only one, my dear. Now stop talking and help me out. I'm like a drag racing car. I can blast out of the pit, but I'll peter out after a short sprint."

Jimenez laughs again, grinning in eerie contrast to the blood wiped across the side of her face. "Okay Pops. Just watch the hand placement. That ain't a cargo pocket you're grabbing."

Crane's face turns red and he grunts, resituates his arm and apologizes.

"Off we go."

Silence echoes inside Everett's head, penetrating with a supernatural serenity that breaks the bounds of science. Not Nirvana, or any state of ascension. Simply, absence of chaos. Complete control. Awareness.

I'll be curious to see if this jacks the boy up or not. I hope not. Can't wait to see what this stuff can do for me.

Everett knows the voice isn't his. Even though he doesn't know the man all that well naturally, he's more familiar with Cambor than Cambor would be comfortable with.

The silence is interrupted by memories flashing. Long forgotten and often intentionally quelled memories float to the surface, the same ones he was ordered, A.K.A. water boarded, to forget.

Growing up he had always been the athletic type. Tall, muscular, and generally healthy despite his poor diet. Regardless, football didn't turn out to be his forte, and with no real-life skills he joined the Army if for no other reason than to serve his country and add to his life resume.

A year into his four-year contract, he wondered if the choice was really the right one. After marrying Olivia, the burden of the service became increasingly heavy. Still loyal to the cause, but miserable, he put in the work, hoping to come out with some sort of trade. Then the unthinkable happened.

Leukemia.

At first, though morbid, he thought the diagnosis might be his get out of jail free card. He rapidly lost weight. More detrimentally, lost strength. Spent over a year in the hospital. Nearly lost Olivia to the stress of it all. The perfect storm bubbled up and pushed him to the brink of insanity.

About a year in, while withering away in the hospital bed, a man in a suit came in for a visit. Clean shaven, professional, and scrupulous, the man never stated who he worked for or explained much of the reason for his visit. Or at least, how it benefitted him.

"Mr. Bailey, please. Call me Mr. E."

The man pulls up the nearest chair and sits rigid, hands on his knees, and looks Everett in the eyes as he talks.

"Today is your lucky day. You have a wealthy benefactor interested in your health."

Everett laughs and looks at his skeletal chest. "All the money in the world can't cure cancer, Mr. E. Trust me, they don't care how much debt I go into and it shows. My diagnosis has me somewhere between metastasized and dead."

Mr. E. smiles and breaths in as he sits up, his energy commanding the room. His face is young for how achieved he appears. Either he was born into riches or is a genius ahead of his time. Or perhaps there really is a fountain of youth.

"Mr. Bailey," the man's words interrupt Everett's thoughts.

"Call me Everett."

The man smiles and continues, "This benefactor has access to technologies that are unheard of in this practice. Technologies that, for lack of a better term, appear miraculous."

Everett's heart bounces and he breaks a sweat. "I'm confused."

"Unfortunately, I can't divulge much information at this time about the technologies."

"No, not that. I'm not surprised about that. I'm sure there's a cure for just about everything, and only the elite have access to it." Everett glares at the man, trying to read his face. "What I'm confused about is, why me? I'm not in that elite class."

Mr. E. holds his smile and lingers on it, long enough to make Everett question whether he spoke the words or merely thought he did.

Finally, Mr. E. cracks the smile. "I can tell you this much. You have a very special type of DNA that plays well with the technologies. Not many do. The Benefactor is interested in helping those in the same pool as you. In fact, it comes as quite a shock that you even have cancer because of the inherent strength of your DNA."

Everett laughs. "Sounds like a Dan Brown book."

The man blinks, as though hiding offense at the flippant remark. "However, I am required to submit to you this disclaimer."

Everett raises an eyebrow, untrusting.

"While we can actually guarantee the outcomes of the procedure, we cannot guarantee you will like it."

Everett turns his head and frowns. "I don't know what that's supposed to mean, but if I'm being honest, I don't like the sounds of it."

Mr. E. stands and straightens, then buttons his jacket. He reaches into the pocket and pulls out a card, sets it on the table next to Everett.

"If you change your mind."

Like a ghost, the man floats out of the room quietly.

Everett flinches. His eyes flutter. The calming silence returns.

"What was that?" a muted voice trickles into his ears.

Everett twitches a finger and remembers where he is.

Somewhere between reality and another dimension, Olivia sits next to his bed. He doesn't see her, but he knows she's there. She takes his hand.

"Everett, baby, everything's going to be okay."

Everett breaths in deep and releases, the connection to Olivia releasing with it.

Reality glitches into memory. The greenish glow flickers white, and he is back in the hospital room, shortly after Mr. E. left.

"Hey, babe." Olivia sits in the same chair. She has gained weight, especially around the midsection. Everett is oblivious to her ruddy eyes and lack of makeup.

"Hey. Hate that you're seeing me like this."

Olivia chuckles and shakes her head, then takes his hand. "I love you."

"Love you too, babe."

Olivia starts to cry, and Everett finally notices.

"Hey, hey. It's okay. I'm going to be fine. I might be here a long time, but the doctors seem to think I'll make it out one day."

Olivia puts a hand to her nose in an attempt to stop the fluids flowing. "It's not that," *she whimpers and closes her eyes. When she opens them, she avoids eye contact like two mirrored magnets.*

"What is it? What's going on?"

Olivia puts a hand on her belly and forces herself to look Everett in the eyes.

"I'm pregnant." She breaks down and drops her head in her hands, sobbing.

Everett goes cold with shock. His milky eyes are wiped blank, where they were once the only lively part of his dying body, they are now integrated into the decay with the rest of him.

Olivia controls herself and looks up at Everett's blank face, turned away and frozen.

"Everett, please say something. I'm so sorry. I'm so sorry."

He picks up the card Mr. E. left, the numbers blurring from the fog creeping into his eyes...

Everett shoots up from the bed with a gasp and grips the flimsy mattress until it rips beneath him.

"Holy…" Cambor mouths on the other side of the Plexiglas chamber and backs up. The doctor standing next to him merely lifts an eyebrow from his notes and sets his pen down, suddenly very attentive.

Everett looks around at the machines, the drip lines, the computers. Then he looks at Cambor.

The doctor next to Cambor turns his head and mumbles something to an assistant sitting at a computer but Cambor puts a hand on his shoulder, motioning him to stop.

I want to see what you can do. Cambor intentionally directs his thought at Everett.

Everett smiles and lifts his hands.

As his hands rise into the air, so does everything else in the cubicle.

He rears his hands back as though winding up for the pitch, and releases.

A Maelstrom torments Quinton's eardrums with an unrelenting pressure as he hovers over the onerous mouth of the earth, situated deeply in the Arctic. His skin tingles at the needling of icy waters fraying from the portent. All the rules he had never completely understood, in government and nature, are now either answered or convoluted by the panorama set before him.

Eternal gray clouds swirl overhead in nauseating perpendicularity to the Maelstrom, making Quinton think of an hourglass. Veins of lightning scatter sporadically, imprinting purple echoes on the underside of his eyelids that flash away like foreign Morse code over a dying radio.

"Why didn't we go directly under to avoid the passage?" Quinton yells at the Eidolon and pushes his wet hair back off his forehead.

198

"I told you there would be a price to pay."
The Eidolon only mutters, but Quinton can hear
his voice as though the creature pursed lips to his
hears.

Quinton looks down at the entrance, this
hole in the earth. All the world's governments
banned travel to the uppermost northern parts for
this most obvious reason. Can't have the public
knowing about an opening in the earth that
connects to the underground civilizations. No, no,
Atlantis must be kept a myth. Deeming Tartarus
as a fairy tale not only helped to disqualify the
Bible but kept dull minds from seeking reality
and therefore – escape.

Not that Quinton wanted to see the demise
of the human population. In fact, he wanted quite
the opposite. To help free the minds of those who
wanted to be free and were willing to sacrifice for
it and help keep those who did not want to see,
comfortable. The masses are too ignorant to
understand the concept that control is for their
own good. Keeping the poor, poor, and the rich,
only richer, all the while keeping the majority of
the population stupid and happy. Or at the very
least, content.

The irony in all this, Quinton muses, is
that the truth is so obvious. Typically extorted
through fiction and once again destabilized by
labels but nonetheless, available. From Francis
Bacon to Suzanne Collins, humans were exposed
to the truth all along. Only a select few have
woken up out of the matrix and those have been

disparaged to mere government stamped conspiracy theorists. Create a label, and let the proles do the rest.

Quinton knew all of this before the opportunity of transmogrification, which is why he chose this path. To avoid the humility of social petrification and denunciation. Join the ranks of the gods, and therefore control the destiny of man.

For their own good, of course.

"Do I understand correctly, then?" Quinton knows the Eidolon can hear his thoughts.

"Yes. If you make it through, your sacrifice will be sufficient for Ascension, and we will accept this blood." The Eidolon gestures at Jason's limp body, hung as though the Marionettist took a smoke break.

Perhaps Jesus was on to something. Diving deep into the earth, into Death, in order to ascend. Just when Quinton thinks he has already performed this duty, the depths increase. He can't help but focus on that little word, *if.*

The Eidolon turns to Quinton, his glowing face flickering amidst the dark sky. "Nyx will be waiting. She will not require payment, but passage will not be free."

Quinton nods. No point in asking what the opposing statements truly mean at the primal level. To understand the primal, one must reduce himself to it. Wallow in the ashes. Eat from the pig's trough.

A portal opens before the Eidolon and he steps through the slit, disappearing into the sideways eye just before it closes.

Jason's unconscious body remains behind.

Heat rises from Quinton's lower glands up through his spine until it reaches his head and pops into a million tiny stars.

The journey was going to be hard without dragging a limp body along. He drifts to Jason, grabs the boy by the nape of his shirt, and dives in.

20.

The hustle of the terminal in Jorge Chávez International Airport roars into the empty air as Rob walks side by side with a slightly awkward version of Helen who has trained her eyes on the floor for safety as well as social buffering. Neither one of them speaks to the other, creating a palpable realm of silence made more apparent by the ever-increasing background noise of the busy airport terminal.

At the threshold, Rob glances at his new friend, desperately attempting to control his fervent interest, balancing his demeanor with a flippant attitude. He knows it isn't working all that well. This is why he works so much. Being put on the spot in the middle of an assignment is natural to him. Having to pull a gun or make a fast decision that could mean someone's life - that's easy. Traversing the complex world of attraction, while on the surface appears to have a similar approach needed, is a danger beyond deciding who gets to live or die.

"That was God-awful." Helen groans as they walk toward the gate.

"I'm sorry." Rob searches for something more meaningful to say.

"Oh, I'm sorry, Rob. I didn't mean it that way. You were delightful. It was the whole, you know." She rolls her hand.

Rob chuckles but cuts its short. "Sure. I know what you mean." He smiles, but she keeps her eyes on the floor.

"So where are you staying?" Helen sighs and looks up at the terminal signs.

Rob's heart thumps in his chest. He didn't expect her to show any desire to continue their visit. *Play it cool, Rob.* "I'll probably just get into the nearest Marriott."

"Marriott's are nice." Helen nods and finally makes eye contact, then smiles. "Aren't you going to ask me where I'm staying?"

Rob catches his breath. *Man, has it really been that long? Am I that rusty?* He forces a laugh, "I was trying to be the gentleman."

"I think you already presented that card with helping me earlier. Am I just not your type?" She winks.

Robs hand trembles as he puts it in his pocket, then takes it back out, unsure of what to do with it. "No, no. I mean, yes. Yes, you are a beautiful young woman."

"We're the same age, Rob. Just about." She laughs and shakes her head, then looks away. "Baggage is over here." She nods to the left.

You're losing her, Rob. Think fast. "Can I pay for your cab?"

Helen barks a single laugh. "I don't think it works like that, but you're sweet." The baggage claim comes into view.

"Let me at least get your bag for you."

She turns and smiles at him playfully, "It's got wheels, I can handle it. But thank you."

Robs face turns red. *Crap. I lost her.*

"I'm staying at the Marriott too, if you really want to know."

Rob chokes. "That's, uh, convenient coincidence."

"But I'll still get my own ride there. Tell you what," she stops at the conveyor, plops her carry-on down and crosses her arms. "I'll let you buy me a drink later. Pretty sure there's a bar in the hotel."

Rob clears his throat. "I'd love to."

"But I'm just warning you now, it'll probably be a soda."

Rob laughs and nods. "Fair enough."

The bell on the conveyor rings and the belt kicks into action.

Rob stares awkwardly at it, trying to find the next natural thing to say but coming up with nothing.

"Oh, it's about time luck turned on my side." She walks to the conveyor and pulls off her bag, slides the handle out, and rolls it over. "See you tonight, then."

"Of course, yes. I'll be there." Rob watches as she walks away and can't help but think about a line he heard once in college describing Marilyn Monroe's strut, *Like two cups of jelly on stilts.* He shakes his head and peels his eyes away as she disappears through the double glass doors.

Olivia reminds herself to loosen up her grip on the steering wheel for what feels like the hundredth time. Bastion sits in the passenger seat, staring out the window with a hollow face. In the middle row Julianna kicks her feet over the edge of the seat, excited to finally sit like a grown-up with no booster. Her glazed eyes are glued to the tablet, bouncing back and forth with her hair as she bobs to the music in her headphones.

"I don't understand why you can't tell me what happened." Bastion grumbles at the window, causing a splatter of fog. He draws a stylized smiley face in it and deadweight drops his hand on his lap.

"You're not old enough to handle certain adult situations, Bastion. I told you this."

"I was old enough to help us escape so you could shoot the guy."

Olivia sighs and loosens her grip again. Of course, he heard the gunshots. He's played enough video games to at least get a hint, even if it doesn't sound the same in real life.

"You weren't supposed to hear that."

"It's not like I was trying."

"I thought you had your earbuds in."

"They fell out as I was running Julianna across the driveway."

Olivia pauses, thinking. "Listen," she rolls her shoulders back. "They were going to get rid of us."

"You mean kill us?"

"Seriously, Bastion, let me explain it my way." She glares at him, daring him to speak up. He does the wise thing and closes his mouth. "I talked with my uncle. You know the one who works over in Dallas a lot?"

"The CIA guy?"

"Yes. That uncle."

"Savage."

Olivia snorts a laugh. "He basically told me to get out. At first, he said to stay put, but after some research that advice changed. These agents aren't really working for the FBI or any government entity. Not directly, at least. He ran an analysis on our whole situation and told me it was dangerous and to get to your grandpa's house ASAP."

"So did you shoot him?" The boy has a little too much enthusiasm.

"I had to. It was the only way."

Julianna leans forward, "Who did you shoot, Mommy?"

"You have got to be kidding me!" Olivia whispers to the side and shakes her head. Bastion fails at holding back a grin and turns his head away to keep from getting caught, putting his knuckles to his mouth.

"Honey, I didn't shoot anyone."

Bastion snorts and then coughs, clears his throat, and takes a sip of an energy drink from the cup holder.

Olivia shoots him a death glare, "Your brother and I were just talking about…" she searches, expressing blank thought with her hands.

"Fortnite." Bastion pipes up. "Finally got Mom to play a round with me."

Olivia's shoulders drop and she sighs, moisture welling in her eyes as she glances at Bastion.

"Oh. Sounds boring." Julianna goes back to her iPad and hums to the song, doing a little dance in her seat as she pulls the headphones back on.

"You owe me one." Bastion half teases and smirks.

"This conversation would have never happened if you hadn't pushed it and manipulated information out of me that you didn't need to know and I didn't want to tell you."

Bastion's smirk fades into a grimace and he suddenly finds the floor mat very interesting.

"And when we get home, whenever that happens and I'm sure it will, you can buy the Season Pass and whatever skin you want, on me."

"Yes!" Bastion hisses, a grin spreading across his face so taught it could split in half.

Olivia smiles as she turns back to the road, reality settling into the corner of her eyes in disparate contrast to the glee seeping from Bastion's.

Dr. Hudson contorts his mouth into an anticipatory wince and holds. All the expensive equipment attached to Mr. Bailey lies destroyed and useless on the ground inside the cubicle. The Plexiglas, however, remains perfectly intact, unscathed.

Cambor's grin expands parenthetical to his bare teeth, his eyebrows raised in wrinkled patterns up his bald head. "Well I'll be! Now *that's* pretty cool. You sure that serum isn't ready yet?" He turns to Dr. Hudson who is still wincing from the recent demise of his medical equipment.

Cambor's phone rings. "Tell me something good." He chuckles as he answers.

Everett fumes in the cubicle, a confused look on his face.

"Oh, yes. Yes. Bring him in please. I believe you're right on time. Thank you." Cambor hangs up.

"That is nearly two million dollars' worth of equipment." Dr. Hudson shakes his head and stares at his clipboard, stunned.

"That's government rate. Take one tenth of that number. I'll get you more."

"We didn't just lose equipment. You realize that right?" Dr. Hudson remarks, writing notes, keeping his eyes on the clipboard.

Cambor hushes and for once gives the doctor a serious look. "You don't have this all on backup? Tell me that doesn't affect the end product." He steps away, studying the doctor.

"I'm going to have to run some serious diagnostics and quadruple check everything to make sure, but I think we can still come up with something."

"You better be right." Cambor shakes his head.

"Might take a few days."

"Uh!" Cambor spreads his hands and drops his mouth in shock. Just as he utters the next word, the doors to the room open, emitting an obnoxious noise.

"Screw you! And you! All of you! I'll dox every single one of you when I get out of here!" Squirrel kicks his legs in a fussy tantrum as two soldiers haul him into the room.

"Eric Willard," Cambor redirects his attention to Squirrel, his arms open as though receiving a guest for dinner and drinks. "I've been expecting you. You, my friend, are a life saver in more ways than one."

"What is going on here?" Squirrel squeaks as the soldiers drop him and stand back. He straightens his shirt and looks around, clears his throat, and assumes a semblance of composure.

"Well, you see," Cambor walks toward Squirrel and puts his hands in his pockets, shaking imaginary keys. "We've been doing this project."

"Wait, who are you?"

Cambor giggles and looks from side to side, hands in his pocket like a grade school bully. "Did you know that all the ancient religions believed that hell was an actual place that existed underground? I was starting to believe it myself, until you showed up. My hero."

"Who are you?"

"So demanding. Whatever happened to chivalry?" Cambor waltzes over, shaking his head and tisking. "As you can see, we are having to shift our perspective here and approach our little project by different means. And you, little buddy, are the answer to my riddle."

Squirrel cocks his head, unsure. "What are you talking about?" The soldiers behind him step back up and grab him by the arms.

"I'm going to be straight with you, Eric. May I call you Eric?" Cambor offers rhetorically. "You're my newest guinea pig. I'm sorry the IT gig didn't work out."

The soldiers grunt and heave Squirrel up and over, dragging him to one of the open cubicles.

"What do you mean guinea pig!" Squirrel yells, squirming in the soldier's grip.

"Look, we get to play again." Cambor turns to Dr. Hudson who only shakes his head in response. Squirrel yells in the background.

"We don't have enough data to run any definitive tests yet. I recommend keeping him confined until we do."

"I really don't want to wait. Can we just jab him with something and see what happens?" Cambor pleads like a child.

"He's your last subject. Unless you want to go with the locals."

Cambor frowns and turns to Everett's cubicle just in time to see the Plexiglas shatter and cascade in awkward chunks down the platform.

Everett steps over the threshold barefoot and looks directly at Cambor.

Cambor holds his breath.

Everett releases his in a guttural scream and charges.

The cheesy glass chandeliers twinkle in the permanent twilight of a hotel bar room, giving the illusion that the hotel is more luxurious than it really is. Rob sits on the edge of his seat, trying to figure out how to stop his knees from rubbing against the bar, when he suddenly realizes he can relax and slides deeper into the chair. He swallows the last of a gin and tonic and sets the empty glass on the counter, then looks toward the elevator lobby.

"Wow, Rob." He mumbles to himself. "Look at you. Chill out."

"You good man?" The bartender puts his hand on the counter and slides it toward Rob's empty glass.

"Yeah, yeah." Rob fakes a smile and checks his watch. Ten past eight. *Did I come too early? Am I that old now?* "Hey uh, have you seen a girl sitting here about my age, blonde hair, blue dress?"

"Probably. There's one right there. And right there." The bartender points out a few other generically descriptive women. He chuckles and picks up the glass, the unspoken refill question in the way he tilts it toward Rob.

"Oh. Yeah." Rob nods, accepting the offer. The bartender gets to work.

"It all makes sense now. Not that I didn't have it figured out before. But that confirms it."

"What's that?" Rob leans over, trying to hear the bartender over the lull of music and nearby drunken conversation.

"You're not drunk off one drink. You're nervous about a girl. That's why I asked if you were alright."

"Oh." Rob nods. "That obvious?"

"Only when you talk to yourself."

Rob laughs and his face goes flush. "Noted. Thanks." He takes the drink and sips, careful not to overdo it.

A purse plops onto the counter next to him as he studies the lime in his glass, causing him to jump.

"Hey there." Helen smiles and sits, then looks at the bartender. "Soda water with lime please. And keep 'em comin'." She winks at Rob and chuckles at her joke.

"I was starting to think the old man in me lured me here way too early." Rob loosens his collar.

"Listen, if you're old, then I'm old. And I disagree with this whole aging practice these crazy people have. We're just…" she pauses a second, finger on her lip to think, "adults. Not teens anymore. That's all." Pleased with her

212

conclusion, she slides her freshly made drink over and stirs the straw before pulling out the lime and squeezing the juice.

"I can get on board with that." Rob smiles, then straightens his shoulders back. A little cozier, a little more confident. Perhaps they are more on the same level than he realized. Not that she stooped to his, but more that he rose to hers. Unless he was there all along and is just now accepting that. Either way, his breathing slows to a normal pace and a real perma-smile settles on his face.

"So, what were we talking about right before I started throwing up?" Helen states as though the sky is blue. "Actually, rewind a little more than that. I'm sorry but I really don't remember much."

Rob takes a sip of his gin and tonic, grunts forgiveness, and smacks his lips. "Let's see. I think it was basically story time, and yours were much better than mine." *That's it, Rob. You got it now.*

By the time he had come to, the pool of blood he lay in had partially dried, sticking Gordon to the tile floor. He groans and rolls on his side, his jacket screeching like wet duct tape pulling off the floor.

Leaning on his elbow, he rips his button-up open and reaches behind his rib cage. With a grunt and a sigh, he pulls the bullet proof vest off and tosses it to the side.

Fresh blood dribbles out as he hoists himself up on onto his knees. Grabbing the counter for stability, he lunges upward with a yell and pounds his fist on the countertop, grimacing.

He hobbles to the bathroom, dragging his right leg and streaking a trail of blood behind. In the bathroom, he wrestles his phone out of his pocket. Blood smears on the screen from his attempt to unlock the phone and he curses, wipes it off on one of the few dry spots on his pant leg, and tries again. After successfully opening the phone he dials a number, hits speaker, and sets it on the counter.

While the phone rings, he tugs off his jacket and peels his shirt down, revealing a missing chunk of flesh from his deltoid muscle. His football player physique may have made him a bigger target and therefore easier to hit, but his sheer mass also helped to protect the more sensitive under layers that would have otherwise been shattered or torn in half.

He pulls the shirt off his left arm, the sloppy sound of blood slurping as it slides. The other line picks up.

"Johnson." A woman's voice grumbles.

"Kat, I need assistance."

"Did your stupid dog get out again?"

"I've been shot." Gordon moves his left arm to check the damage from a second bullet strike that riddles down the side of his forearm.

Must have struck as he dropped the grocery bags in order to make that kind of a mark.

"Oh. You okay?"

"Still breathing. I'm at the Onassis house. She took the Tahoe."

"That wench." Johnson stabs the word as Gordon touches at his wound. He grimaces and catches his reaction in the mirror, unsure of to what degree it was in response to the pain or the word.

"I'm on my way." The line goes dead.

Gordon grabs the hand towel and turns the cold water on, then soaks the towel. He dabs at his shoulder, shaking his head.

After cleaning up the best he can, he eases down and picks up his bloody jacket. Holding it clumsily with his bad arm, he fishes in the breast pocket. After a minute, he pulls out a forest green crayon. He turns it in his fingers for a second, grunts, and drops it into his pants pocket.

*Little **Quinton** **shivers** on the front porch, rubbing his arms for warmth, teeth chattering from the burning cold wind. He has been sitting on the concrete for over two hours, since 4 a.m., as punishment for writing the wrong character of a Kanji symbol. Inside, his mother is doing the dishes by hand, frowning through the window where she can see Quinton trembling.*

The sun pretends to look through the clouds and sees Quinton. Almost out of embarrassment for Quinton's mother, the sun retreats behind a snow cloud, turning a blind eye. He notices and curses the sun for its cowardice.

His mother dries off the last plate and sets it to the side, beyond the border of the window. Silently, she disappears, and like a scene change in a stage tragedy, reappears through the porch door.

"You will write it perfect now. Come." In an impossible act, she deepens her frown and turns into the house.

Quinton sets his eyes hard. He has suffered this type of punishment enough. "Why are you doing this to me, Okasaan?"

His mother stops, hands gripping the side of her dress. "I do nothing. It is Hariti who punishes you for misbehavior."

"Hariti isn't real." He stays unmoved, defiant.

"It is Hariti who possess you now. How dare you defy me?" His mother looks over her shoulder and scowls.

He huddles in on his knees and turns his face toward the frostbitten streets. A car slides down the black pavement, brake lights undulating an anxious pace.

The blunt numbness of the freezing concrete pushes through his tailbone and up his spine, but he ignores it.

The porch door closes behind him.

His mother peers out from the window, partially silhouetted by the dull yellow light bulb of the undersized kitchen. A stubborn tear pushes

Before he shot himself, Quinton assumed a shroud of darkness would envelope him. He thought death, even temporary death, would be tangible. That darkness wasn't merely absence of light. It was presence of nothing. A blanket of asphyxiation, clinging more deeply than mold in the lungs, like breathing wet air. He didn't anticipate the light. Blinding, painful light.

This juxtaposed place is more than death. A darkness so deep he can only conclude that he is part of the darkness. Just as mass breaks down into elements, and elements into atoms, he is separated at the smallest juncture and synthesized into the shadow. Where he once thought passage brought illumination and death brought culmination, he now floats trepid through the murky waters of self-denial and effacement, unsure of any conclusion but disturbed by the peace that ignorance brings.

There is no light here.

He used to think that emphasis was made by contrast. The more the dark, the more the light. In this place, not only does light simply not exist, but dark bellows a mocking *I AM* from the black flames of an all-consuming guttural tar.

Swirling with a black so deep it is incandescent, he struggles to keep hold not only of Jason's fortuitously unconscious body but his own sanity. At any moment, the mind can break hold and release all those precious chemical connections into a thousand tiny shards of bestial impunity, returning to a primitive state of survival with no real conceived consequence of a determined end. The reversal of primordial muck standing bipedal from the mire, the once conglomerating evolution of man turned on his heal and dispersed back into bedlam.

He feels carved, like coal etched into the thick surface of parchment. His form sketched by some brutish heavy hand, churned into an oblivion reserved for the damned, struggles to remain existent against the brawling reverberations of eternal chaos fighting to swallow itself into nothing.

A shadow appears, contorting his mind beyond limits. What type of shadow could be so dark as to make this current darkness appear bright in its presence? The form takes shape in his mind, though he's sure it always had a shape before he was capable of perceiving it.

Slender yet gargantuan, perhaps the height of a common house, the form reaches out a hand to him. He recoils in his spirit, but his body remains suspended, confused, steeped in what must be the underside of quicksand as far as he can comprehend.

"I… I know you." Quinton stutters, his voice crackling out a fluttering origami swan, crumpling into the dark. The fraying water of the maelstrom seeps into his bones, but it doesn't matter anymore. He is the water. He is the darkness. He is the dispersion of mass ejaculation from the existential womb of dualistic reconciliation. In this place, futility is king and he is kneeling to His Majesty.

The form orbits closer, taking the lustrous shape of a woman. Her curves flitter in the dark, pulsing with the confliction of amorous energy and death, should the two be faultily considered separate. In this realm, sex, death, and life are one and the same. The brooding crunch of frozen dirt beneath the boot that conceives orgasmic awareness of life in contrast with dormancy. Palpable dissention that agrees with itself by merely exposing its cooperative existence.

"And I," she whispers, her voice a rake over hot coals, "know you. My dear Quinton."

21.

The last thing Everett remembers is the sound of a single gunshot. His sandpaper tongue sticks to the roof of his mouth. His side throbs with a deep soreness, combined with the burning itch of healing.

He hears a knocking sound and wrestles his head up high enough to look around.

"You really didn't think I'd be ignorant enough to not have a backup plan, right?" Cambor smiles through the Plexiglas and gives a little wave, mouths the word "hello" as though Everett can't hear him through the shield.

Everett shoots up and slams his body against a metal harness, screams, and drops back down. The barbaric coffin rests like a piano hand over his entire body, cross-hatched for air circulation but tight enough to keep him secured. He pulls his arm up, searching for a way to unlatch the device, and groans at the odd pain, a feeling akin to striking the funny bone.

"Have you ever read the Bible, Everett?" Cambor paces just inside Everett's peripheral vision, rubbing his chin. "Weird question, I know. Me, personally, I'm not a religious guy. And truly, if it wasn't for Mr. E practically forcing me to conduct research on the book, I would have never thought to look there. Lot of interesting things in that story. If you keep your eyes open for them."

Everett cautiously feels around the coffin to no avail. He closes his eyes and focuses in on Cambor's energy.

"Not this time," Cambor smiles and chews the corner of his lip. "Nuh uh, no mind reading. It's the copper. Such a strangely simple and useful tool for guys like you. That's where the Bible research comes in, by the way. Amazing, the kind of nuggets hidden in that cryptic text. And to think, I once believed it was all 'a bunch of bologna' as my dear Pop would say."

Everett stares at the coffin metal, laced over his body. He thinks of apple pie, then grunts at the thought. He must be the apple filling.

"From what I hear, it's a weird feeling, being hit by copper. Or touching it. For you, anyway, not me." Cambor pulls a handgun from his side and checks the chamber. "One pure copper bullet in the side took you down quicker than a rubber duck at the fair. I always liked those little duckies. Oh, and don't worry. I have other worst-case-scenario means of keeping you right where I want you. So don't bother too much with trying to figure a way out of this one."

"What do you want from me?" Everett grumbles, fidgeting with his side.

"It's amazing, really. The copper would only kill you if it struck you in the head. Otherwise, it simply renders you completely weak with contact. *Painfully* weak. In addition, and fortunately for me, it also inhibits your cognitive abilities. Which is great, because the Doc here has given you a little somethin' to enhance all those abilities that I need caged at the moment. Something to get that blood flowin', if you know what I mean."

"What do you want from me?" Everett repeats the question, this time with a guttural emphasis.

"The Hebrews in the Bible figured out something very fascinating. Did you know that all those clans they fought against were actually Giants? Well, most of them anyway. Isn't that crazy?" Cambor pauses for effect. "They don't teach that in Sunday School. Not that I paid attention anyway."

Everett sighs. "What does that have to do with anything?" The claim sounds farcical, but Everett humors him.

"What do I want from you…" Cambor paces, thumbing his chin. "Well, you have this gene. Actually, it's a protein. In fact, you have a magical composition of genetics in general. Negative blood, IGF-1, ten percent more brain mass than the average bloke, just to name a few. Bet you didn't know that when you signed up for the Army, huh?"

Everett closes his eyes and focuses on his breathing.

"No? Anyway, at the risk of being blunt, I want your blood. I want those genes. Now, I know this is supposed to be some sort of special military operation where we do the whole *super soldier* experiment and I'm supposed to create this unstoppable army and blah, blah, blah. And, I mean, I'm going to do that. Eventually. But you can't blame a guy for wanting a little bit of that first. Since that idiot Viggo got himself and most of the crew killed, I'm going to do what I want with the little time I have left.

"So here's what I'm going to do. I'm going to synthesize all those little goodies in your blood into something a little more potent, more condensed. And then I'm going to infuse myself with it and become, basically, a god. Like good ole Nebuchadnezzar. Of course, you wouldn't know about that because you don't seem like the Bible thumping type. But those ancients, man, they were on to something. Smarter than we contemporaries give them credit."

"Sounds dangerous." Everett grumbles.

"Oh it is. That's why I'm testing it on your little buddy here first. Hope you didn't get too close on the journey here." Cambor looks over at the adjacent chamber where Squirrel lies on a bed, hooked up to machines and drip lines.

Everett jolts and syphons the air through his constrained nostrils, clenching his fists.

"Oh, you don't that like I see." Cambor frowns in surprise. "Interesting. I didn't think you'd mind. Don't worry. If it all goes downhill, we'll euthanize him and put him out of his misery. And in the likely case of success, we'll just add him to the Super Solder ranks!" Cambor claps his hands as though he just announced an exciting piece of news.

"You're sick. It'll never work. You are playing with fire."

"I really expected something less cliché from you. Man, I hate clichés. Oh, and one last thing." Cambor motions someone from the darkness.

Everett turns his head to see and squints as the form walks out of the shadow.

Daniels steps into the light, zombie-eyed and breathing hard. His body has been stretched to its limits; unnatural muscles rippled by uncomfortably large veins looking like they might pop any second.

"Daniels!" Everett screams and jolts against the coffin. His body hits the copper and immediately drops back down, the abating pain reverberating throughout his body like a fading jolt of electricity.

"I thought you two might know each other." Cambor nods in approval. "One of my other fail-safes. He's programmed to obey me, and only me. And if you get out of line…" Cambor wags his finger, then looks at Daniels. "Use lethal force."

"You won't get away with this!" Everett screams from his coffin, careful to keep away from the surface.

Cambor turns to Dr. Hudson. "What's the status?"

"Should be ready in a few hours." Dr. Hudson keeps his eyes on his computer screen and makes a note.

"Ahead of schedule. Daddy likey."

"Mother of God." The words drop in manifested essence as Agent Johnson trots around the side of the Escalade. Gordon grunts in return. "We need to get you to the VA."

"Not the VA. I'd like to survive this round."

"We're not going to-"

"Yes, we are." Gordon whistles through his teeth as he snatches the door open.

"That dude's a chop and you know it."

"You believe all the gossip you hear? Get the door for me, will you." Gordon eases into the passenger seat, squinting his eyes.

"Aw man, you're getting blood everywhere. Where are you hit?" Johnson inspects the mess, her hand on the door.

"Just get in. Let's go." Gordon nods his head toward the driver seat.

Johnson frowns at the seat and slams the door, cursing under her breath.

Gordon watches Johnson as she hustles around the front of the car, thinking. She jumps in and slams the door, fumbles the gear shift, and squeals out of the driveway.

"They can't know about this one."

"What you mean they can't know?" Johnson slaps the steering wheel. "They know everything. Man, they probably know more than I do and I'm here with you now."

"They couldn't possibly know. I'll take care of it anyway." Gordon stretches his leg out and groans, pain throbbing up into his hip.

"Yeah, yeah. You'll take care of it. Where did she get the gun? Was it yours?"

Gordon glares at her.

"Just asking!" Johnson puts her hands up and looks back at the road. "Maybe we can slip a bill to the doc at the VA. I've done that before. Haven't been written up yet."

"We go to the Barber." Gordon sighs, catching up to his breath.

"You mean the Butcher?" Johnson laughs and shakes her head. "Dude's got a nasty reputation. You know he stitched a crack spoon inside McCabe's leg once?"

"McCabe is a coward and a liar. Take me to the Barber or pull over and I'll walk there myself."

"Your funeral." Johnson tongues her cheek, staring at the road. "You really like her, don't you?"

Gordon stays silent, eyes on the road.

Johnson chuckles and shakes her head. "Never thought I'd see the day."

The walk outside is surreal, and surprisingly pleasant. In a bit of a drunken stupor, Rob had convinced Helen to take a little walk in the fresh air. Subconsciously, he knew he needed to walk off some of the alcohol. He also knew she was stone cold sober and could see right through his failed attempts at handling the alcohol like he used to be able to do in high school.

The bustle of the night life in Lima shimmers in restaurant patio strung lights and passing traffic, blurred with the fuzz of passing laughter and conversation.

"Want to get a bite?" Rob offers, gesturing at a passing restaurant.

"Oh, no. I had a little somethin' before meeting up to settle my stomach."

"Oh, right." Rob thinks, slower than he realizes. "You feeling okay?"

"Yes. Good as new. Just not hungry. But if you are, I'm totally down to hang out still."

Rob slurs, "No, no. Wanted to uh, make sure you were good." He knows he's running out of steam and conversation. "I do think I'd like some water though."

"It's free at the hotel." Helen offers. "Hey, I've had a good time with you tonight. And that's saying something, coming from a sober Helen."

"Same here." Rob turns the corner that heads back to the hotel and Helen follows. "One of the best nights in a long time, actually."

"I like to hear that."

"So," Rob misses a step and regains his balance, pretending like it didn't happen. Helen raises an eyebrow and does the courteous thing by not acknowledging it. "You starting up research early tomorrow morning?"

"Eh, when I want. I have a lot of lenience." Helen emphasizes the words, drawing them out long enough for Rob to fully hear them.

"Ah, I see. Well, maybe we'll run into each other at the hotel sometime."

The hotel comes into view, "Think we're about to right now." Helen drops the hint, leaving Rob to decipher exactly what way she means it. He laughs and leaves it alone, hoping the response will suffice.

"What time is it?" He mumbles as they approach the hotel.

Helen checks her phone, "About ten."

"Wow. That's earlier than I thought."

"I wasn't about to call it a night if you weren't." Helen slides the phone back into her purse as they walk through the automatic doors. "In fact, now that I've had some space away from that horrible flight experience, a glass of wine sounds pretty great. Might help me sleep, too."

"You have a hard time sleeping?"

"Little bit of insomnia. But I think it's just my personality. Always working on something."

"Well, let me buy you a glass. If you really do want one, that is." Rob gestures at the bar.

"Ugh. Those chairs are miserable. But my suite isn't top notch either. What about yours?"

"Um, yeah. Mine's decent." Rob stammers, "Probably the same though."

"I'm willing to take my chances if you're comfortable with that? Plus, I'd love to hear the rest of your story about working with that White House threat that you never did finish earlier." Helen points at him, teasing.

"Sure, yeah." Rob can feel the heat coming up out of his shirt and restrains the urge to fan it out. "I haven't dipped into the cooler drinks yet either. Pretty sure there's wine in there."

"Perfect." Helen slips her arm into the crook of Rob's elbow, "Lead the way, sir. I'm excited to hear about this White House breach that the news apparently didn't cover."

"There's a reason for that." Rob flips into Agent mode to cover his insecurity and the two disappear into an elevator.

It doesn't take long for Crane to realize he wouldn't be able to get Jimenez to a legitimate practitioner. The entire base echoes the silence of a ghost town. No personnel in sight. Not that there were many in the first place, but Crane always had a knack for feeling energy. In this corridor, the only energy came from him and Jimenez, but he could tell they were close to something.

"I'm fine now, Pops. Really. I can walk." Jimenez clutches the makeshift bandage around her waist and slides her arm off Crane's shoulder.

"Don't overdo it. I don't like the feel of this."

Jimenez grunts and does a poor job of covering up the gimp in her step, then unlatches her holster and pulls out a 9mm. "Told you to let me have that AK. Sure you're not going to shoot your foot with that machine there, old man?" She shakes her leg out and walks a little smoother but still slow.

"I know a thing or two." Crane's eyes scan the stark hallway and land on a door to the right. He motions toward it as Jimenez racks her pistol and readies the weapon.

Crane slinks to the side, rifle poised, and nods at Jimenez. She returns a confused look and shrugs her shoulders. *"That's locked man."* She whispers, *"What are you doin?"* She gestures at the fingerprint reader, then glances up at the security camera.

Crane rolls his eyes and digs into his pocket. He pulls out Viggo's amputated thumb and puts it up close to the reader, then looks to Jimenez for approval.

Jimenez drops her jaw to her chin and in her shock gives a slow thumb up, shaking her head.

Crane presses the finger onto the reader and a loud clack is heard as the door unlocks, then throws the door open as Jimenez rushes over and trains her pistol on the opening.

"What the ffffhu..." the word trails off into oblivion as Jimenez lowers her pistol and walks into the room, Crane close behind with his rifle drawn.

"Oh, Lord." Crane lowers his rifle.

The room opens up larger than anticipated, camouflaged by the nonchalant placement and demeanor. Big enough to house a fleet of C130's, the room gapes open revealing row after row of Giants lying in cylinders, still in stasis. One large cylindrical machine sits idle in the center, a hundred stasis chambers circling around it like rays from the morning sun.

"What is all this?" Jimenez stalks further into the room, perusing the chambers in awe.

"You know," Crane walks parallel, carefully examining the room and all potential dangers, "I always knew these monsters were Biblical, and real. But I didn't know they were still alive."

Jimenez stops at one of the chambers and stares at the chest of a giant as it gently rises and falls in a deep slumber. Red, curly hair mats the muscular body and his finger twitches, causing Jimenez to jump back and point her pistol at the creature. She releases an overdue breath and lowers the pistol back down. "You say these things are *Biblical*? As in, the Bible talks about them?"

"Oh yeah. You remember King David and Goliath, right?" Crane edges up to the cylindrical machine.

"Refresh my memory. I slept through Mass."

"Well, Goliath was a giant, standing about twelve-foot-tall and twice as wide as any normal man."

"Impressive." Jimenez joins Crane at the machine and studies the controls.

"He was the smallest of his brothers." Crane looks at Jimenez and raises an eyebrow.

"Oh." Jimenez looks back out at the chambers. "There must be at least a hundred of them."

"And I think we've only just scratched the surface." Crane points to a sign above the controls that reads *Level 12 Stasis Holding.* "and I mean that literally."

22.

Olivia rolls up a steep, wooded driveway with caution. The term driveway being a pleasant overstatement. Gravel would be an upgrade. The road twists and turns, threatening to high center the already high-profile vehicle with neglected ditches and jutting rocks.

"When we get there, stay in the vehicle."

"Why?" Bastion smarts.

"Do what I say, okay?" Olivia glares at him and grips the wheel, her knuckles white from keeping it jerking side to side. "Listen, your grandpa is kinda…"

"Angry mountain man?" Bastion jams a button on his Nintendo Switch and drops it on his lap, "Lost reception."

"I guess he is kind of an angry mountain man." Olivia rolls down her window. "Which is why you need to stay in the vehicle until he realizes who we are."

"You think he's going to shoot us?"

"No!" Olivia yelps, "Well, I mean, maybe. It's not out of the realm of possibilities."

"Sounds like a stand-up guy."

"Yeah. He's a survivalist." Olivia apologizes for her father.

"You mean a prepper."

"What do you know about preppers?"

"Other than the fact that they're typically angry mountain men holed up in the middle of nowhere with canned food and guns, quite a bit actually." Bastion retorts, impressing himself with his knowledge.

"Where did you learn about all that?"

"Mom, the internet is a thing."

"But why are you…" Olivia searches for the words. "Never mind."

The road takes a sharp turn and forks, one side turning into more of a quad trail and the other staying generally the same as before but with more of an opening of trees on either side.

"How come grandpa never comes to visit? I haven't seen him since I was like, three."

"Two. And that's a question you'd have to ask him. Though I wouldn't recommend it."

"Great." Bastion stares out the window.

Olivia looks in the backseat at Julianna who is passed out despite the bumpy terrain, a stuffed unicorn strangled in her arms and her head cocked painfully to the side. By the time she looks back to the road, it has opened into an obvious property line with a hint of a house tucked behind a patch of trees. She slows the vehicle down and puts her hand out the window.

A water tank appears on the side and Olivia pulls up to it, then stops the vehicle.

"Is this it? Looks like a house over there."

"Stop talking." Olivia puts her hand up and makes a gesture with her fingers while Bastion watches in confusion.

"What are you doing?"

"I said stop talking!" Olivia barks and stops the gestures, keeping her hand raised and searching the surrounding woods.

A figure appears out of the nearby trees on Bastion's side and steps up to the door, causing Bastion to jump.

"Son of a-!" Bastion scrambles at his mother who pops him on the mouth before he can even finish the statement.

"Don't you ever say that again!" Olivia points at Bastion and grinds her teeth.

The figure laughs, exposing itself as a live human. "I told you they'd start talkin' after you if you ain't gonna stop that mouth of yours."

"Bastion," Olivia sighs and gestures at the man. "This is your Grandpa Adams."

Bastion stares at the man, still bent toward Olivia and leaning on the center console as though the man might break through the window and grab him.

"Good to see yah 'gin, son. Why don't you come out and give your Grandpa a hug?" The man shows a big, toothy grin that is surprisingly white considering the lack of other obvious hygiene.

Bastion looks at Olivia and raises a worried eyebrow.

Olivia smiles and pushes him. "Go on."

Two gangsters stop talking to each other as the mint black Escalade rolls around the corner and into the trailer park. One of them whistles as it passes, leaning back as though getting the better view of a voluptuous set of curves strutting by. They watch as the vehicle eases over the speedbumps and rolls deeper into the park.

The Escalade parks in an unmarked lot that sits in front of a lime green shack with shuttered windows and an ancient antennae threatening to slide down the roof. The screen door sways in the wind, so warped and weather worn it no longer latches. The number on the front door reads 2 3 (blank) 6.

The gangsters look at each other and suddenly think of a better place to be, glancing back every few seconds as they walk away.

The passenger door of the Escalade opens and Gordon eases out, struggling with his own weight as he hobbles to his feet. He slams the door behind him and walks to the driver side, knocks on the window with his knuckle, and waits.

The window rolls down.

"You're coming in with me." Gordon says, leaning his shoulder up against the door.

"I'm not going in there. You gon' die. Crazy old man's prolly going to kill me too, just for being here."

"Get out of the car."

"You lost your mind."

Gordon opens the door quicker than anticipated and stands to the side. "I'll die here waiting before I'll ever die in there."

236

"Why you want me in there so bad? I can stay out here and keep watch."

"No one messes with the Barber. Nothing to watch for."

Johnson steps out of the vehicle and straightens her jacket. "You know we ain't gonna have tires when we come back out, right?"

"It won't be touched."

"Dude must be the Devil himself. Why you want me there in so bad anyway?"

Gordon sighs and shifts his weight. "I," he pauses and looks at the ground. "I uh, need your support, Kat."

Johnson cocks her head and stares at him. "You did not just say that. I'll be, the great Gordon Pierce needs *my* support to fix his owies."

"Fine. Stay in the car." Gordon waves her off and hobbles toward the shack.

Johnson shuts the door behind her and smiles, sticks her hands in her pockets and walks behind Gordon. "Nah, no. Not now. The table's turned. I can't back off that."

Gordon struggles up the first step, wincing as he pushes his weight on his leg. Johnson hops up and offers herself as a crutch.

"I can do it."

"You already showed me that soft under layer. Let me help you." She carefully puts an arm around his waist and encourages him to lean on her. He only grunts in return, but gives in.

At the top of the short stairs on the porch, Gordon stops. "Listen," he says, looking her

directly in the eye. "And don't laugh." He
whispers.

Johnson grins and raises an eyebrow.

"Seriously. This isn't a joke, but it sounds
like one." Gordon warns. "Tell me you're not
going to laugh."

Johnson glances at the front door, then
back at Gordon. "Sure man. I won't laugh." She
nods, furrowing her eyebrows in curiosity.

"You can't say anything about horses."
Gordon whispers again, glancing at the door.

Johnson snorts and puts a finger to her
nose to cut it short. "I'm sorry, what?"

"Horses. Don't even say the word. Avoid
any sort of conversation that could lead that way."

"You realize how crazy that sounds, right?
Is this guy mentally stable? You sure this is a
good idea?"

"Just," Gordon puts out a hand and closes
his eyes, takes a breath, and looks at her again.
"Just trust me."

Johnson tilts her head to the side and
watches as Gordon steps over and knocks once on
the door.

"That it?" Johnson says. "He heard just
that one knock?"

"Yeah."

"This is worse than the movies."

Gordon grins, "Where do you think they
got all that from?" He glances at her, then looks
back at the door. She chuckles and looks behind
her shoulder, just in case.

A moment crawls by. The distant sound of a baby crying from a nearby single-wide ebbs into the air then flows right back out. The screen door smacks against the wall, rattling on its way back out as it floats.

"Dude's not here. This is a waste of time." Johnson slaps her leg and turns to the stairs.

A lock clicks open on the other side of the door and Johnson turns back. The door cracks open, revealing a dark interior.

"I seen your mother's face in my dreams last night." An old voice crackles out from the darkness.

"You've never met my mother, Barber. She died when I was little. I need your help."

"Oh, the things you think you know. What'chu done this time, little brother?" The door opens a little more, revealing only a dark silhouette.

"Need some stitches. I've got pay."

The door opens more, and an old black man with sputnik frizz hair frowns at Gordon. He hunches, hanging a brown, oversized shirt off his shoulders like a dress trying to slip off a small hanger. He nods at Gordon and looks at his pockets, then pulls his bare upper lip into his mouth.

Gordon reaches into his pocket and pulls out a large, ping-pong ball sized marble. He holds it up for the Barber to inspect.

The Barber gasps and reaches into his breast pocket, pulls out a monocle, and plops it in front of his eye. He motions for Gordon to hand over the marble then snatches it from his fingers like a starving animal stealing food.

"Where you find this, boy?" The Barber studies the marble, holding it up to the light.

"In a common place."

The Barber glances an eye at Gordon, then looks back to the marble. "Mint sulphide. Charcoal Lapis Lazuli sun in center. One of three in the whole world. You know that, right?" He continues his examination.

"I figured something like that."

The Barber looks back at Gordon again, then pockets the marble in his sweatpants. "Well, what'chu waiting for? Come in, come in. Don't know why you're standing out here." He opens the door and steps to the side to let them in. Gordon looks at Johnson, who stares back in shock and mouths a *WTF* at him as they walk inside. He waves it off and ushers her in.

Rob wakes up and grimaces at the sunlight pouring through the open hotel curtain. Empty beer bottles litter the nearby desk, with a few plastic cups. He groans and rolls over, a cheeky smile on his face.

An empty hull greets him with a punch in the gut.

He jumps out of bed and pulls on pants, cursing. His hands shake as he attempts to button the fly until he gives up and leaves it open.

He scrambles to his satchel and flips the latch open, then pilfers through the compartments, cursing under his breath. He shuffles through them again, grabs the satchel and dumps it upside down on the bed.

"She took it. That little…" He catches himself, takes a deep breath, "She took the tablet." Rob pushes his hands on his temples, his thinning hair in disarray. Were it not for the seriousness of the situation, he may have even laughed at himself had he seen a mirror. Bare pot belly flopped over unbuttoned pants, Einstein hair, and purple bagged eyes.

Rob sighs, accepting the obvious fate. The tablet, and all the information connected to Kelim Tekhnologies, is gone.

He staggers to the bathroom and slaps cold water on his face, grabs a towel, and dries off. No time for a shower. Action must be taken, and now. Something catches his eye on the edge of the counter.

A note, written on a hotel paper.

Rob, duty calls. In more ways than one, unfortunately. If you haven't discovered already, you will soon. I hope you know it's not personal, only business. Orders are orders.
I had a great time last night.
I hope we can both move passed this when all is done.
Don't bother trying to find me. I'm already gone.
I'll find you.

Rob crumples the paper and throws it at the trash can, shaking his head, then releases a built-up yell from the pits of his gut.

A warm hand engulfs Quinton, stretched from the core of the goddess, intertwining not only with Quinton's structure but the space between the atoms that hold the structure together. His mind splinters into a dozen different rays of vortex, causing him to forget all about Jason and therefore releasing his grip. Jason's unconscious body floats down into oblivion, torn apart by the voracious freezing teeth of the maelstrom.

One fracture of his mind notices for a split second and panics. The grip of Nyx tightens, knowing his thoughts. He lets the concern go and watches as it falls from his mind and into the maelstrom to follow Jason to his shredded demise. The grip on his soul loosens but remains, alarming in its deep and uncannily familiar comfort.

"Hariti," Quinton forces the name out. "It is you. I know it." His words become a creature of their own as they pass his lips, iterations reduced to cenobite exposition, now vulgar in display.

"Shhhh." Nyx's voice is a lullaby in his head, caressing tortured nerves. "I have been watching you from the depths, Quinton. Waiting for this moment. I knew you would find me."

"Were you there? In my darkness?" Quinton stays in his mind, avoiding the ugly procreation of inadequate low-frequency utterings.

"I am always in the darkness, my love."

"They call you Nyx. Are you one and the same?" Quinton's body relaxes in her open palm, his shoulders rolled over the curve and his head lulled back. The arch relieves the pressure on his back, stretching out the years of anxiety that seeps into the darkness.

"I am." Nyx responds. "Are you ready, love?" Nyx's voice rolls like velvet over his mind and trickles through his spine, spreading out into his extremities with a warm tingling sensation.

"I don't understand." He revels in the warmth of her hand and closes his eyes.

"You will." She clamps her hand shut as though snatching a fly, her energy emulsifying with his as he dissipates into her essence.

He jolts, the pressure from the clap overpowering him, causing him to lose his breath. The splinters in his mind conjoin into one and spin, becoming the gaping open mouth of tunneled vision, blinding light pulling him into the lower dimension that is earthly memory.

Trees flutter. Sunlight flickers through the leaves. Quinton steps onto the grass, the low crunch solidified in his hears. The pungent smell of crushed green blades rises to his nostrils, triggering a strong olfactory response.

A figure moves in slow motion, blurred by the backlight.

Kendra.

Quinton's heart skips. He reaches out a hand.

"You've known me longer than you realize, my love." Nyx's voice rolls in his head.

"Is it…" He hesitates, unsure. "you?"

Kendra's form sharpens. She is wearing a white sun dress printed with red carnations and carries a book in her hand. She smiles at Quinton, then walks past him.

Quinton turns to see himself, a teenage boy, walking toward Kendra.

"You understand?" Nyx says.

"She was only seventeen." He bites his lip and watches the scene. "Why did you take me here?"

"I know this was a hard moment, but it was an important one."

Kendra's blonde hair bounces as she approaches young Quinton and puts her arms around his neck. He smiles and wraps her in his arms.

A tear drops down Quinton's cheek.

"I can't look." He groans.

"You have to, love. Be strong."

As Kendra's lips touch young Quinton's, a different form appears, dark and blurry. It grabs Kendra by the arm and snatches her away, causing young Quinton to stumble backward.

"I never saw them coming." Quinton trembles.

"YOU WHORE." The words echo from the shadow, bouncing off the walls in the memory chamber. Young Quinton grabs the shadow and pulls.

"Let her go!"

The shadow sharpens into a young man who elbows young Quinton in the jaw, knocking him back. Young Quinton trips and falls, holding his mouth. More shadows appear behind him, laughing.

"Shut up, jank. Go back to China." The first shadow laughs, wrestling with Kendra.

"He's Japanese, idiot!" Kendra barks and pounds at his chest. The shadow is too big. She can't wrangle free.

"Same thing." The shadow says.

Young Quinton pushes to his feet. "You let her go!" He cries again, unaware of the group behind him.

"Or what? You gonna go Jackie Chan on me?"

"Shut up, Nathan! Just let me go. This is ridiculous." Kendra squeals.

"I think we need to understand something here, Kendra." Nathan, the shadow, grins, "You don't have sex with chinks. He doesn't belong here."

"He belongs here as much as you do!"

Young Quinton steps at Nathan and is intercepted by the group behind him. "Whoa little fella, whaddya think you're doing?" One of the shadows says, grabbing his arm.

"Lay off me!" Young Quinton throws the arm off.

"Oooh, tough guy." The shadow responds, instigating laughs from the other blurry shadows.

Quinton winces as he watches the scene, biting back tears. "You were the only light in my life."

Nathan pipes up, "Hey guys, this slut says she hasn't jabbed the jap." The group laughs in mockery.

"Shut up, Nathan. You're just mad because I dumped you for him and never gave it up to you." Kendra struggles more, to no avail.

Young Quinton puts out a hand.

"I knew I was outnumbered." Quinton says, watching himself. "But I could have done more. I could have at least stopped…"

"You could have done nothing but also gotten yourself killed." Nyx whispers. "You have to confront this now or die in the maelstrom. There is no passage without sacrifice."

Wallow in the ashes, Quinton hears his own thoughts float back to him.

Nathan snatches Kendra closer in. "You're right, Kendra. I am a little ticked off. And if I remember right, you were a virgin when we met. Which means there's a way to find out if you *have* slept with this jank or not."

"That's not funny, Nathan. You wouldn't dare." Kendra glares at him, challenging.

"Hey, we can walk away from this." Young Quinton interrupts, taking a step forward.

"Don't get too close." One of the shadows grabs his arm again, warning.

"Listen, if it comes down to it, we can stop seeing each other. I'll disappear." Young Quinton begs.

"Don't let him fool you, Quinton. He's not going to do anything. He's going to let us go, and we'll be on our merry way." Kendra squints her eyes at Nathan. "Cause he knows who my dad is."

"Is that right?" Nathan smirks and nods, then looks to his support group. "Hey guys, who do you think the Judge will believe more? Me or the jank?"

The group laughs in response.

Kendra spits in Nathan's face. "Let me go. What're you gonna do? We're in public."

Nathan slowly wipes the spit off and grins, then backhands her. The shadow group sharpens into view as they groan in encouragement.

"In public, huh?" Nathan nods his head, squeezing Kendra's shoulders tight. "Don't look like anyone's around to me! This park is always empty. Which is why you meet here, isn't it?"

Fear and confirmation settle in Kendra's moist eyes.

Nathan smirks and jolts her body around, grabs her by the waist, and pushes on her back to force her down.

Young Quinton jumps and grabs at Nathan, quickly followed by the group who pulls him back. He yells, "Get off her!" but is swallowed up in the arms of the entourage.

Kendra kicks at Nathan and slaps his hands, but it only makes him mad. He punches her in the back of the head, knocking her dizzy and weak. He pulls up her dress, and unzips.

Quinton trembles as he watches the scene. "I can't…" He shakes his head.

"You must, because you did not the first time." Nyx whispers. "Until the end."

23.

Helen crosses her legs as she settles into the
recliner of a private jet. She sets her purse down
on the table in front of her and shifts her briefcase
onto her lap.

"Chardonnay, miss?" The attendant
flashes a plastic smile as she presents an
expensive bottle wrapped in a white towel.

"Oh, no thank you. I don't drink."

The attendant nods and walks away. Helen
slides the briefcase onto the table and pops it
open.

Inside, in neat array, sits a small stack of
manila folders, one non-descript smart phone, a
laptop, mystery cables, and a tablet. She picks up
the phone and turns it on.

As the phone boots up, she slides the
tablet out and sets it on the table, followed by the
laptop and a few cables. Her demeanor is
reminiscent of a proper tea party, with every
move being intentional and tidy. She closes the
briefcase one latch at a time, slides it off the table,
and secures it at her feet.

The phone lights up, ready to use. Helen
picks it up, enters in the passcode, dials a number,
and calls. As the phone rings, she opens the
laptop and fires it up.

The other end picks up.

"First stage complete. Permission to move
to second?" Helen says, tapping the top of the

tablet. She nods, *mhm*, "Of course. The jet is very comfortable. There have not been any snags."

The computer screen turns on. Helen bypasses the password with her fingerprint.

"Booting up the system now." She pulls out a Bluetooth earbud from her purse and affixes to it her ear, then transfers the call to it and sets the phone down. She unravels the cord and connects each end to the laptop and tablet, respectively.

"Sir, I mean no disrespect, but I've never seen an automatic program that could hack into even a WordPress blog efficiently. I'm not trying to toot my own horn, but I believe I can do a more efficient job-" She pauses, mouth open, listening. She tilts her head to the side and taps the table. "Understood. I will use the program."

Helen whistles out a sigh and navigates to a program on the computer screen, then clicks on it. The screen goes black. In the center, a single word fades into view, a touch of gold color amidst the blurred edges of letters. The word sharpens, comes into focus, filling the center of the screen.

DOMAIN

A ding is heard from the cockpit. The flight attendant struts out from the back, pearly teeth tingling in the sunlight that peaks through the windows. "Time to buckle up for lift-off." She giggles and sways back to her spot.

Helen stares at the screen and mumbles under her breath. "What kind of program *is* this?"

The jet lurches forward.

Pressure releases pure oxygen from the main Collider Chamber on Level 12 Stasis Holding in the Operation WhiskerChew quarters located at the edge of the world, where Samuel Crane struggles with the slow realization that he may very well be standing in his grave.

Jimenez stares at Crane, a hardened soldier who's seen more than her fair share of death and destruction, fear in her eyes. "What's happening?"

"I don't know, but I think it's time we leave." Crane nods and shuffles away from the machine, motioning for Jimenez to follow.

The couple passes a row of sleeping Giants, eyes locked on the only visible escape. A low hum rumbles the floor, emitted from the Collider Chamber, making a sound like a massive laundry washer kicking into spin mode.

As Crane and Jimenez pass the second row of Giants, the stasis covers in the first row snap and release another round of high-oxygen into the air. Crane turns and looks behind him.

The glass covers sweat with fog from the hot breath of the giants lying in them. "Faster." Crane kicks up into a jog and Jimenez copies. Behind them, the stasis chambers on the first row pop and ease open. The second row snaps and releases more oxygen, following suit with the first.

"Come on old man!" Jimenez shifts into a run, attempting to keep the distance between her and Crane as long as possible without outrunning him. Crane huffs, saving his breath.

The third row pops.

A groan ripples through the room, followed by a thud. And another thud. And another.

Jimenez is within throwing distance from the door and glances back. Her eyes widen, and she blasts into a full sprint.

Crane winces at a cramp working into his side but pushes through, his rosy cheeks glistening in comical mimicry of Saint Nick.

"Run!" Jimenez shimmies backward, beyond the threshold, her eyes hopping from Crane to the room and back.

Crane wheezes and grabs his side, his knees burst into inflamed balls of fluid as his joints grind on each other like deer grappling antlers. He limps as he runs, keeping a 'do or die' pace. Mere yards away from the door, his knees finally give up and he collapses to the concrete ground, busting his elbow as he breaks the fall with his arm.

Jimenez yells in the background. The ground rumbles below Crane at the stomp of the giants stumbling out in mass. Crane scoots back and leans up, then looks out toward the main collider. One of the first awakened Giants stretches rock hard muscles and kicks his legs out, then looks at Crane, and smiles. The monster stands to full height, pops his shoulders back and rolls them out, then rubs his bare stomach.

Crane takes a deep breath and looks behind him to see Jimenez rack her pistol with visibly shaking hands. "Find Bailey." He nods.

Jimenez raises her gun and balances her weight. "Come on pops! I can't carry you, but you can crawl. It's only a few feet!" She sways back and forth, working up the courage to cover him.

"You have to help Bailey out of here. He's important." Crane grimaces and scoots toward the open door.

Jimenez keeps her eyes on the target. "Understood. Now let's go!"

Crane grabs the bottom edge of the door and swings it shut, locking Jimenez out of the room. He army-crawls to the door, props up in front of it, and wedges the rifle into the crook of his arm.

The door rattles from Jimenez pounding on the other side of it, her muffled screams broken by the thumping.

On the other side of the room, the first giant licks his lips, then takes a step forward.

"In the name of Jesus Christ of Nazareth, I command you, devil, to go back to the hell you came from." Crane grinds his teeth and unloads the rifle, aiming high.

Gordon winces as the Barber pulls the last stitch a bit tighter than the previous ones and ties it off. The Barber smacks his lips and drops the needle on a nearby dinner tray amidst an array of basic medical tools, a bottle of liquor, gauze, and a small metal tray that holds a splintered, bloody bullet.

The windows are covered in sun bleached sheets that droop from neglect. There is a single box television in the corner, a rocking recliner, a bookshelf, and a loveseat sofa where Johnson sits on its edge, elbows on her knees and hands clasped.

"So, you cut hair too?" Johnson breaks the silence with a grimace.

"Nope." The Barber pushes away from Gordon and massages his old, bloody hands with a towel.

Johnson nods as though she agrees that the answer makes sense.

"Back in the day, barbers were also doctors, of a sort. You've never heard that history?" Gordon reaches over and grabs the bottle of liquor, then takes a large swig.

"Right, yeah the whole red and white pole thing. But uh, weren't they also *barbers?*" Johnson spreads her hands at the suggestion.

The Barber laughs and walks to the kitchen. "Go 'head and tell her, son." He disappears around the corner.

"Barber came from a long line of barbers, but never took on the profession." Gordon grunts

254

and pulls a t-shirt over his head. "Instead, he decided to break the mold and go to school. He was one of the small group of black men in his era to get a medical degree at Montreal Neurological Institute." Gordon sighs and looks over at the mess on the dinner tray. "He goes by Barber simply because of the irony."

"So, he's a neurosurgeon?" Johnson bounces her knee.

"Yeah."

The Barber hobbles back in, drying his hands on a towel. "You didn't tell her the good part."

"Not my story to tell, Barber." Gordon smiles, picks up the smashed bullet on the tray, and studies its expenditure.

"Well, I suppose, unfortunately, we don't have the time anyway." The Barber grunts as he flops down in his recliner. "You need to get to your destination, and I need to get to mine."

Gordon frowns. "Busy schedule?" He pushes the bullet into his pocket and grunts.

The Barber looks down and says nothing.

Johnson looks at Gordon, trying to read his face.

"What's going on, Barber?" Gordon shifts on the chair, staring at the old man.

The Barber sighs and reaches into his pocket. "I ever tell you how much I *hate* horses?"

Gordon relaxes his shoulders and shakes his head. "Come on, old man. What are you trying to do?"

The Barber turns and looks at Johnson. "I don't just hate horses. I *despise* them." The word drips with black tar as it falls from his lip. "I HATE horses." The Barber shakes a little as he says the word, fidgeting with something in his pocket.

Johnson flinches at the sudden outburst but otherwise remains calm, outwardly.

Gordon stands up. "I think we better get going."

The Barber shoots a glance at Gordon. "You better listen to your mama. She's lookin' out for you, and the trouble you tryin' to get in."

"My mom is dead. You must be thinking about someone else."

"She say to mind your own, and your own mind you." The Barber freezes, his wide eyes locked onto Gordon.

Gordon hesitates, then shakes his head. "Anyone could come up with that statement."

"You on the Blacklist now. Or about to be. You tell your partner here that?" The Barber gestures at Johnson.

"Wait, what is that? Doesn't sound good." Johnson barks and sits up.

"It's not stamped. This isn't a John Wick movie."

"It is when you work for Mr. E." The Barber sits back and rocks in the chair. "And then you do somethin' Mr. E. don't like. You know what that means."

"Who's Mr. E?" Johnson demands. "Wait, you're a double-agent?"

"We'll talk about it on the ride."

The Barber *tisks* as he rocks and shakes his head, hand still in his pocket.

"Let's go." Gordon walks to the front door, followed closely by Johnson. "Thanks again, Barber. I'll try not to come back." He opens the door and walks out.

"What was that all about?" Johnson pounces down the stairs after Gordon.

"I said *we'll talk about it in the car*."

"Don't you get that tone with me! I'm your partner! I'm supposed to know everything already!"

Gordon opens the passenger door and eases a foot in.

The front door of the shack opens and the Barber steps out, then whistles.

Gordon looks up at the Barber just as the old man throws something at him. Gordon twitches a stitch as he automates a catch and taps in to old, forgotten baseball skills to catch the marble.

"You always take payment." Gordon looks at the marble, confused.

"You know what it means to aid the Blacklist, son. The crows, they caw. Many crows 'round here. Now follow your mama's advice, and stay outta trouble. He comin'. You better get." The Barber shoos them off with a hand and closes the door.

"Get in." Gordon drops down into the SUV quicker than he probably should considering his wounds and slams the door. Johnson follows suit, turns the engine, and peels out of the parking lot.

24.

The hallway rumbles under Jimenez's feet as she races down the stark corridor, ignoring the tears streaming down her cheek. She pants and bites her lip, then rounds the corner and crashes straight into a solid heap of a man, knocking them both across the tile. She scrambles to her knees and rushes to grab the gun that flung out of her hand from the impact. She swoops the gun up, swivels around, and points it at the beast of a man as he stands and puts his hands up.

Hare, the groundskeeper, stares back at her, deep purple rings under his eyes.

"Come on, man." Jimenez lowers the gun and lets out a breath.

"I heard something loud coming from a place it shouldn't be coming from. What happened?" Hare drops his hands and leans up against the wall, exacerbated.

"We gotta keep movin'." Jimenez pushes to her feet.

"Sounds like all hell is breaking loose. Were you just in the stasis chambers?" Hare glances back toward the hallway.

"Yeah. Someone turned on the machine in there, and now a whole army of giants are waking up and not happy about it. If we don't get out of here, we're dinner." Jimenez turns and shuffles off.

Hare catches up and keeps pace. "How did you get in there?"

"Long story."

"You know there's only one way out of here, right?"

"Why am I not surprised?" Jimenez cocks her head. "And let me guess, it's crazy dangerous too?"

Hare raises an eyebrow in agreement.

"Old man told me we had to get to Bailey. Maybe he knows a better way out."

Hare stops.

"What are you doin? Let's go!" Jimenez motions with her gun hand.

"I – I – I don't know about that. He's not uh, well…"

"Would you stop the stammerin' and just tell me!" Jimenez stomps a foot.

"He's in holding. I'm not really supposed to know that but I see everything. People always underestimate me." Hare sulks, his face downturned.

"Take me to him." Jimenez turns. "Oh, and help me find a better gun. You better get one too."

Hare nods, takes a deep breath, and follows.

"We have a problem." Dr. Hudson hovers over a monitor, typing furiously.

Cambor sits back in a nearby chair, kicked back, one leg crossed over the other revealing a ridiculously bright colored dress sock, smacking on a tuna sandwich.

"What now?" Cambor whines and lags his head back, rolling his eyes. He rolls his head to the side and looks at Dr. Hudson, then sighs.

"Someone has turned on the colliders."

Cambor chuckles. "That's not possible. There's only one other person beside me and you with access to that passcode and if I remember right, he's dead." Cambor takes a lazy bite of his sandwich and plops his hand on his lap.

"Well, someone found a way in. Looks like the transmission came from…" Dr. Hudson squints at the screen. "Peru."

Cambor sits up, his mouth half open, a slop of tuna on his lower lip. "Oh, that sly S.O.B."

"I can't shut it down." Hudson drops a bead of sweat onto the keyboard.

"It's not – did he…? Clever bugger, that man. I didn't think he'd do it." Cambor giggles.

"This is serious, Cambor. The subjects are waking up."

Cambor points his sandwich at Dr. Hudson, "Then shut it down! You don't need special permission to do that!"

Dr. Hudson hunches closer to the screen and scrambles away at the keyboard. "Our access has been overridden. I can't do anything." He throws his hands up and breathes in deep.

"Also not possible." Cambor stands up and flops his sandwich down on the nearest counter.

Chickens cluck in disapproval as Grandpa Adams shuffles through their pen with a basket, collecting the eggs and humming. Olivia stands just outside the pen, hands on her hips, looking around the property.

"It's what you always wanted." Olivia stares in wonder at the tall pines camouflaging the property.

"What's that?" Her dad's voice muffles out from inside the pen and he follows it, brushing debris off his hair.

"This place. The seclusion. The whole setup. It's everything you always talked about doing. I never thought you'd do it."

"No one did." He latches the pen door and sighs. "And that was the point."

"You always planned years in advance, didn't you?"

"Is there a better way?" He smiles and walks past, heading toward the house. "A good prepper ne'er lets anyone know what he's doing. Except, family, of course. Maybe a few trusted friends."

Blue birds chirp from tree to tree as the two walk toward the house. A cloud of smoke puffs out of the chimney, topping off the already homey cabin. The place is more modern than expected, sporting a nice wood finish and brand new, double-paned windows. In the background sits a large storage shed with a green metal a-frame roof, the kind that keeps the snow off.

"Never thought I'd have to come here." Olivia puts her hands in her pockets, her own comfort at the thought surprising her.

"Then you weren't listening' very close, were ya?" He chuckles, that all-knowing dad demeanor puffing his chest up.

"I guess, I mean I never wanted it to be a necessity." Olivia explains. "But it's not for the reasons you always said it would be. Don't get too arrogant." She points, teasing.

He laughs, "How do you know?"

Olivia climbs up the stairs to the front porch and stops, letting the question hang in the air. He chuckles and smiles, then walks inside. "I'll make some brunch. Fried eggs and tomatoes. Hope you still like that." The screen door swings shut behind him.

"Yeah, of course." Olivia stares out at the forest, distracted. She crosses her arms and rubs them even though the weather isn't cold.

The trees stare back at her, hiding something. She shivers.

What if the old man is right? What if the end really is near, but it's just her end and not the end of the world?

What if…

The door busts open behind Cambor, catching him off guard and causing him to trip and stumble to the ground. Jimenez steps into the small control room and points an AK-47 in Cambor's face, sweat dripping down her cheekbone. Hare follows suit and closes the door behind.

"You're gonna let them out of those boxes right now." Jimenez steps in closer, pushing the muzzle uncomfortably close to Cambor.

Cambor puts up his hand and chuckles, keeping his eyes on the ground. "Okay, no worries. We can make an arrangement."

"The arrangement - is you let them out or I blast your face off your skull."

In the background, Dr. Hudson makes a slow move to a nearby drawer.

"Nuh uh," Hare steps over, stopping Dr. Hudson. "Back to your corner. Don't touch anything."

"Well," Cambor sighs, "I have to get up, if you don't mind."

Jimenez nods and backs up, giving him room to stand. "No funny business. I ain't stupid."

He keeps his hands up and slowly moves to the controls, smiling.

"You think something's funny?" She steps to the side where she can see his face better. "Let him out of that little cage first."

"No problem." He pushes a couple buttons and types in a code onto the monitor.

In the cage, the copper coffin top pops open and slowly eases up. Everett slides out and tosses the hospital gown off then stands at the door, staring up at Cambor in only his boxers.

"Now the doors. To both of them."

"Whatever you say, boss." He pushes each release button at the same time, unlocking the doors.

Everett moves into a bracing stance. Squirrel sits up in his bed as far as his restraints allow and shoots a worried glance to Everett.

"Something's not right." Hare shifts his weight and re-grips the rifle, looking from the holding floor to Dr. Hudson and back.

"What did you do?" Jimenez barks at Cambor, a command more than a question.

"Just doin' what the lady asks. Nothing more. I promise." He steps back from the monitors, hands up.

Below, in the holding room, Everett emits a guttural war-cry as he bursts out of the chamber and clashes with a beast of a man hiding in the shadows, knocking the giant back up against a wall hard enough to rumble the control room.

"Holy-" Jimenez stares in disbelief at the scene.

Cambor steps and throws an elbow, connecting with Jimenez's temple and knocking her dizzy. She trips and grabs onto the wall, slipping down, desperately attempting to regain vision and clarity.

Hare yells as he moves to aim on Cambor, leaving Dr. Hudson to make a move and jump to the drawer. Dr. Hudson scrambles out a handgun, cocks it, and shoots Hare in the back just before Hare gets a sight on Cambor.

Hare drops to his knees, staring at the bloody patch on his shirt, and drops the rifle to his side.

In all the hustle, Cambor manages to slip out the door and disappears down the stairs, Dr. Hudson following close behind.

Jimenez crawls over to Hare, "Oh no. Ah, man!" She puts pressure on the wound but the blood pumps out regardless.

"They took everything from me. My business. My family." Hare's pale face stares into oblivion. "Wish I'd never come to this place."

"You're gonna get them back. Is there a med kit in here somewhere?"

"My wife and kids. Don't even know where they are right now." Hare slips off into delusion, ignoring her.

She jumps to her feet and searches the room, pulling out supplies from every cabinet and throwing it out in search of a med kit. "There's gotta be one in here somewhere. Hold on, man." She throws open another cabinet and yelps at her luck, pulling down a med kit and slamming it on the counter. "You're in luck, buddy. I think I can at least limp you by." She grabs out a large wad of gauze and turns to Hare.

His cold, empty gaze stares at the ceiling, mouth ajar.

25.

Cambor snatches the doors of the research room open and rushes in, focused on a particular machine in the corner that holds a collection of vials. With a grin on his face, he punches in a code and presses his finger on the reader, unlatching the glass paned door. He grabs a handful of vials and a case, carefully places the vials inside, and latches it shut.

"They might not be ready yet!" Dr. Hudson gasps as he steps into the room, out of breath.

"Ready enough. We gotta go. This place is going to be Armageddon in a hot minute." Cambor tucks the vial case close to his side and speed walks out of the room.

"How are we getting out of here?" Dr. Hudson follows, a paranoid glance over his shoulder.

"Well, there's only one way. Keep up, Doc. I'm your ticket to paradise." Cambor smiles and laughs, a twinkle in his eyes.

The jet powers down, causing Helen to bump forward and brace herself on the table's edge. "That's odd."

The program on the computer screen scrolls in a tech language riddled with symbols Helen has never seen. *Trust the plan*, Mr. E. said. *All you have to do is give her a little push, and*

she'll take over from there. Once she is done,
she'll let you know.

When Mr. E. hired her on, he claimed his draw to her was based on her tech skills, namely, her ability to hack. The covert emissary history was merely a bonus, and the fact that they knew each other since high school of course played a part. She wonders if the main reasoning was true, considering the lack of need for her programming skills in light of this obviously far-advanced program. Either way, the paycheck always quells any questions. Not to mention the world class treatment.

The flight attendant hustles out of her corner and stops next to her. "My apologies, miss, but we have been delayed."

"What's going on?"

"I'm not entirely sure," the flight attendant folds her hands. Her eyes confirm the statement, glossed with ignorance. "but Traffic Control mentioned something about an anomalous weather pattern that requires us to stay grounded until further notice."

Helen looks out the window.

Clear, blue sky.

"What does that look like to you?" She points at the sky, tapping the glass with a jab.

The flight attendant nods, "I understand. I'm sorry miss, there's nothing either I or the captain can do. Would you like some water?"

She ignores the woman and stares out the window, perplexed. The attendant takes the hint and slinks away.

On the computer screen in front of her, the program flickers, then slows. The characters come to a halt, each line disappearing into the previous one as the scrolling wraps up its work.

"That must be it, then. I guess." She shrugs and glances out the window again.

In the distance, off in the mountain range, she notices a strange blue light. As the light grows larger, she can see it take the form of a massive swirl shape.

"Is that…"

The computer screen goes black.

She cocks her head. The screen shouldn't go black. The program should merely close out, leaving her at the normal background. Normally, a black screen means something went wrong.

A number pops up on the screen in the same greenish hue as the DOMAIN program lettering.

10

And then another number to replace that one.

9

"Okay…" She recognizes a countdown when she sees one, but to what? As though déjà vu kicked in via Hollywood programming, she subconsciously remembers the famous tech self-destruct scenes from the *Mission Impossible* movies.

6

"No way." She chuckles to herself and breaks a modest sweat on her forehead. She stands up and straightens her jacket. "It's just shutting down. You've seen too many movies, Helen."

3

She shakes her head and steps away. "I need to use the restroom anyway." She takes one more glance at the strange blue swirl in the sky outside, then once again at the screen.

1

There were moments in her life when she knew better - knew to listen to her instinct. Most of the time, it was innocent. The kind of instinct that tells you to fold on a certain poker hand, or bluff, but then you ignore it and regret it. The kind of regret that only costs a few dollars, or an embarrassing moment, or an awkward conflict when something shouldn't have been said. She knows the feeling well, but never thought she would end her story on earth with it. At least, not this way. Not taken advantage of. Not tricked or subdued, blindsided or outsmarted. No one outsmarts Helen.

No one, but Mr. E.

She squints at the bright light as it flashes from the computer screen and throws her arms up as a shield, but to no avail. Considering the extremely advanced operations of the inherent program in the computer, she isn't terribly surprised at its capacity to also be an explosive. The only surprising element is her ability to disassociate from her situation and automate into work mode, thinking about the abilities of modern technology instead of her demise.

She had always thought she would be a little more… well, irate, if someone she had trusted not only deceived, but also assassinated her.

But none of that matters anymore, not now that the plane is disassembling into a million tiny shards, conflated with the many separated pieces, of Helen Beretta.

"Where you gonna go?" Kat stands in front of the Rent-a-Car, hand plopped on her cocked hip, a sly grin on her sunglassed face.

"To find her." Gordon adjusts his new button up shirt to allow for the bandages beneath it.

"And what, profess your undying love?" Kat chortles and lowers her sunglasses. "Not a great plan, my friend. Especially not in your condition."

"I'll be fine." Gordon cinches up his tie and grimaces.

"Suppose you don't have many options anyway, if this E fellow is onto you. What'chu gonna do? Track the vehicle?"

"Yeah. She's smart but I don't think she's that clever."

"Might have something to do with the fact that she's just a normal human. Not really the first thing they think of."

Gordon grunts in agreement and walks to the back of the Escalade, then pops the latch open. He slides over a small black suitcase and eases it out, wincing at the pressure on his wounds.

"You sure about this?" Kat watches him from the side, a disapproving look on her face.

"I'll be fine." Gordon growls and slides the rolling handle out.

"Sure." Kat shakes her head, chuckling quietly to herself. "Is all that stuff true? About Mr. E.?"

"Of course." Gordon hobbles to the rental car and opens the trunk, then wrestles the small suitcase inside.

"Then I better get my distance. You think he'll know about me helping you?"

"I think you can plead ignorance if it comes down to it. He's not evil. It's all business. I was in charge, not you. It all falls on me."

"Not to mention this whole AWOL plan of yours." Kat leans up against the Escalade. "Hey."

Gordon slams the trunk down and looks at Kat.

"How did the Barber know you were gonna do this?"

"Oh." Gordon waves off the statement, "He always knows more than he should. He's just a good people reader."

She squints, seeing through the lie. Something Gordon isn't saying, or admitting, one of the two. He always was such a practical, down to business sort of man. Not much for speculation.

"Well, since I'll probably never see you again, it was a pleasure workin' with ya." She steps over and holds out her hand.

He takes the handshake and nods. "Thanks for everything. Until next time."

She laughs. "Right. Till next time." She waves him off and hops into the Escalade, then slowly drives off, leaving Gordon propped up against the side of the rental car. He wrangles out a pack of cigarettes, bites one out, and lights it.

Like he's got all the time in the world.

26.

Edgar Cofield sets a Nokia 3310 dark blue cell phone down on his bathroom counter and looks in the mirror. He turns his face to one side, then the other, studying the horrific caterpillar of a moustache on his upper lip. He nods to himself, as though a conclusion was met in his mind, and picks up a beard trimmer. He turns the small machine on and proceeds to erase the eyesore on his face.

After cleaning up with a close shave and a shower, Edgar places his feet on the bathroom scale. Down ten pounds since last week, right on time.

Edgar walks on a grey and white marble floor to his master closet and picks out his costume for the day.

Security Guard. Replete with royal blue baseball cap and utility belt. The name on the breast pocket reads *E. Cofield* in blue stitching on white. Below it is embroidered the words *Kelim Tekhnologies* in a clever pyramidal design, with the *el* having emphasis. He dons the shirt and performs the finishing touches of the usual: deodorant, aftershave, and a dash of cheap Wal-Mart cologne to sell the whole look.

Not that he needs to anymore, but appearances may still be important. One can never be too careful. But that moustache – it had to go.

Edgar strolls down the custom tungsten plated stairs into the open floor plan of a kitchen and living room combo surrounded by wall-to-wall vaulted windows that overlooks the valley from a thousand-foot-high hill. He pours coffee into a tall green thermos, secures the lid, and walks into the garage.

The garage opens into a span as large as a normal house, revealing a dozen cars. On one side is a Tesla Model S Long Range Plus, plugged into the wall next to a Porsche Taycan. On the other side is a 1962 Ferrari 250 GTO, paired with the lower priced but equally as sharp Mercedes SL 300 Gullwig in pearl black with a golden interior.

In the center, closest to the main garage door (of which, there are seven) sits a 1997 Toyota Corolla with 267,000 miles, a broken side view mirror, and sun damage that would make your grandma's skin look plush. He walks to the Corolla silently, unlocks the door, and sits down. The garage door opens, and he backs out, tapping on the steering wheel.

The vehicle rolls around a cobblestone round-about driveway with a fountain statue of Poseidon surrounded by mermaids in the center, water gently flowing from the mouths of arched fish splattered in artistic array to the basin below.

At the gate, he pauses to let the automatic rotors roll the cast iron out of the way, then continues down the long driveway that twists and turns down the hill, neighbor-less.

Seventy minutes later, he pulls up to what once was Kelim Tekhnologies and parks in the furthest spot away possible, even though the lot is empty. He muses on the drive, understanding it may be one of his last, if not the very last indeed. He had always appreciated the time to think. The Corolla's stereo is broken, and though he always had the means to resolve the issue, he chose silence instead.

His mind, like a playbook, needed no entertainment. His plans, goals, and strategies came naturally. Almost mechanical. It was like he didn't even need to try, which was quite distressing to him at times. Like playing a game of chess with a child, unless you love that child dearly, boredom sets in after the first few rounds.

The thing that keeps him going isn't the money, or the elusive infamy. Deep down, the drive in Cofield's actions is revelation. Things coming anew. The world needs a change. A drastic one. Sometimes, you have to destroy the thing you love the most in order to give it the opportunity to rise from the ashes and grow into something greater.

He steps out of the car, pulls his cap on, shuts the door, and sticks a thumb in his belt. While naturally cool and quiet, he has learned that in order to pull off this scheme properly, he needs to be someone else entirely. So once again he puts on a smirk, jiggles his jowls, and throws a little over-confident pep in his step, just for old time's sake. Oh, but what he would give to lose the accumulated belly fat. The gut that changed his appearance not only in the midsection, but his face as well.

He would give the world. Just as he is about to.

Kelim Tekhnologies sits on the edge of the lot, gated off and shut down. He passes a large black stain on the "Reserved for Management" parking spot without a second thought and pulls out a set of keys.

He unlocks the deadbolt from the main gate and slides the chain out of the links, swings it just wide enough to step in, then returns it the way he found it.

At the front door, a new scanner has been installed. He lifts his hat and props open his right eye, letting the scanner do its job. The front door lock unlatches with a crack, and he walks into the foyer.

When the bosses had their little mess with the whole suicide/car bomb "accidents", the CIA came down hard. They knew something beyond government capabilities was happening at this place and tried their best hand at confiscating the entire site. Fortunately, or more likely, strategically, Cofield happened to be in business with the Director, and many clammy hands suddenly turned dry. The local authorities stepped down right quick after only one phone call, leaving a little mess for him to clean up.

For a while, he kept some of the employees, mostly for the dirty work. A few needed to disappear, but he wasn't the psychopath type to just off people in order to make his life easier. Except for Byron. That one brought him joy. The man abused his position for far too long, unknowingly being watched by the real boss all the while. Quinton, well, he was a strange phenomenon that man. Very unpredictable, though doubtless organized and reliable. Whatever that poor soul was up to never bothered Cofield much. He had every intention of keeping him on in various ways. The man could have been useful. But, no good chess player spends too much time fretting over a lost pawn. Bailey, now he needed to go. Too smart. And his history, a fascinating read on his profile, suited him perfect for the little experiment over in Antarctica.

Then of course, there is the issue of little miss Helen. If the computer he gave her hasn't blown up yet, it's about to. Any second. Perhaps he did get a kick out of killing off the problem children. Is that psychopathic? Or just taking care of business? Either way, it doesn't matter. A lot of people are probably going to die.

He walks across the foyer, just like any other day minus the hubbub of activity and checks the monitors. No signs of disturbance.

On the walk to the experiment rooms, he stops for a second to admire the art Quinton had pinned up on the wall. The one that catches his attention most, that he could never figure out its meaning but always felt close to it, is the Tree of Life. Why that painting? Why the mysterious little swirls for leaves? Could they be artistic clues to portals? How did it relate to everything? Quinton was not indiscriminate. There must be a relation. He must have known more than he gave off. But now is not the time to crack that puzzle. The DOMAIN program is likely finished, which means the colliders should be at least warming up.

The set in Peru has been ready to go for years. Quinton made sure of that. Reliable, that man. Fortunately, Cofield didn't *need* Quinton in particular to man the colliders there. Those were of a specific technology that didn't even look the same. Something a little… out of Cofield's realm, admittedly.

He steps into the room that holds Marlene. As suspected, the machine is humming, moving from the warm-up phase to initiation.

He walks to the monitor and punches in a code. At the end where the cylindrical opening meets the container, the circular door fans open. He nods in approval and looks at his watch.

A loud crack is heard from the collider, and static electricity sputters out, electrocuting the interior of the large cubicle.

This time, instead of a form pushing its way through the dimensional curtain, an entire door opens in the shape of a large, blue swirl. The veil between worlds is torn in the shape of a large, peering eye. A passageway. A birthing canal.

A Giant steps through, his massive feet thudding the ground and shaking the whole room.

Cofield smiles and sets a timer for the chamber door to unlock.

Fifteen minutes.

That's all he needs to get from here to the car, and well on his way, leaving all hell behind him quite literally breaking loose.

On the way out, he pulls out a smartphone and scrolls to his private pilot contact.

"I'm on my way. Is everything ready to go?"

"Yes sir. Just waiting for you." The pilot responds.

"You ever been to Peru before?" He officially drops the security guard façade. Nothing to worry about anymore.

"Only once. Looking forward to it, sir."

"Me too, captain. Me too." Cofield hangs up and picks up his pace, leaving the facility a little quicker than usual.

Quinton lies in a heap on the ground, sobbing, unaware of his location. He pulls at his hair, contorting his body into a shell, holding in the convulsions. His mind scrambles to keep some form of confinement after the extreme pressure of the passage through realms. More than realms.

Transition.

Evolution.

No, *Ascension.*

He crawls to his knees, his eyes still closed, and grips the foliage in his fingers.

"I can feel you there." He pants out in spurts, acclimating to the climate. He can feel the sun on his back, it's energy seeping into his cells. More than that, he can feel his cells receive the energy and circulate the precious light throughout his glorified body the way it was meant to at creation.

Creation? He questions, the once dismissed theory now relevant somehow. Subconscious. Intrinsic. *Divine.*

"Yes." The Eidolon responds. "We were here at the beginning. We will be here until the end, and until the new beginning, and for every revolution of time. And you will be with us, *Qemu'el,* for once you were destroyed, and now stand forever resurrected."

Qemu'el stands to his feet and takes in a deep breath, all the earth below him expanding with his intake. "It was you all along, my love. My Darkness. My *Nyx.*" He opens his eyes, a stark blue contrasted with long white hair. His stature has changed from average to tall and lean, muscular and glowing. The man who was Quinton remains only a hint in Qemu'el's true form.

A dark sun shines behind him, hovering beneath a strange canopy of emerald firmament, casting a silvery light on the ancient metropolis below. The city bustles with technology reliant not on petrol nor crude nuclear, but balance. A kind of energy that appears magical to all but the adept.

Nyx steps to Qemu'el's side and puts a hand on his shoulder. "You did it. Our children are free to reclaim what is truly ours. It was *your* human suffering that saved us. The Emulation worked." She peers at him through silver hair.

"I remember everything." Qemu'el returns her gaze. "It is time for war. We will reclaim our domain."

27.

The trees hum a sleepy song beneath a perfectly clear night sky. The crisp air wafts in short puffs, just enough to need a jacket but not requiring a blanket. The thought of snuggling up in a blanket on the front porch in the middle of nowhere like a frontier woman never bothered Olivia, despite the lack of necessity. Perhaps it is necessary to be entirely comfortable and not just sufficient.

Inside, the kids *should* be sleeping. Bastion should have no problem, after spending a day splitting and stacking wood with grandpa and an evening playing cards. Olivia is coming to love this whole no wi-fi, back woods type of lifestyle. Between the simplicity of daily activities and the nourishment of home-grown foods, she hasn't felt this good in years. If ever.

Grandpa Adams steps out the front door, swinging the screen with his foot, and sets a hot cup of cocoa down beside her. He takes his place in an adjacent wooden rocking chair with a grunt and motions at the cup.

"I know you like that sugary garbage." He teases.

"Thanks, Dad." She smiles, somehow managing to snuggle deeper into the comforter as she pulls the cup to her face.

"Any word on Everett while you were in town?" He asks.

"No. But I did bring back a bottle of Jack." She winks.

"Ahh. My girl." He takes a sip of tea and clears his throat. "Sorry about your man."

"I guess I haven't really confronted reality yet."

"What's that you mean?" He throws a perplexed look.

"Well, I don't…" She stutters to figure out how to express her thoughts. "I don't think he's coming back." A tear burns out of the corner of her eye and she sniffles.

"How so?"

"The lady agent. She said, when they took us, she said that men on missions like his don't come back. And I wouldn't be surprised. The government literally stole us from our homes. Just the way the whole thing went down looks as though they have no intention of fixing it. We never got our phone calls like we were promised. I don't know, Dad. Something is wrong. I can feel it. A constant, sick feeling in my stomach. I don't think they planned on returning him. I think they were going to eventually get rid of us too, when they were done with him. Holding us as collateral for the ends of their means. That's why I came here." She wipes the tears off her cheek.

"Honey cakes, that can't be. I ain't heard of any procedure like that. And you know my history."

"Dad, you're old school. Times have changed." She looks out at the property and blinks the tears back.

"Yeah, ain't that the truth." He nods, choosing his words carefully. "Gotta keep up hope. He knows where we're at. He'll come find us when he figures it out."

"He knows where you live?" She snaps her head his direction.

"Course he does. I told him myself."

"Last time he saw you, you still lived at home."

"Well, I made plans, dear. This wasn't no impulse buy." He smiles, a little twinkle in his eye from the moisture.

"Wow." She frowns, unsure of what to say. "I mean, that's probably the best news I've heard yet. But I don't think it changes the circumstances."

"You always were a little cup half empty. It's alright. Sometimes, I think that's a good thing, that way when your cup fills up, it's a pleasant surprise."

"I'd sure like to think so." She looks back out at the property, her eyes adjusting to the darkness.

Down the road, a figure stumbles out from beside a tree.

Olivia shoots to her feet, spilling hot cocoa on the blanket.

"What?" Grandpa Adams quickly but carefully sets his tea down and stands.

"Out there. Someone is here." Her heart skips a beat. Could it be?

He reaches into the house and pulls out a rifle, then aims at the movement. "It's a man. I can see him. Stumbling like he's hurt. Don't know how in the world he got past my trips." He bolts a round.

"What are you doing!" She rushes over and puts a hand on his shoulder.

"Just bein' safe. Hold on." He peeks out from the scope and yells, "WHO GOES THERE?" He readjusts the rifle and looks back through the scope.

She holds her breath, a glimmer of elation suppressed behind her eyes.

The man shouts back, "My name is Gordon Pierce and I have a gun, but I come in peace."

Oliva's shoulders drop and she looks at her dad, who looks back.

"You know this man?" he says.

"Unfortunately, I do. And I think you should shoot him."

The amount of strength pulsating through Everett's muscles surprises him. This is different than a rush of adrenaline, like no other physical expenditure he's ever felt before. The feeling is sparkly, invigorating, almost… addictive, if he didn't know any better. Compared to extreme sports or racing a car, the hormones flashing through his body are crack-cocaine without the harm and withdrawal.

Daniels' face is a blank slate, a monstrosity of what it used to be, nearly unrecognizable. His features show no expression as his arms lock into Everett's in a death grip meant to break the bones. Like an arrested arm wrestle, the two hold each other in a vice tight enough to splinter any average human bone.

Everett closes his eyes and searches Daniels' mind, but it's like beating down a closed vault door after failing to crack the entry code. A vault that very well may be, unfortunately, empty.

Everett growls and pushes his weight to the side, tango-stepping out of the way as he thrusts Daniels across the floor. The centrifugal movement whips Daniels to a tumble and he crashes into the chamber where Squirrel sits, still attached to the bed. Squirrel takes cover as best as he can but is smashed up against the wall after Daniel's tumble knocks a broken sheet of Plexiglas into the room, creating an A-frame that traps Squirrel awkwardly between the dumped bed and the wall.

Everett hunkers down, elbows on his knees, and strains his mind. While he doesn't quite know exactly *how* he's doing it, he understands that there is something more in his brain. Some sort of organic device or perhaps a gland that may have been there all along but is now activated in a way that makes him think it should have been like that from the beginning. Something inherent, potential, subconscious.

The blood in his brain swirls around the center-back portion, creating pressure on his nasal cavity and splintering throughout the rest of his brain. An orb like a lightning rod accumulating energy in a plasma ball shoots out from the base of his brain to the front and center, behind his forehead, and he screams, rising to his feet.

In the chamber, Daniels pushes to his feet and steps toward Everett, brushing off debris from the carnage. He snaps his neck and grunts, bloodshot eyes blistered from extraneous straining. He stomps forward, rattling the ground with each step deliberately.

Everett opens his eyes and concentrates the energy orb in his mind, then releases it at Daniels. He can feel it travel, like watching a dog run across the yard, a strange sense of peace connected to the invisible wave. Maybe not peace but perhaps, confidence. Confidence in knowing it will do what it needs to do. What that is, he will have to find out in this new learning curve.

Daniels takes another step forward, and the orb that he can't see strikes him in the forehead, paralyzing the man-made Giant.

For a moment, the two stand quietly in what appears to be a standoff, each breathing heavily, moving only at the lull of the blood racing to catch up to the adrenaline in their veins.

Everett mentally controls the orb, like listening in to a private conversation on the other end of a closed door, tapping into Daniels' stunned mind.

Kill me. Kill me. Kill me. Kill me. Kill me. And over. And over. A short, simple mantra.

For a second, Everett remembers the old Daniels. His cheesy grin when one of the squad mates told a dirty joke. His stories about home life and the good ole days. The way he would wink as a sign of support, *I got you brother.*

But he's not here anymore. The man who was Daniels has left, and only a remnant of his soul remains trapped in a machine.

Kill me. Kill me. Kill me.

Daniels tenses his body and grits his teeth, then bursts into a rush.

Everett discharges the orb by cutting it off from his own mind.

Daniels' skull blows apart, casting chunks of flesh and splatters of blood into a dozen different directions, leaving a gored body as it flops heavily to the ground, spluttering blood.

The strange artifacts in the Room of 10,000 skulls at the Museum of Anthropology stare at Rob in mysterious expanse, a plethora of untold histories either long forgotten or well-hidden. One skull in particular stands out, almost literally, as he walks by, its elongated crown uncomfortably large, suggesting not just a different kind of humanoid, but an entirely different species altogether.

Rob can't help but giggle at the thought of the Tsoukalos "Aliens" meme. Every good joke has an element of truth.

For a moment, he wonders if maybe this is a museum Helen might visit. But what would he do if she did happen to show up here? Cuss her out? Or maybe forget about the whole thing and move on? In reality, the tablet wasn't his to begin with. He really had no business owning it. Shoot, he couldn't even get into the dang thing. Maybe that's what he gets for stepping out of protocol and taking matters into his own hands.

He was being selfish, and he knows it. This Helen character has him distracted even still. That note though… it suggested something more. The whole tablet theft thing wasn't personal, only business. Maybe there really was something to pursue there.

Either way, it doesn't matter. He will stick around for another few days, or until the office checks in to see what he's doing in Peru. Of course, he'll give them the usual run around. Chasing a lead, gathering evidence, etc. He has enough clout in the work force to get away with it. Not that they won't suspect anything is off, but more so that they won't do anything about it if they even care.

Time to move on. Whatever happens, happens. Or doesn't.

He pulls his cell phone out and checks the time, then immediately forgets it. He walks, bored. More skulls. More placards of information he doesn't really care to read. A stand of postcards.

Olivia.

What happened to Olivia? How could he have forgotten about her situation?

Helen – that's how he forgot. How incredibly selfish. And for what?

He pulls his phone back out and searches for the number she called from. When they had their last conversation (how long ago was that?) he made sure to save the number just in case.

He scrolls down to her name and calls.

No answer. Perhaps he'll try again later. As long as she stayed put and followed the agent's directive, she's fine, until he can get her anyway. Time is of the essence, however, since she'll likely be collateral damage at some point. Can never trust those covert safe house missions. The government does not like leaving evidence behind. Maybe that's the next mission to get his mind off Helen.

"Excuse me." A man nods as he squeezes by. He stops to inspect a showcase and adjusts a blue cap on his head.

Rob looks at his phone again and bounces it in his hand.

"Weather's looking pretty grim out there." The man mumbles.

Rob raises an eyebrow at the odd fellow, trying to figure out if the guy is talking to him or his imaginary friend. He looks out the window.

Clear, blue sky.

"I don't get it." He blurts, annoyed.

"You know what they say." The man scoots a little closer, still studying the display.

"It's Peru. If you don't like the weather, wait five minutes."

"They say that everywhere." He snorts and shakes his head. "You local?"

"Nope. Just know a bad storm comin' when I see one." The man turns his head and smiles. "Anyway, good day." The man tips his hat and walks out.

The hat.

Rob double takes the emblem on the hat.

Pyramid design made of words, white etched on blue.

The man disappears out of the museum.

"Hey! Wait!" He rushes out after him to a busy street, but he is nowhere to be seen.

The crowd on the street is stopped in a chatter, pointing. He follows their gestures to a mountain just outside of town.

A massive blue swirl warbles on the mountain, causing a low hum.

He cocks his head to the side and looks back at the crowd for the strange man.

No luck.

28.

Some dumb schmuck must have set off an alarm somewhere, causing a loud and incredibly unnecessary siren to blare down each and every hallway. Cambor jogs, not used to exerting himself in any way really, huffing as he goes, with Dr. Hudson keeping pace. He points at a turn and the two round the corner.

A door comes up on the right and they slow to a halt. Cambor pulls out his phone and opens a security app.

"Level 12 Stasis Chamber status." He speaks into the phone and a screen pops up, a security video feed on the top half with status information text on the bottom. "All the holding pods have been opened and it looks like…" He squints at the phone. "They all did as they should have."

"They went through the collider all on their own?" Dr. Hudson looks at the door as though he might see through it.

"Portal, Doc. It's a portal *created* by the collider. The Neanderthals know what a portal looks like. Did you read *any* of the research I gave you?" Cambor smirks and shakes his head. "Either way, we're good to go. Hasn't been any movement in this room for a while, and you know those monsters were hungry. Thousands of years without food. Torture." He shucks and puts his finger on the reader.

The door unlocks and the two enter cautiously. The room is eerily quiet except for the low hum of the still active collider. Cambor unsheathes his gun, his eyes popping from side to side. They stalk the walkway and approach the collider control panel.

"Keep an eye out." Cambor sets his phone down on the panel and adjusts the digital settings. "I think they went to Georgia, according to these coordinates. That Kelim place probably." He moves a few more settings and a read comes up on the screen. "Oh. And Peru. Hometown, baby. I bet they're having fun over there. Now, strangely enough, and you're never going to believe this, the safest place to be with this mess is actually in…" He adjust a few more settings and the collider kicks back up. "Israel."

"Sounds biblical." A gruff voice rumbles out from one of the stasis chambers.

Cambor jumps, gasping and grabbing his gun.

"Nuh uh uh, no sir." Crane sits in the closest stasis chamber, rifle barrel locked in on his target. "You can put that down, young man. And when you're done setting it on the ground and kicking it this way, go ahead and keep that little thing-a-ma-bob set right there on Peru. God's got some hellfire to rain down, and you, boy, are going to be the wailing prophet in this book."

A woman screams as she watches what is most likely her husband almost escape the grip of a Giant, just before being ripped in half at the waist. The Giant stomps as he takes a bite of the man's torso, unconcerned about the woman's incessant screaming. Blood oozes down his red beard and he takes another bite, growling in intense pleasure at the long-awaited meal.

The woman finally passes out and busts her head on the concrete as she is passed by a crowd of frantically sprinting people.

The streets shiver with the barrage of Giants as they descend faster than a streetcar down the mountain and into the ancient town of Lima, Peru. Buildings crumble from the clumsy, bloodthirsty beasts as they shoulder the erections, greedily chasing down their prey. Horns honk, the desperate cries of panic from scared drivers trying to escape the carnage, unaware that these monsters aren't just looking for destruction but also – food.

A Giant swoops down on a car and smashes it with his heel to stop the noise, splattering the occupants inside. The city floods with the beasts, bellowing rampage, pent up aggression now explosive and untamed with no real hindrance to their whims.

A squadron of police vehicles blocks a road, and the officers step out, yelling and aiming shotguns and rifles at a Giant as he stomps down the street. One officer loses self-control and

shoots, causing a flood of shots to rain down on
the Giant from the other scared officers.

The Giant jolts from the blows, chunks of
flesh peeling off with the bullets. The wounds
heal in an instant and the Giant continues to step
forward, growling in anger with each new
penetration.

Some of the officers scatter, the more
valiant ones staying to fight as the Giant gets
closer. The Giant swoops his arm down, too quick
to duck, and grabs an officer by the legs then
whips the man to the blacktop, exploding the
man's body like swatting a fly. The rest of the
officers take the hint and run, forfeiting the
position.

In a little electronics shop down the street,
a television projects the local news on the other
side of the glass display wall. A woman
newscaster stands at a distance in front of the
mountain, gesturing at the massive swirl. The
video feed shakes and she looks off camera,
screams, and covers her face. The camera falls to
the ground and tumbles, then lands, pointed at the
brutally decapitated body of the newscaster, then
goes blank.

Gordon leans up against the railing to the old
man's front porch, struggling to maintain his
breathing. He keeps his eyes on the ground but
can still see the old man narrowed in on him with
his rifle. The wound in his side burns, throbbing a
deep pain that wasn't there earlier in the day.

With the long drive and the walk and having to dodge a few archaic traps in the woods that nearly skewered him, the wound only got worse.

"Boy, you look like trash. What's your business?" The old man crackles at him. Gordon glances at the man then looks back down, breathing heavy. The man acts a little older than he looks, almost as though he's trying to trick Gordon into thinking he may be weaker than he truly is. Smart man. When you think you have an enemy, let them think they have the upper hand. That way, you can blindside them and gain an even bigger advantage.

"I came to talk with Olivia." Gordon sighs, each word dragging out a little more energy.

"I told you to shoot him." Olivia says to the man.

"Sit down, boy. And before you do, toss that gun out right there." The old man nods at the gun in Gordon's waist holster.

Gordon nods and eases his hand into the holster, unsnaps the leather button, and slides the gun out. He sets it on the top stair to the porch, stretching his arm a little too much for comfort considering the stitches, and drops down to the lower stairs.

Olivia grabs the gun up and checks the chamber. "It's empty."

"I told you I came in peace. That's my favorite gun. I wasn't about to leave it behind."

"What do you think you're doing here?" Olivia snaps at him and slams the gun down on the porch railing.

"I said… I need…" Gordon sways, his vision goes blurry. "to talk." His vision goes black, and he drops onto the stairs.

Olivia holds still, frozen by overdue shock. This man, *this man*, took how many bullets? And still chased her down, with no intention of harm as far as anyone can tell, then collapses at her feet. What did he expect was going to happen? What is it that he *wants* to happen?

"Well," Grandpa Adams breaks the silence, "help me lug this big boy inside."

"What?" She shakes the shock off her face.

"You heard me. Grab him by the shoulder there, and be careful. Looks tender." He kneels down and gestures at Gordon's side.

"I'm not doing that. This man is the sole cause of my entire world falling apart. If you had only seen the way-"

"Sole cause, huh? That's a lot of power to give one man." He grunts and glances up at her. "Listen hun, we all got torment. Which means we all got torment*ors*. Harboring bile in your gut will only make *you* sicker. Sometimes, you gotta puke up the sickness to heal from it. Get it outta your system."

"That's disgusting." She frowns.

"More disgusting to harbor. Plus, I don't really want this man to die on my front porch. Don't feel like diggin' a grave tonight."

She sighs, then looks down at Gordon and frowns. "Seriously, Dad." She hikes up her sweats and squats down, wrestles her arms under his shoulder, and heaves at her Dad's queue.

They drag Gordon through the front door and into the back porch sunroom and situate him on the couch. He lifts Gordon's shirt and inspects the wound with a grimace and a whistle.

"Looks like he's patched up just fine. Just disheveled. Think he only needs rest."

Olivia stares at Gordon, his big, square jaw slumped to the side. Why the man still chose to wear the same type of suit is a mystery. Perhaps the kind of man who doesn't know how to separate work from personal life, consumed by duty. She notices Gordon's jacket pinching him in the arm, looking extremely uncomfortable, especially considering his injured state. "Help me get this jacket off." She smacks her legs, succumbing to altruism.

He nods and wrestles Gordon's torso up as Olivia pulls the sleeves one at a time, then yanks the jacket out with a little extra vindication, just to make sure her intentions aren't misunderstood.

"I'll get a blanket." He smiles and walks into the house, disappearing around the corner.

She folds the jacket neatly, out of habit, and drops it on a nearby table. Something falls out of the breast pocket and rolls across the floor. She quirks her head and leans down to pick it up.

A forest green crayon, now personalized with a splatter of blood.

Everett snatches off the restraints on Squirrel's wrists with such efficient quickness that it startles the already distraught man. Squirrel rockets out of the cage, devolved into an animalistic survival mode, and stops short in the dark.

"What the… holy crap. I mean, oh man." Squirrel puts shaking palms to his head, staring at the dead giant. "There's no amount of movies that can prepare you for this." He nods, agreeing with himself.

Everett speed-walks out and stands beside the poor guy. "I think that's the most accurate thing you've said this whole trip." He slaps Squirrel on the back and avoids looking at Daniels' corpse as he walks away.

In the back, a door busts open, followed by a frantic Jimenez. "He got away!"

"Where'd he go?" Everett growls, clenching his fists.

"I'm not positive, but I think I have a clue." Jimenez eyes up and down Everett. "But I think you need some pants first. Better make it fast, we're running out of time." She points her gun at Everett's midsection and turns, then stops. "In fact, I know where you can find a pair. I have some less-than-fortunate news."

300

Crane drops down, his rifle impressively trained on Cambor and Dr. Hudson consistently as he maneuvers. He grunts and hobbles closer, squinting beady blue eyes at the two.

"Ya know, I didn't exactly understand why the good Lord sent me here but you don't question authority when the message is clear, even if the reasoning isn't so clear. You perform your duty." Crane sniffs and glances at the collider. "And all things make sense in retrospect."

"What do you want, old man?" Cambor steps back, his hands up.

"Me? Oh, it's not about what *I* want. It's about what needs to happen. 'Cause I can tell you right now, what I'm about to do is not something that I want, personally. But I know better than to tell God any different. Been down that path before."

"You're one of those Bible thumper loons, aren't you?" Cambor chuckles and shakes his head. "You people are the reason we are in this mess in the first place."

"Perhaps. But we aren't alone." Crane gimps in closer. "And if I heard right, and understand, you know a little more about our Lord than you'd like to admit. I'd ask if I'm right, but I know I am."

Cambor scowls, disgusted. "You kidding me? There's a HUGE difference between logically researching and blindly believing in something ridiculous."

"True," Crane nods, not disagreeing. "But which one are you?"

Cambor scoffs, then looks away, considering. He snaps back and digs in his heels. "I know what I am, and what I can be, and I don't need any higher power to give me permission for anything."

Footsteps clatter through the open back door.

The collider opens a portal and kicks into high gear, causing a loud hum.

"Looks like a party." Cambor smiles as Everett rushes in with Jimenez and Squirrel.

"Pops!" Jimenez yells, "What the?" Confusion interrupts her excitement as the trio marches down the aisle.

Cambor glances at Dr. Hudson and winks.

For a second, Crane loses focus and turns to greet the interruption. Cambor nods at Dr. Hudson, grabs the serum case, and jumps into the portal with Dr. Hudson right beside as Crane turns back, yelling.

29.

It's like nothing he's ever experienced, in a fantastical but scary way. His body feels torn apart at the seams, disconnected atom by atom, the energy between molecules stretched to a thin wire and exposed at their basic level.

It's wonderful.

Cambor drops onto a triangular stone platform and tumbles to the side into a plot of dirt, fumbling the serum case. Dr. Hudson follows close behind, stumbling to the opposite side and rolling up against a stone wall.

Cambor scrambles to the case and grabs it up like a lost child, then flips over to his back and sighs.

"You think they're going to follow?" Dr. Hudson climbs to his feet, shaking off the dirt.

"Probably." Cambor sits up and unzips the case, looks at the portal, then thinks better of his position. He jumps to his feet and rushes off, careless about whether Dr. Hudson keeps up or not.

"Where are you going?" Dr. Hudson stammers. "Wait, where are we? Is this Israel?"

"You people. No class. No taste. You don't recognize this?" He presents the scenery with a roaming arm. Mountains surround ancient ruins, green and patched with a mysterious fog. The platform they stand on is made of perfectly stacked stones of various sizes, creating an angular curved blend with an open top. "Didn't have the time to change the destination to Israel but this'll do. Machu Pichu. And if I'm not mistaken…" He looks around at the ruins, fumbling for the syringe in the case. "This is the Sun Temple."

"The what?" Dr. Hudson catches up.

He giggles, then whispers, "*I don't think we're supposed to be here.*" He teases, a sly grin on his face. "But! Who cares, huh? I'm about to become a god, so it doesn't matter. Maybe to you. Mere humans aren't allowed in the temple." He plugs the serum into the syringe and taps it. Not because it does anything, but because it looks good.

A man steps out from behind a wall, "Is that what this has all really been about, Cambor?"

Cambor jumps and grabs his heart, syringe poking awkwardly at his chest. "Geez, Rob. Why you gotta scare me like that?"

"You know," Rob laughs, then coughs. He looks torn up and dirty, like he just got done with a street fight. "It wasn't easy getting up here with all the mess you let loose. Also wasn't easy figuring out this whole plot, but I'm smart. I got it." He taps his head.

"Okay, Rob. Congratulations." He smiles, then pockets the extra vials and drops the empty case to the ground.

"Thanks." Rob retorts with a forced cheer, then pulls out a gun and points it at Cambor.

"Whoa, whoa." He backs up and puts up his hands, syringe pocketed between thumb and forefinger. "Take it easy, Rob. What's all this about?"

"She used me." Rob snaps his neck, his thin hair flopping awkwardly.

"Who?" Cambor frowns, recognizing Rob's delusion.

"You used me. Oh, I see it now. I see aaaaaall of it. And I'm a little sick, and TIRED of being used."

"Calm down, Rob. I didn't use you. We were a team. Still are!" He laughs.

"Shut up!" Rob jabs the gun at him, his finger dangerously clamped on the trigger. "Now, I don't know what you're doing. I admit that. Haven't figured out your ploy yet. All I know, is that there is some strange business going on and it all points to *you*."

"Listen, I know I've done some really questionable things, but nothing to do with you. No offense, Rob, but you're not really on my list of concerns." He shrugs. "In a good way." He backs up, right next to Dr. Hudson who stands still with hands in the air.

Behind them, the portal makes a crackling sound.

"What is that?" Rob shakes the gun at Cambor.

"It's a… portal." He makes the statement as though being asked what type of tea he's drinking.

"What's it doing?" Rob keeps the gun on him and his eyes on the portal.

"How did you know I'd be up here?" Cambor says.

"Don't change the subject. Tell me what that thing is doing."

"Really, I don't know Rob. I know a lot of things, but not that." He lies.

Rob sighs, then looks back at Cambor. "I didn't know you'd be up here. But I'm not blind. Anyone can see that huge blue thing from down in town. I figured either A – get eaten by Giants on the streets of Lima or B – figure out what this thing is and hopefully not get eaten by Giants on the way. Easy decision. So I got close, jacked an SUV, and drove the thing up as far as I could until I had to hike. How about that?"

"Fair enough." Cambor relaxes his arms a bit, keeping a keen eye on Rob.

The portal cracks and whirls, causing Rob to instinctively turn his gun on it.

Cambor reaches over and grabs Dr. Hudson by the shirt and shoves him at Rob who responds instinctively by shooting, connecting the shot right into Dr. Hudson's torso as Cambor clambers away and out of sight. Dr. Hudson grabs at the wound and slumps to the ground, bewildered.

As the shot rings out from Rob's frantic miss, Everett tumbles through the portal, followed by his entourage in spurts.

"No!" Rob yells, frantically looking for Cambor. He gives up and leans over, hands on his knees, still catching his breath from the hike.

Everett jumps to his feet and rushes over. "Uncle Rob, what in the world?" He puts a hand on the man's shoulder, perplexed.

"Don't even ask. I assume you're after that worm too?"

"Cambor? You know him?"

Rob waves him off. "He went that way." He grunts and settles down, plopping on the ground.

Crane appears at Everett's side, "Small world, huh?"

Everett shoots a glance at Crane and looks in the direction Cambor left. An orb forms in the back of his mind and he closes his eyes.

You know I'll find you. He throws the thought out.

Come get me. I have a surprise. Cambor's thought floats back at Everett, and he tenses up.

"Here." Rob hands the gun to Everett.

"Don't need it." Everett nods, then walks away.

Rob looks at Crane, then at Squirrel and Jimenez staggering up behind. "What in God's name is going on?"

"You could ask Him. He's the only one who really knows, trust me." Crane glances at the sky, frowns, then watches Everett as he walks beyond the temple walls.

Little Julianna watches her mother pick something off the floor in the sunroom as she hides, tucked behind the door. She wonders who the man on the couch is for only a second before her impeccable memory kicks in.

That's the man in the suit. The nice man who used to visit us at our new home and bring us food. She snuggles a stuffed unicorn tight and bites her lower lip out of habit, something her mom is constantly getting on to her about. But Mom doesn't know she's there, because she's supposed to be asleep.

Mom puts her hand to her face and wipes her cheek, then walks over to the man. She squats down and looks the man in the face, then reaches over and brushes a lock of hair off his forehead.

For a long moment, Julianna watches her mom as she watches the man breathe, waiting for something to happen. She doesn't know exactly what, but surely something will. People don't just sit and watch other people sleep, do they? Unless they love that person very much. That's what Mom used to say anyway, whenever Julianna would catch her watching. Sometimes, in the middle of the night, she could feel her mom watching her and would wake up and ask. The answer was always the same.

"I just like to watch you sleep 'cause you're my precious little girl, and I love you."

Was it the same with grown-ups? Do grown-ups watch each other sleep? Maybe that's why they sleep together, so they don't have to stay up and watch. They can just be together.

But the couch isn't big enough for Mom and the man in the suit to sleep together. Maybe that's why she's watching him.

What about Dad? Did she ever watch him sleep? When he comes home, will she watch Dad *and* the man in the suit sleep? It's all very confusing.

A loud noise blasts out from the woods, startling Julianna. She jumps and squeaks at the sound, backing into a dark corner.

Mom rushes out of the room, almost running right by Julianna.

"Hey, hey, what're you doing up?" Mom leans over and pulls Julianna into her arms.

"I heard a noise." Julianna snuggles the unicorn tighter.

"I know baby. I hear that too. It's just a siren."

"Like an amboolense?" Julianna's doe eyes stare up at her mother.

"Yeah, kinda like that. But much bigger." Her Mom nods. Julianna can tell she's not saying something but doesn't know how to call it out.

"Like a bigger amboolense?" She says, confused.

"No, honey. It's like…" Her Mom searches for the words. "Like an emergency call for the whole city. You know, like how they do when tornadoes are close?"

"Are there tornadoes?" Julianna tenses up, gasping.

"No, no, honey. It's not tornado season. Come on, let's get you back to bed. I'm sure it's nothing to worry about." Her Mom picks her up and kisses her on the cheek.

Bastion stumbles out of bed, rubbing his eyes. "What's going on? Is that a siren?"

"Shhhh." Mom puts a finger in front of her lips and points at Julianna. Julianna knows what that means. *Not in front of your sister.* The grown-ups always think she doesn't see those things, but she does.

Mom takes her into the room and tucks her back in. The room has two beds, one for each child. Julianna still wonders why Bastion was so mad when he had to sleep in here but all Mom would say was he's just 'being a boy' and not to worry about it, but she does. She doesn't want her brother to be mad, especially not at her.

Mom sits on the edge of the bed and puts her hand on Julianna's cheek, a glistening sadness in her eyes.

"Just go back to sleep, baby. It'll all be okay."

Julianna nods but doesn't believe her. She's probably doing that grown-up thing where she keeps a secret because it protects her kids.

Mom leans over and kisses her on the forehead, pulls the sheets up tight, pats her on the belly and walks out, taking one last glance before closing the door.

Julianna turns to look out the window at the dark night sky. A light flashes in rhythm with the ebb and flow of the siren. She shivers and closes her eyes and tries to think of something else like Mom always says to do when she has bad dreams.

Everett climbs down the ancient stairwell, far too big for any human use, and drops to an opening. The scenery is breathtaking, and under any other circumstance, Everett would pause a moment to take it all in. The fresh, crisp mountain air. The view of the valley, overlooking the layout of the city below. The strikingly green grass growing over stacks of stones, leveled to perfection despite the oddity in arrangement. No human hand could have done this. At least, not without help.

He walks out to the center of the open arena covered in grass like an empty park, the Huayna Pichu peak towering imperious behind him.

Cambor stands on the other end, propped up against a lone tree, his legs crossed casually. He pushes off the tree and strolls out into the fading sun, hands in his pockets, looking up at the sky and scenery like a typical tourist.

"Lovely day, don't you think?"

"You took the serum, didn't you?" Everett walks slowly toward Cambor, forming an orb in the back of his mind.

"Of course I took the serum. And you ruined my surprise." Cambor snorts. "All three vials. Feelin' a little… good."

"Just good?" Everett shakes his head.

"Well, of course, a little more than good. A little, uhh, fit, I guess you could say." Cambor lifts his shirt and slaps his trimmed-out stomach. "I don't really know what to expect, honestly, but so far I like it."

"All that for a six pack?" Everett prods.

"Oh, that's just the start. You know that. I know what you can do. And, according to my math, I should be able to do about three times that starting any second now." Cambor coughs and stops, then stretches his legs. "Don't mind me, just a little sore."

"I bet." Everett closes in but is still half the field away.

Cambor blows out a breath, then leans over, his hands on his knees. "That's odd." He jolts, then gags. His shoulders pop and he lets out a holler, then straightens up. "That sun. It's a little warm." He unbuttons his shirt and flaps it out, sweating profusely.

"Doesn't look comfortable." Everett picks up his pace but not too quick. He needs Cambor to stay put. Just a few more feet, and this orb worked up in the back of his brain should be at full capacity.

"I'll be alright. Hey, you know somethin' crazy?" Cambor waits a second for a response, then continues when Everett ignores him. "All those Giants down there, causing a raucous, that's just the top level Giants. Nuts, right?" Cambor laughs.

"Doesn't matter. I'll take care of them." Everett keeps walking.

"Oh, I know you're capable of that much. My question is-"

"Let me guess, you don't think I can handle you too?"

Cambor laughs and takes his shirt off, revealing an impressive eight pack as he tosses the shirt to the side. "No. I'm just curious if you can handle me *and* levels one through ten Giants. 'Cause I opened up all those chambers and colliders too."

The portal in the background crackles, causing Everett to pause and look.

"Level eleven went somewhere else, in case you were wondering. Somewhere a little close to home."

"What is that supposed to mean?" Everett growls, pointing a finger as he turns back to look at Cambor.

"Hey, it wasn't me man. That was done before I got to it." He puts up his hands and his stomach lurches, making him cough again. "I wanted all of them to come here."

"Tell me where they went."

"Because you're my brother, I'll tell you." Cambor turns on fake empathy.

Everett grits his teeth and ignores the statement.

"They went to a little town in Georgia. Somewhere in the country." He puts out a halting hand as Everett picks up his pace. "I'm just the messenger." A vein pops out in his neck, pulsing a rush of blood as his body prepares for transformation.

The portal emits a thunderous snap in the background, stopping Everett. He turns to look and sees the inner portion of the swirl gloss over like a mirror.

"Should be here any second. And with my superiority…" Cambor barks as his muscles rip, his deltoids pushing out like wings on his shoulders in tandem with his entire frame enlarging. "There is only one God, Everett. And you're looking at him."

Everett turns back and stares at the beast who was Cambor, now over twelve feet tall and proportionately balanced in muscle and strength, approximately three times his size in girth.

A roar crashes through the portal, followed by the footstep of a Giant. Gunshots fire off immediately.

Everett releases the orb in his mind, letting the built-up energy explode from his aura as it blasts toward Cambor.

Cambor stomps toward Everett and embraces the impact of the orb, letting it crash into his chest. The energy knocks him back a step and he grunts, looking down at his gut.

Everett waits, forming another orb in his mind, bracing his feet for impact.

Cambor looks up and smiles. Then, in a deeper voice, "I really hope you've got more than that." He charges with a yell.

314

At the last second, Everett dodges out of the way, letting Cambor tumble in his own velocity into the stone wall behind, breaking the stones loose.

Everett releases another orb then races after it, screaming. The orb hits Cambor in the back, knocking him down, and Everett jumps onto his back, swinging his fists. Though diminished in size by comparison, the hits from Everett's empowered faculties still crack the bones as he strikes, rewarded with cries of pain from Cambor.

Cambor pushes up and wobbles to his feet, clumsy with his new physique, like a baby learning to walk. But learning fast.

Everett keeps his grip on the beast, arms wrapped as far as he can reach around the back of Cambor's neck. He opens his mouth and sinks in his teeth, clamping down as hard as he can.

Cambor yells and grabs at Everett, barely catching a hold of his heel and snatching him off, slinging him across the field.

Everett rolls, his hair flailing, until he bumps up against the stone wall. He pushes to his hands and knees, reeling for breath.

Cambor jumps, crossing a humanly impossible distance, and lands right in front of Everett. He reaches down and picks Everett up by the nape like a puppy dog and raises him up to look him in the face. "That wasn't very nice. We don't BITE people. You need to learn some manners." He scolds Everett, who winces at the pinch in his back, unable to speak from the pressure. With a flick of his wrist, he flings Everett to the side. The thrust is powerful for such a simple action, surprising even Cambor. He frowns in approval, raising his eyebrows at the distance.

Everett flies through the air and collides into the front wall of the Sun Temple, right next to Jimenez.

"Hey." She says, pushed up against the wall, cradling her gun. "You're holding up pretty good for a small guy."

"Small guy, huh. That's a first." Everett grunts as he pushes to his feet. Cambor stares at him from the lower level, anticipating the next move.

"Well, comparatively, you know. It's nothing personal." Jimenez nods, sweating.

"More giants come through?" Everett leans over to catch his breath, grateful for the break Cambor is giving him in this lovely game of cat and mouse.

"Yah. That handgun Pops got from this psycho down there is better than this thing." She lifts her rifle, then pulls it back. "I don't know how, but he's killed four of them and I think they've stopped coming through because of it."

"He has Cambor's gun?" Everett looks at Jimenez, hopeful. *Pure copper bullets.*

She shrugs, "I think it's his. He's up there." Jimenez points toward the portal.

Everett looks down at Cambor who squints, curious. Then realization strikes his face.

Both of them jet toward Crane with equal speed.

"Crane!" Everett jumps into the temple. "The gun! Shoot him!"

Startled, Crane whips around and points the gun at the speeding Giant causing him to fumble the gun and drop it.

Cambor jumps, careening through the air, just as Everett slides to the gun and grabs it. Everett rolls to his back, Cambor descending down on him, and pulls the trigger, perforating Cambor's neck.

Cambor timbers down on top of Everett, dead-weight pinning him to the ground. Everett struggles for breath beneath the hot body and works his arms into a position to finally push the beast off. Cambor's body rolls to the side, his face limp against the stone floor.

"I could've done that." Squirrel peaks from behind a stone wall, his broken glasses topping off the whole frayed look.

Everett sits up and sighs, hands on his knees.

Crane walks over and pats his back. "Good shot. Thought you were a pancake there for a second."

"Aim high." Everett brushes his hands off on his pants and stands up. "Now what are we supposed to do about this?" He nods to the portal, hoping to God nothing comes through. "There's probably a hundred Giants waiting on the other side."

"Well, I think our friend here has a cell phone with a special program." Crane nods at Cambor's body.

"On it!" Squirrel hops-to, for the first time in the whole trip getting the opportunity to play with a gadget. He climbs down the stairs, headed for the shredded pants that were left behind after Cambor's transformation.

"Hey, where's Rob?" Everett looks around.

"You mean that random guy?" Jimenez nods toward the dead Giants. "He really tried, but he was too close. I told him to back up but he didn't listen to me. Think he was a little looney, if you ask me."

Everett drops his head. "Oh no." He puts a hand to his mouth and glances over, trying not to look too hard at the smaller corpse amidst the pile of dead Giants.

"How'd you know him?" Jimenez softens her tone, catching a mystery in the story.

"He was uh," Everett clears his throat. "My wife's uncle. Don't know how he ended up here."

"I'm sorry to hear that, brother. It is odd. Small world." Crane nods and keeps his eyes on the ground, giving Everett space to think.

"He was a good guy. I didn't know him that well but Liv will be upset." Everett steps

318

forward and shakes it off. "Let's get down here and see what Squirrel comes up with."

The crew agrees by following Everett down the stairs to a very excited Squirrel, swiping and texting ferociously on a smartphone.

Cambor opens an eye and takes a long, low breath in.

30.

The chop of a helicopter machine-guns the dark sky over Gainesville, Georgia, breaking up the chaotic noise of carnage below. Emergency vehicles skid around street corners, frantically searching a way out of the maze of fires and abandoned vehicles. A police car races through a street, blaring a message over the loud speaker:

GET TO YOUR HOMES
EMERGENCY
GET OFF THE STREETS AND GET HOME
THIS IS NOT A TEST
EMERGENCY

A man in a sedan blazes down the street and pulls to the side with a halt as a Giant blasts through the front of a butcher shop, chewing on a skinned cow torso. The man hops out of the car and pulls out his phone, flips to Instagram, and goes 'live', then faces the camera at him with the Giant in the background.

"I'm here in downtown, Atlanta, where you can see the Giants have overrun the city." Gasp. "This is probably closer than I should get, but the world needs to know! This isn't a joke! That thing-" he points the phone more directly at the Giant, catching the beast ripping a large chunk of meat off the carcass like a stubborn piece of jerky. "Is NOT CGI!"

With the last excited yell, the man unintentionally gets the Giant's attention. The Giant snaps his head the man's direction and drops the cow carcass.

"Oh crap!" the man fumbles the phone as he scrambles to get back in the car. The Giant shakes the ground and sprints at the man, grabs the car door just before the man can close it, and wrenches it off, tossing it to the side.

The man crawls to the passenger seat and grabs for the door, dropping the phone on the seat, still live. He screams as the Giants grabs him by the ankles and pulls him out, clawing the leather apart as he is dragged, breaking his fingernails.

The Giant dangles the screaming man over the windshield where the phone is able to capture a small slice of the action.

"Stop! Stop! Please stop!" The man screams, to the Giant's amusement.

The Giant takes one leg in each hand and rips, splattering blood all over the windshield of the car. Amused with himself, he licks the massive wound like a lollipop and then takes a huge bite, reveling in the fresh meat.

On the other side of the nation, a teenage girl watches in horror with her girlfriends as the video plays out on her phone.

"Ew. That's disgusting." One of the girls frowns and shakes her head.

"It's totally fake. Get over it." The girl on the other side retorts. "I mean, it's a good fake but its fake."

"I don't know. That looks awfully… realistic to me." The main girl holding the phone raises an eyebrow and then glances at her friends. "Kinda crazy."

"Totally crazy." The believer girl says.

The doubter shakes her head, "You guys watch too much T.V. if you think that's real. Hey, send me the link. My brother would *eat that up*." The girl explodes a laugh and falls backward on her bed.

"You're a dork." The main girl double clicks the video, liking it, and then sends it to her friend. "Speaking of dorks, did Henry ever text you back?"

"Oh, no, don't remind me!" The girls all giggle as the main girl locks her phone and tosses it on her desk.

"Spill the tea, sis." The doubter says, a twinkle in her eyes.

I was a god, if only for a moment. The pain… that's what it's like. I was only able to describe it indirectly before but now, I can feel it. I know it. One more moment to rest, and it'll be gone. The bullet must have exited, or I'd be dead. Yes, that's it. I can feel the hole in my neck closing up, the pain receding. I can hear their voices. Unaware.

Good.

Cambor flutters his eyelids, blinking at the blinding sunlight. Everything looks purple from the deep darkness his mind went to while he was dead. The bullet struck his spinal cord, severing it in two, shutting down his entire nervous system. However, something about this DNA doesn't give up. His cells immediately targeted the injury and repaired, pulling his spirit out of purgatory and back into this shell of a body.

The humans, yes, that's what they are, they walk off, proud in their false victory. Cambor moves while their backs are turned, relying on the loud hum of the portal to cover any noises.

He dashes behind the nearest wall and hunkers down, planning his next move. The walls are short and have holes, so the moves need to be quick. If he can catch Everett by surprise, perhaps he won't think quick enough to aim high again. A bullet to the stomach, even a copper one, won't be as bad as the neck. But what if it gets lodged? The gun is powerful enough, it should go through, but that's for a normal human, not a three-times as thick Giant.

Cambor has to make a move anyway, or he's dead.

He slinks down the side wall with more finesse than he thought possible. Being a Giant is a lot different than what he thought it would be. Better. It's almost like he's cheating, how easy it is to maneuver. No wonder these beasts were so feared in biblical times. Not the dumb, clumsy monsters the movies always made them out to be. Quite the opposite.

Cambor gets close, close enough to jump. At least, one of *his* jumps. His previous launches weren't even full power and that would be sufficient.

He peers around the edge of the wall, his sharp vision another welcome phenomenon he didn't expect.

Everett stands with the gun hanging lazily at his side, circled with the group, all staring at the smartphone.

Time to act quick if he wants that portal to stay open. That Eric kid was taken on for a reason. He'll figure out the SHIVA program in no time.

Cambor moves into sprint position, one leg cocked behind him like a gun hammer, and takes a deep breath, then jumps.

The only sound he makes is a whistle as his body cuts the air.

Eric looks up from the phone, the only one who could possibly see Cambor from his angle, and double takes, then drops the phone, stumbling backward. The whole group splits, Everett turning around with the gun waiving in all directions, unsure of where the threat is.

Cambor pounces down, jarring Everett into whiplash as his massive hands grab Everett's shoulders and drive them into the ground. Everett manages to keep hold of the gun but is knocked loopy, flopping his hands around. Cambor growls and reaches down, grabbing the gun from Everett's hand and flinging it over the cliff.

Jimenez shoots, pelting Cambor's side, but he ignores her.

Everett punches Cambor in the chest with surprising force for his stature, but it's not enough to do any lasting damage. The poor man wrangles under Cambor's grip, unable to break free. Cambor stares him down, smiling.

"I've got you now." Cambor can't control a spurt of giggles. "I've never before wondered what human flesh is like, but suddenly, I have this insatiable craving." He grins and opens his mouth, two rows of jagged teeth lining his gums.

Everett goes limp for a second, then swings his arms inside Cambor's, knocking his grip loose and causing Cambor to fall on top of him.

"Get a taste of this!" Everett wraps his arms around Cambor's head and pulls in close, forehead to forehead, as tight as a clamp.

Cambor pushes up and yells, the pressure on his forehead stunning his brain, and stumbles backward with Everett dangling down his chest.

His brain swells, making his muscles spasm. He can feel a strange sort of energy pushing through his skull like a drill, severing the connection between the two halves of his brain until it bores all the way to the base of his brain and connects with the pineal gland. The energy balls up, bigger and bigger, pushing all matter aside in his skull until his ears and nose bleed.

He screams and flails but Everett clamps on, refusing to let up until the entire orb of energy is transferred.

Cambor can see the orb in his mind, a brilliant white filling his vision and turning him blind. He drops to his knees, and the orb explodes, turning his brain into soup.

Everett releases his hold and jumps back, letting the corpse of Cambor fall on his face, a bloody, fleshy bubble of gore protruding out the back of his skull.

Below the ancient ruins, the city of Lima, Peru is spotted with pillars of smoke as the city burns to the ground. The screams of the people as they are chased down as prey travel up to Machu Pichu, carried on the wind in an eerie echo.

"We have to shut the portals down." Crane shakes his head at the demise below, empathetic pain etched on his face.

"No." Everett grunts and turns away. "Not yet."

"What do you mean not yet?" Crane gruffs.

"Those people down there are already a lost cause. And I'm sorry for them, I really am. But there's a bigger problem and shutting down the portals will only trap us here. It won't take those Giants down there back." Everett walks toward the portal at the top of the ruins.

"But we have to shut down the portals so none of the others come out." Crane follows Everett. "It's only a matter of time before they try again."

Squirrel and Jimenez give each other confused looks and follow, a little more hesitantly.

"I know. But I have to get home." Everett locks his eyes on the portal.

"Wait, wait," Squirrel pipes up, "How exactly... do you plan on doing that?"

Everett points at the portal and climbs up the first stair.

"You do realize there's probably Giants on the other side of that thing, waiting to see what happens, right?" Squirrel catches up. "Or to see what comes through."

"I know exactly the chances I'm taking."

Squirrel frowns, thoroughly confused, and looks at Jimenez. She only shrugs in response.

Everett crests the top of the staircase and stops, staring at the portal. "Here's how this is going to go down."

"You can't be serious." Crane drops his hand to his leg, slapping it in frustration.

"I'm going to go through that portal and take care of whatever lies on the other side." Everett points at the portal like he's discussing a power point. "When I'm done, I'll come back through and get you."

"This is crazy." Squirrel laughs.

"Eric, I need you most." Everett turns his finger on the man who seems shocked to hear his real name. "Because when I come back, you're all going back through to Antarctica with me, and then we're going home. You're going to get us there." Everett glares at Squirrel and nods.

Squirrel nods timidly in return.

"If I'm not back by nightfall, it's safe to assume I didn't accomplish my task." Everett turns to the portal.

"What do we do if that happens?" Squirrel whines.

Everett glances over his shoulder. "Get the hell away from here." He steps up to the portal, takes a deep breath, and walks in.

His mind stays stable through the passage, like stepping through a waterfall. A little invigorating and disturbing at the same time, being unable to really see what lies beyond but seeing well enough to get an idea. As his foot sets onto the tile floor of the stasis room, the scene comes into view.

Down below the collider platform, a group of Giants surround a bloodied mess on the ground, eating. At first, they don't notice Everett as he gently steps into the chamber. He prepares the orb in his mind and hands, controlling his breathing, moving into a meditative like state.

One of the Giants feels the energy shift and looks over his shoulder, revealing the meal. Another Giant is ripped apart on the floor, cannibalized, his pale face the only recognizable flesh on the hollow corpse.

Everett sees the horror and ignores it, focusing on his task at hand. The first Giant stands up and smiles.

"Milseog." The Giant grumbles and laughs, alerting the others to Everett's presence.

"Alright," Everett pumps his shoulders. "Let's see if I still got this thing under control."

The Giant cocks his head and furrows his eyebrows, curious about this little man. His eyes widen at a foreign feeling in his brain and he grunts, stumbling backward.

Everett straddles the air, his hands shaking from the immense amount of energy charging from his body. The electric veins of the portal snap out and connect to him, becoming a power source, a charge port.

The Giant bellows below, pushing his palms to his head, "Draíocht! Tá draíocht aige!" The other Giants scramble to their feet, staring at the first Giant as though he's gone mad.

"Ní féidir draíocht a bheith aige. Tá sé marbh!" One of the Giant's yells at the first one, just before his head explodes.

The blood and brains splatter across the second Giants face and he recoils in shock, looks at Everett, then at his brothers, and bolts at Everett, wasting no more time.

Everett acts quick and throws out his hands, lightening shooting from his fingertips, stretched through his body from the portal. The portal swirls faster and thunders, flickering with the abuse.

The lightning hits the second Giant and canon-balls him across the massive room, slamming him against the concrete wall and dropping him to the floor. Another Giant follows quickly, this time getting blindsided by a catapulted stasis chamber to the torso that pins him to the wall, splitting his body in half.

Nearly a hundred Giants pause and survey the situation. Everett breaths in deep, his cheeks quaking with the pent up energy, and releases again.

"Tell me again," Jimenez sits on top of a stone monument, chewing on a piece of jerky. "How you didn't die."

Crane sits across from her, his back propped against the stone wall. "Well, you see, I started blasting off rounds at that first Giant, and then the portal opened up. And I'm not joking, the thing quite literally looked at me, grunted, waved me off like I was a pest, and walked into the portal. I'm telling you, it was the name of Jesus. He knew he couldn't touch me."

"B.S. I don't believe it." Jimenez points her jerky at him and laughs, shaking her head.

"I'm here aren't I?" Crane raises his voice and his hands.

"Then why didn't you call on Jesus just now?" She gestured at the war torn field, topped with the bodies of Giants.

Crane's face crumples, "Honestly forgot about it."

"Hey, where'd you get that jerky?" Squirrel looks up from Cambor's cell phone and squints at Jimenez. She slaps a cargo pocket on her leg and winks. "Can I have some?" He asks like he shouldn't have to.

"Say please."

"Nevermind."

The portal snaps louder than usual and flickers, the humming sound warbling like a dying fan.

"What do you think is going on in there?" Jimenez nods at the portal.

Crane raises an eyebrow. "Phew. I don't even wanna know."

"Think we should maybe..." Squirrel studies the portal, "move a little further away, just in case?"

The other two nod in approval and hop up, then walk down the stairs with Squirrel and settle in a more comfortable position.

As another giant's head explodes, the rest rush all at once instead of waiting to see what happens.

Everett throws his hand one after the other, throwing lightning bolts with one hand and empty stasis chambers with the other, holding the line at the front and piling up the carnage. The Giants yell and clamber over the mess, knowing it's either fight or die.

One Giant slips through the barrage, darting in the air, and rolls on the ground in front of Everett. He kicks Everett's feet out from under him, knocking him to the ground and causing him to release his control of the energy shooting from him and the portal.

The Giant jumps over the top of Everett and pounds a massive fist, just missing Everett's skull as he ducks out of the way. Everett undercuts the Giant in the chin, knocking it's jaw loose. The Giant howls and grabs at his face, popping the jaw back into place. Everett throws an orb, striking the Giant in the chest and knocking him backward.

The Giant tumbles away and regains his balance, pushing to his feet.

Everett meets the challenge and stands up, then reaches for the energy from the portal.

The portal is down.

The Giant steps forward and chuckles.

Everett feels a strange pressure in the base of his brain. Not his own energy, but something else.

The Giant squints his eyes at Everett and licks his lips. "Is dóigh leat gur tusa an t-aon duine. Ah." The Giant shakes his head and walks forward, keeping the pressure on Everett's brain. "For you, this wretched English." He points at Everett, his voice rumbling. "You think you're the only one. How do you think you can, *little brother?*"

"I'm not your brother." Everett keeps his eyes on the Giant but notices the rest of the room. The explosion of the portal annihilated everything past him and this last Giant.

"Oh, you don't know. Now, you do. You may not have our body, but you have our *blood.*"

"I will not be associated with you monsters." Everett braces his feet. The inherent energy he was able to conjure has been spent, but not his muscles.

The Giant laughs. "You have no choice."

Everett clenches his jaw and breaks into a sprint, catching the Giant off guard. The Giant reacts by swatting, catching Everett's move just in time to knock him to the side. He pounces at Everett, his heel aimed for Everett's head.

Everett throws his arms up and catches the Giant's heel, surprising the beast, then twists the ugly foot, throwing the Giant off balance and knocking him to the ground.

"You really are," the Giant lies on his stomach in push-up position, "one of us." He springs his arms up, throwing his entire body into a standing position, and turns, ready for another attack.

Everett lunges, his fist making contact with the Giant's face, his other fist following right behind before his feet even hit the ground.

The Giant takes both hits before he can react and stumbles back against the wall. Everett stays on him, hammering the beast in the chest, moving too fast for the Giant to get a headlock on him. The Giant wheezes, his arms spasm, blocking him from covering himself as Everett knocks blow after blow into the same exact spot on his chest, right over his heart. The Giant chokes and his eyes roll back into his head as he slides down the wall, unable to stand.

Everett is rabid, hyperfocused, a machine gun stuck on auto. His fists splinter with pain as he breaks through the Giant's ribcage but he doesn't give the pain his attention. The flesh on the Giant's chest tears, ripping open into a mangled hole.

Everett's fist sinking into the Giant's cavity is the only thing that stops him from his volley, the bones partially trapping his wrist inside the dying Giant's chest. He feels the beasts heart bump up against the back of his hand in a slow pulse and spreads his fingers out, staring into the Giant's face.

The Giant lulls his head down and with a pale glare looks back, barely conscious. "You are still... brother."

Everett frowns, wraps his hand around the Giant's heart, and squeezes, busting the organ open like stepping on a ripe cherry.

The Giant squirms and grunts, puts a hand on Everett's shoulder for stability and squeezes, then goes limp.

Everett guides the body down, slowly pulling his hand out of it's chest, until it drops on the floor.

The collider kicks back in to motion, whirring with action. Everett steps back from the dead Giant and watches as the portal swirls back open.

Crane steps through, waving a gun wildly in his hand.

"Whoa whoa, calm down." Everett yells, putting his hands up.

Crane swings the gun across the room, taking it all in. "Dear God." His eyes are as wide as saucers. "I'd ask how, but I don't want to know."

"So you drew the short straw, huh?" Everett slings the blood off his hand and walks to the portal.

"I volunteered." Crane grunts, unable to peel his eyes off the massacre.

"What a gentlemen."

"Don't swoon. The old man sacrificing himself always makes the most sense."

"Thanks." Everett teases, his nerves still jittering from the adrenaline.

"Well. Looks like you've got this taken care of." Crane nods. "Shall we get the others?"

"Probably a good idea. I think you should go though. My appearance might be a little startling."

Crane looks up and down Everett standing there, shirtless and bloodied from head to toe. "Yah. Good thinkin. Be right back."

31.

Crane walks back through with Squirrel and Jimenez stumbling one after the other behind him.

"I warned them."

"Ruined all the fun." Everett sits on the ground, resting.

"What in the devil's dirty -" Squirrel blocks Jimenez from entering the room, frozen in place. She puts her hands up in WTF pose behind him, then gently moves him out of the way. "I don't know what you're about to say and I don't want to, but move!"

Jimenez nods at the scene, takes a bite of jerky, and looks at Everett. "Good job." She hops down the stairs and plops down, putting her elbows on her knees.

"Thanks. I would've saved one for you, but they were impatient." Everett squeaks out a little smile.

"He's got jokes." Jimenez looks at Squirrel as he dawdles down the stairs toward the collider controls.

Squirrel shakes his head, snapping out of his trance, and gets to work on the controls. "So, where we goin'?"

"Can you take us to Gainesville, Georgia?"

"With how intuitive this system is, I don't see why not." Squirrel smiles and fidgets with the controls. The portal flickers, powers down slightly, then powers back up.

Everett nods, then pushes to his feet.
"Well, is everyone ready?"

"Why not." Jimenez finishes off her last
bite of jerky and wipes her hands off on her pants.
"What're we doin' in Georgia?"

Everett drops his hands and looks up at
the crew. "Killing more Giants."

Everyone groans.

Everett steps into a quiet side street in
Gainesville, only a short walk from his house.
The rest of the crew follows behind, careful to
keep quiet. A dog barks in the distance as the
portal closes down, leaving a strange imprint on
the otherwise dark midnight sky.

"I love this thing." Squirell whispers at the
phone in his hand and pockets it.

"This way." Everett motions them on
toward his house.

"I mean, it's got it's limitations but I've
still never seen anything like it. The portal back
there was much more-"

"Shut up, Eric." Everett and Jiminez
respond in unison, limping as their wounds catch
up to them.

"Uh," Squirrel coughs and watches the
ground as he walks, silently.

A few minutes later, they arrive at the
house. Everett walks up to the front door and tries
the handle. It's unlocked.

Olivia never leaves the front door
unlocked at night.

338

He turns to the crew and puts a finger to his lips. "Stay here a moment."

"Why are you being wierd about your own place?" Jimenez whispers back.

"For one, I have a ragtag entourage of strange looking people with me. And two, Liv never leaves the front door unlocked."

Jimenez frowns at his explanation but keeps quiet.

Everett pushes into the dark house and creeps around the corner. He reaches under the hallway table and releases a hidden 44 mag, racks it with ease, and stalks the house, room to room.

Nothing.

At the front door, he turns on a light and opens the door the rest of the way, motioning the crew to come in. "No one's here." He says, unhappy.

"Where do you think they are?" Crane reads his disappointed look.

"I'm not sure, but I have a pretty good idea." Everett stares back at Crane, his face hardened. "But it's going to be a long drive."

"Ahem." Squirrel interrupts, flashing Cambor's phone. "I mean, it doesn't have to be."

Edgar Cofield thumbs his chin as he watches the portal at the top of Machu Pichu dissipate. The sun sets in the distance behind the peaks, casting a sudden twilight. A cloud of fog rolls by, slithering through the mountain range's crevice, trying to sneak up on the night.

He steps out from what looks like it used to be housing and walks across the field. He pulls out a non-branded smart phone, now a third phone in his repertoire, and unlocks the screen by pushing his thumb on a tiny needle. The needle pricks his skin like a diabetes monitor and checks the blood, then affirms his identity, and opens up the main screen.

He scrolls over and pops open the DOMAIN app, of his own design. Not even the government has this one. He gave them SHIVA, letting them think they got the best. But this program... there's nothing like it. The face behind the face. The grey pope of scientific software.

The language on the program riddles foreign, but not to Cofield. He maneuvers a few icons, restricting all devices but his own.

He swipes to another screen and clicks on a little blue swirl icon. Different commands pop open and he clicks one.

In the distance, the portal opens back up. He looks up at the portal.

"That didn't go the way I thought, but I couldn't have planned it better."

Cofield smiles and walks to the portal, the night sky closing in.

END

As you might have guessed from the subject content in this novel and how it is represented through the various character's perspectives, this is not something I just made up out of thin air. King Solomon said, "There is nothing new under the sun." and it couldn't be more true. All I have done is taken truth and made it fun with fiction, using a very generous amount of liberties with a multitude of topics and stories.

The main plot was inspired by the "Giant of Kandahar" told by anonymous soldiers in an interview with a man named L.A. Marzulli. I stumbled upon the video after spending way too much time on YouTube pilfering through all the top five weird creatures caught on camera or something equally as silly but thoroughly entertaining. That was years ago now, and you will be hard pressed to find the original Kandahar story on YouTube without also having to type in Marzulli's name. Of course, I recommend watching the video even if just for entertainment purposes. The story is fascinating at the least. And whether or not you believe in the fantastical, you have to admit, it makes for a good story.

For copyright purposes, and other legalities I'm probably not even aware of, I must reiterate how much of this story is genuinely fiction. All of the characters, especially those in Everett's flashbacks at Kandahar with the other soldiers, are *purely* my imagination. The names and likenesses of his squadron are entirely made up. I have no inside scoop on this story whatsoever. In fact, if you watch the above-mentioned video and compare the story to my fictionalization of it, you'll notice a lot of discrepancies. That is absolutely one hundred percent on purpose. I cannot emphasize enough how much the Giant of Kandahar story is merely *inspiration* and nothing more.

There are many other "conspiracy theories" riddled throughout this story, many of which only the adept would catch on to. I'll leave most of those up to your own research and imagination, but I wanted to give inspirational credit to the story that Marzulli and the unnamed soldiers shared.

That being said, I cannot go without mentioning one of my favorite clichés, *there is truth in fiction*. What those little truth nuggets are, dispersed throughout the story, I'll leave up to your own deduction. However, a few honorable mentions are in order.

The "collider" concept comes from the infamous CERN project.

Yes, there is more than one giant (Goliath) in the Bible. For a great resource on that, read Gary Wayne's book "The Genesis 6 Conspiracy". If I could think of a stronger word than *comprehensive* on biblical giants, I'd use it for this book.

The Hollow Earth is a real theory, and it is what I am suggesting with Quinton's epic descent.

As for the more normal stuff, there are a few other things I'd like to mention.

Copyright has it so that I can print small quotes without having to cite, however, I'd like to do so anyway.

"Sticking feathers up your butt does not make you a chicken" is a quote by Chuck Palahniuk, the author of Fight Club which is a great book and strangely enough, while it is my favorite movie, it is not my favorite book. I am also fairly certain the quote is not entirely original to Palahniuk, as I have heard similar idioms in my life before Fight Club that utilizes feathers and orifices in like-manner. Palahniuk just said it best.

The statement I use "…only the curious have something to find" is a quote from the band Nickel Creek, one of my favorites.

The Bible is quoted in several places, almost exclusively by Samuel Crane and often paraphrased.

In Everett's dream-like state in chapter one, there is a small quote from the show Black Mirror. There are a few more easter eggs that I can't remember off the top of my head so have fun finding them.

I hope you have enjoyed this story and are looking forward to the sequel.

Yes, I said sequel. Originally, I had no intention of writing this story as a series. At just after the halfway point, I discovered that I kept on finding more subplots which expanded the story. I intended to stop the story much later, but because of the nature of the newly (at the time) developed subplots, I decided to end it on a lovely little cliffhanger to keep you on the lookout for what happens next. At this moment, I plan to write a trilogy, but time will tell as the story unfolds and dives into some more fantastical and epic rabbit holes. In the meantime, keep a lookout for "Egress", book two of the Domain series!

Thank you for purchasing my book. If you would like to stay up to date on the sequel and other projects I am doing, the best way to do so is on my Instagram account @douglasalsmith. I have a tendency to post inside scoops on my IG stories more than anything (oooh, the mystery) so be sure to keep up!

See you there.

-   Doug

Made in the USA
Las Vegas, NV
23 November 2022